MARBLEFACE

"Full packed with reckless deeds and hairbreadth escapes...no fan will be disappointed."
—*New York Times*

A writer of legendary genius, Max Brand has brought to his Westerns the raw frontier action and historical authenticity that have earned him the title of the world's most celebrated Western writer.

In *Marbleface,* a one-time middleweight contender needs to rest easy or his bum ticker will take him out. But since a man can't survive in the Old West without defending himself, Marbleface trades his gloves for a gun and a deck of cards. Winning comes easy to the wily gambler, but soon every desperado, cowboy, and lawman is itching to bring him down for the count.

MARBLEFACE

LEISURE BOOKS NEW YORK CITY

A LEISURE BOOK®

June. 1995

Published by special arrangement with Golden West
Literary Agency.

Dorchester Publishing Co., Inc.
276 Fifth Avenue
New York, NY 10001

MARBLEFACE

CHAPTER I

The First Three Rounds

THERE are two ways of telling a thing. You start at the beginning and go straight ahead or else you begin in the middle. I'd rather begin in the middle. That means cutting out everything before my fight with "Digger" Murphy, beginning with the fourth round of that fight, when he pasted me and knocked me cold.

The events preceding that don't count.

I mean, of course, it would be pleasant and a lot of fun to commence at the very beginning and tell about how I started out and loved using my fists when I was just a kid; how I grew up and kept using them; how "Dutch" Keller saw me using my fists, one day, on a couple of the boys and decided that he could use me in his string of fighters; how he kept me in his gymnasium and made me like it while he put me through the ropes for three years, worked my head off, and never gave me a chance at money; how he finally uncorked me and how I started to make good; how I fought my way up until there was nothing between me and the champ except Digger Murphy and Digger was only a set-up for me.

I would like to tell all of those things, because the taste of them is still mighty sweet in my mind. But you know how it is. I have to explain how I came to be out here in the West, wearing chaps, packing a gun, daubing ropes on cows, and all that sort of thing. And the explanation of that is the fourth round of my fight with Digger Murphy.

That fight was as easy as any of the set-ups that Dutch had found for me when he started me in and gave me the soft ones to break my teeth on. He used to say that fighters have to find their teeth, and that gymnasium is important, but it's only gymnasium. The ring is the ring, and that's a lot different. He was right. He used to say that many a man was great for a show and no good for the money, and he wanted me to bring in the cash. He made me do it, too.

He got me when I was seventeen. He kept me till I was twenty-one. He gave me three years of hell in the gym. Then he gave me one year of glory in the ring, and, believe me, I would have worn the middleweight crown if only the crash hadn't stopped me. It wasn't the fists of another man that did it, but a thing that nobody can figure on. It was fate.

When I was a kid, just coming on, Dutch used to throw all kinds against me. One day it would be a big, hard-boiled heavyweight who only hit me once a round but, when he connected, what a song and dance there was in my brain!

"That's what it feels like when you're socked," Dutch used to say. "You gotta get used to it. That's nothing to the way you'll be socked when you get up against the fast ones."

The next day he'd throw in a fast, snappy little light-weight, all feathers and fluff, who would bang me from the belt to the part of my hair, fists going so fast that you couldn't see them.

"That's a real boxer," Dutch would say to me. "Until you can box like that, you'll never be fit to go up against a classy middleweight."

The next day it would be someone of my own weight, some old, cagey guy, who was going downhill, but was still full of tricks, who knew how to seem "out" while he was on his feet and then would drop a ton of bricks on your chin just as you were stepping in to finish him.

Well, everything went fine. I climbed right up in the

profession. And in those days it was a profession. But I pass over those days. I pass over the headlines they began to carry about me in the papers after I knocked out Jeff Thomas in three rounds. That made me.

For the rest of the year, I kept on growing. Thomas was the first hot one that Dutch fed to me. He made me study him hard. He told me that he was a tough nut. But after the first round I saw that he was easy, unless he was faking and keeping something back. In the second round I got to him and plastered him black and blue. Then I knew that I had read that book from cover to cover. It gave me confidence. But still I waited. I waited till I could walk in behind a perfect fence in the third round and then I poisoned him.

Brutal? Sure it was brutal when I saw his hands go down. But I didn't feel like a brute. I just felt pretty good when I stepped in and rose on my toes and dropped on my heels and cracked him on the button. He fell forward on his face. They're done when they do that. And I felt pretty sweet, what I mean to say.

Dutch told me a lot of bad things I had done in the fight, but I looked him in the eye and grinned, because for the first time I knew that I was good, and how!

After that I had confidence, and confidence is worth a horseshoe in your boxing glove. It adds fifty pounds to every punch. And it makes the other fellow know that you're going to get him. I smiled when I was stung. It was that way with "Soldier" Baker. He was fast. He was tough. He nearly turned out the lights for me in the fifth round, but I only laughed, and so he held off a little, thinking that I hadn't been really hurt. Finally, when he made up his mind to step in, I did the stepping first and dropped him off the map. That was sweet, too.

That was the fight, in fact, that cinched me to go up against the champion. He didn't want me. He'd seen me and he knew that I was poison. So he just threw in the name of Digger Murphy. If I beat Murphy, he would take me on.

Well, Murphy was nothing. I'd seen him and I knew that he was my meat. I knew all his tricks. He had a hanging guard and he liked to step in with his head and body weaving and sock for the body. Well, I knew all about that.

When the first round came and he tried that, I let him weave until he was right close in and then I took the cork off the bottle and let it hit him under the chin.

He stopped weaving after that. When he tried it, the old uppercut always stood him up as straight as starch. He tried to box, but he couldn't. I kept getting him with a straight left and a right cross that traveled high and dropped with a jerk on the side of the face. Once it connected with the chin, he was gone, and Digger knew it. He began to open his eyes; he was seeing his finish. I saw it, too.

Then I started feinting with the left. When he jerked his guard up, I stepped in and socked him with a swinging right to the body. I could feel the fist sink in. I could feel it jar on his backbone. That was sweet, too!

In the third round, he was going fast. I knew that I could finish him any minute, but I was in no hurry. All of the big sporting writers were there at the ringside watching what I did, and so I gave them a show. I mean, I showed them perfect straight lefts, heels and hip, shoulder and fist all in line. I lunged like a fencer, because I knew that I wouldn't have to recover too fast. I pulled uppercuts from my hips. I looped hooks and crosses over his shoulders, and with each punch poor old Digger Murphy sagged.

Still I kept walking in behind the perfect fence that Dutch Keller had taught me to build. Every time Digger Murphy socked, he hit my elbows, shoulders, and nothing else. I began to catch his punches. I caught them at the elbow and laughed at Digger, then jerked a short jab into his middle section and saw his face convulsed as though he'd had an electric shock.

Yes, it was a good show.

Things were going along like this when the end of the third round came. At the finish of that round, I'll bet that every man in the house was putting the middleweight crown of the world on my head. I was, for one.

Then, as they fanned me, one of my seconds threw half a bucket of cold water over me and changed my life.

CHAPTER II

The Finish

I SHALL never forget that moment, of course. I remember that Dutch—good old fellow—was calling up from under my corner. He was like a happy boy, laughing as he looked up at me.

"I've had 'em fast, and I've had 'em with the kick of a mule, and I've had 'em foxy," he said. "But you got all three together."

I leaned back on the chair and felt the rubbers working on the inside muscles of my legs, and said nothing. I didn't need that massage. My legs were as strong as iron posts. They could stand anything. Road work accounted for that.

But I was luxuriating in things and taking everything that came my way. Then that half bucket of cold water splashed over me.

I don't know what happened. It seemed to freeze me all the way through. Afterward I couldn't catch my breath. I felt as though I had been running a mile uphill, and I still felt that way when the bell rang.

Well, I stepped out, confident, easy, in spite of that trouble with my wind. That would pass, I was sure. It was only like a catch in the side.

There before me was Digger Murphy, serious, his face set and pasty white. He knew that I was going to knock him out. And wasn't he ripe for it?

His eyes were uneasy in his head, shifting a bit from side to side. His legs were so far apart that I knew that he was bracing himself for the shock that he expected me to give him.

Well, I stepped in and gave him the left jab, an easy, light one, to feel him out. That jab found its mark, as though he were a man made of putty. He saw what I was going to try and blinked, but he couldn't make his hands move fast enough to block the punch. I hit him, but what I noticed, most of all, was that there was no lead in the wallop. I had expected to daze him a bit, so that I could shoot across the right, which I was holding my hand high for. That right was to end the battle. To show them the real wallop that I carried up my sleeve, you see. To show them that I could take a man fresh out of his corner, after a whole minute of resting, and sock him cold, for keeps. That was what that right was poised and ready to do.

But the left didn't work. There seemed not to be a fist, but just cold mush inside of my glove.

That punch made no opening for me. I could see the surprised look in Digger's face. He was waiting for the sock, and it hadn't arrived. I grinned at him, as much as to say that I was only playing. But it wasn't playing. There was something wrong with me. You see, my breath was still gone. I was sick. I wanted to sit down on that stool again. I wanted to lie down—lie flat. I couldn't breathe. I was out of wind. Yet at the end of the third round I had been ready to do a toe dance!

I would have liked to cut that round short, but I couldn't. Every move of it hangs in my mind. I was the winner. Digger Murphy was finished. I had only to hit him once, yet I couldn't hit.

He was a game one. When that left of mine didn't faze him, I hauled off and socked at him. No, he wasn't ready to lie down. He socked at me, and I put up my right to block the swing. I had the arm there in plenty of time. I should have stopped that punch. I should have been ready to step in and poke him with my left. But the arm I put up seemed to be made of feathers. His sock went straight through it, and he hammered me on the side of the jaw.

I back-stepped, a little groggy, grinned and nodded, as though to invite him to step in and try the thing again. Only I wasn't inviting. I knew that something was wrong. I tried a glance at my corner and could see Dutch looking puzzled and shaking his head. Still he was smiling. He was so sure of that fight!

So was I. I was only waiting for the change, waiting for the wind to come back, waiting for the thing that wouldn't happen.

My legs were bad. My knees had turned to dough. There, where the mainspring of a boxer's action is centered, I had nothing but pulp! In boxing, you do your feinting, your hitting, all with the legs. The arms don't count so much. The feet are what get you out of danger and bring you back into position to hit, throwing the vital weight behind the punch. But my feet were dead under me!

Digger was coming in.

I flashed a left at him. It hit his forehead and bounced! There was nothing to it. He came right on through that feeble barrage and socked me. My perfect fence was full of holes!

His blows went home now and how they came! My body, mind you, was ringed with cushions of hard fighting muscles that were guaranteed to soak up all sorts of shocks and punishment. But the cushions were gone. He seemed to be hitting right into the core of my being. I felt the blows sink through to the backbone. I was jarred; I was sick.

Then I backed away and I saw on Digger's face a look of dull astonishment, almost as though he had received the blows. In the preceding rounds I had been sliding away from or shedding those punches like water.

He was amazed one moment, the next, he was at me, hammer and tongs. He knew the taste of that pleasure of

13

old. He knew how it felt to sink your fists into a pulpy, weak, fading body. I was learning for the first time.

He came at me and he hit hard and with growing confidence—that confidence I was speaking about, which puts a lump of lead in each boxing glove. The lead hit me. It hit me in the sick body and made me sicker. I was thinking yards ahead of anything that my hands could do. They were helpless. And there was no strength in my elbows, where a man needs it for blocking. They were like my knees, just pulpy.

I knew that I was going. I knew that I was sliding. I'll never forget the roar of the house, when I backed away from Digger and the people could see that the smile on my face was frozen. I'll never forget Digger's manager— he'd been silent up to now—jumping up and down and screeching to him to stop me—to knock me for a row of loops! And I knew that he could do it!

I still tried to smile—the foolish lesson that I had learned. And the words of Dutch came drilling into my mind. He was telling me to back away and cover up; that I was all right; that nothing would happen; that Digger was pie for me!

Well, Digger was pie, all right, such pie that I had cut the slice already, so to speak, and could have eaten it at any time during the three rounds before.

But now the case was different. He picked me up and carried me before him like dead leaves before the wind. He hit me in my perishing body. He slammed me on the head.

Then I went down. I felt a blow between my shoulders. It was my own head, jerked back before his smashing fist!

And I went down, sinking, crumpling. I seemed to be made of sand. There were no legs under me, to hold me up. I just went on falling, and telling myself that this was ridiculous, and that such a punch never could hurt me in the world. Ten thousand harder ones had glanced from me like water when I was stepping on the sweat and blood-spattered canvas of the gym.

But down I went.

I got up again, but I had to fight to get up. I laughed

14

at myself. I was maddened, because there was no breath in me. But I got up somehow. I put my will power under my knees and pushed myself up, rose and met the shrieking of that crowd. I was the favorite, five to one. They had bet that way on me. I heard them calling me a dirty dog, a yellow traitor, and a lot of names that look even worse in print.

I could still feel my face stretching in the same foolish, idiotic grin, the pretense of not being hurt.

I knew that the sham was no good. I knew that I was a fool to keep on wasting effort on that smile. But it wasn't really effort. It was only the effect of the old gymnasium habit—to sneer at the other fellow when he has hurt you the most!

I saw Digger, with his head cocked wisely to one side, thinking, preparing himself, ready for a great effort. Still, there was an air of amazement about him. He was still feeling the work of my hands. He still felt me right into the core of him. But now he came, side-stepping, sliding, glimmering before my eyes.

I knew what he was doing. I read his mind, miles away. A feint of a low, swinging left to the body, and then a smashing right-hander to the head. I tried to forestall the blows, but it was no use. I was made of paper, wet pulpy paper.

I saw the feint start and end, hanging in the air.

I saw the right begin and the high, sudden arching of the arm to get over my sagging shoulder, then the sudden drop of the clenched fist. But the guard that I put up was no good. The sock came home. I felt it like a hammer stroke in the back of my brain. All the yelling in the house became nothing. I dropped into nothingness.

CHAPTER III

Recovery

WHEN I came to, a voice was saying dryly, with only a slight sneer: "I had half a grand on this bird. I stood to win a hundred. That was all!"

Then I opened my eyes and saw a doctor leaning over me, with what looked like a trumpet pressed against my breast.

He stood up, straightened, looked down at me hard.

"Auricular fibrillation," said he. "Why did you ever let this fellow step into a ring?"

The last part of his speech was addressed to Dutch.

Poor Dutch! He was standing by with a set smile, like a fighter's when he's gone, waiting for the knock-out, as I had waited for it in that last, fourth round.

"Auricular—what you say?" asked Dutch, wrinkling his fleshy forehead.

"His heart's no good. It never could've been much good. Never for years," said the doctor. "You knew that. Don't lie to me!"

"His heart's got something wrong with it, eh?" said Dutch quietly.

"Of course it has. Listen to it yourself, jumping like a rabbit with the hounds at its heels!"

I felt it myself then, the flutter and the failing of it.

16

The pulsation seemed to be in the center of my lungs, thrusting out all of the life-giving air.

"His heart's gone!" said Dutch, whispering to himself.

I pushed myself up on my elbow. There was an ache under my right eye. I could see the swelling, the discoloration of it. But the pain didn't bother me any.

"Dutch," said I, "I've been knocked out!"

He came over, hurrying. He put his arms under my shoulders.

"Aw, that's nothing," said he. "You slipped. That was all. You give your head a rap on the canvas. Just an accident. You're going to be better than ever. All you needed was a lesson. Now you got it. I always told you that only fools took chances."

I stared square up into his face and saw the frown of reproval fade away. An empty, bewildered look came into his eyes.

"All right, Dutch," said I. "I didn't take any chances. You know that. I played the game, but the game beat me. I don't know what happened."

He looked away from me suddenly, like a scared child. He looked at the doctor, as though asking for an explanation. And the doctor was biting his lip and glowering thoughtfully at me.

"The heart's like the mainspring of a watch," he said sourly. "Sometimes it just gives way. The watch begins to tick out of tune. That's all! You understand that? Just begins to flutter."

"What cures this?" asked Dutch, grabbing at me and holding hard.

"Nothing," said the doctor. "This boy will never wear the gloves again."

"You lie!" screamed Dutch, while that bad heart of mine froze and was still.

The doctor took a step and put the gloved forefinger of his hand on the chest of Dutch. "Listen to me," he said. "I've seen every fight he's fought. I've backed him every time—after the first. I'm not taking you for a ride. I'm telling you. That's all. Quinidine might bump his heart over the hill and put the rhythm straight again. Nothing else will turn the trick. The poor kid!"

He looked at me, as he said that, then frowned suddenly and left the room.

"All right," Dutch said. "That's easy. Quinidine. That's the thing that fixes you, kid."

It didn't though.

No, it only made me sicker, for a while. I spent six days lying flat, and for six days, they shot the pills into me. Then the doctor gave it up, when the heartbeat had been shoved to a hundred and sixty.

I tried it a second time, and a third time. Three times, they say, quinidine is worth trying. Each time I was beaten!

You know what it meant. I was only a kid of twenty-one. I had been on tiptoe. I was going to be a champion. Suddenly they told me that I was an old man. I had to go slowly upstairs. I'd better eat only one meal of meat a day. Better lie down an hour after every meal. A sedentary life, that was preferable, so they told me.

Me! I'd never pushed a pen across ten pages of paper in all my days! Well, I thought it over for months. I saw doctors all the time. I got so that I was willing to trade the rest of my existence for one year of real life, the sort of life that I had known, the life of a champion, knocking them out.

Digger Murphy came to see me. He was straight. He gave my hand a squeeze. That old has-been had met the champion, on the strength of his win over me, and he'd landed a lucky punch in the second round and now he wore the crown himself!

Digger Murphy!

"You were taking me, kid," he said. "I never got such a slamming. I thought you were all dynamite. What happened anyway? Were you doped? Did the stuff quit on you cold?"

I told him. I told him word by word, no word more than one syllable. He kept listening and he kept nodding. He couldn't look me in the face. It made me sick to see how he took it, like a slam in the chin.

18

Then he said: "Look here. I've made fifty grand through that scrap. I'm going to make more, too. Any part or all of that is yours."

That was pretty good, I'd say. He meant what he said. He was white.

Finally I said: "Digger, you take and salt the coin away. I'm going to be all right. Don't you think about me."

Digger grinned. "You mean that I won't be champ long?"

I shook my head. "You never can tell, Digger. You're a good old sport and a grand fighter, but you take care of your coin so it can take care of you, one of these days."

He kept on grinning and looking at me askance.

"I know," said he. "I'm not much good. I've only happened on some luck. You could've beaten me in the third. I know that. I'm only a ham, when it comes to the real class. Only I've just had some luck. Kid, let me give you a hand."

I said "no." He got up and left. For three months, I got a hundred dollars in cash mailed to me every week. The sender's name was not given, but I mailed all of that money back to Digger, and finally the coin stopped coming. He was a good fellow, as Irish as they make 'em. Then up came that fellow "Tug" Whaley and knocked Digger for a row of loops, took the crown, and wore it fair and square for five years.

Anyway I got no more money sent to me from old Digger!

By that time I was ready to look around at the new life and the rotten world that I found to live it in.

What a world! An hour in bed after every meal; one feed of meat every day; no running upstairs—I couldn't do anything fast and hard; no running uphill, or running upstairs. Everything must be slow and easy; no emotion. Keep your heart locked up. Smile at everything. Play poker all your life.

That was what I had to learn to do. And that was just how I happened to go wrong. Rather, you can't say that it happened. It was inevitable. What else was there for me to do? I couldn't be a clerk, somehow. That wasn't in

19

me. I couldn't join a profession because I didn't know enough. And I couldn't sponge on my old pals, because I wasn't that cheap.

It wasn't fun. The doctors told me to live like a snail inside a shell. But then along came a physician with a new hunch. He said that the heart was a muscle and, even though it was a damaged muscle, it ought to be worked regularly. He gave me graded exercises, and I was thankful that I had met him when I began to build up—a step at a time. Pretty soon I could ride a horse all day. I could climb a mountain. I could dance, if I didn't speed up, for half an hour at a time. I could even go into the gym and lug around a little at the fixings there.

I had to get rid of nerves; that was all. Every time I got a nerve shock, my heart went smash. But at the end of three months, you could let off a blast of dynamite in my room while I was sound asleep, and I wouldn't be shocked. You could snap your fingers under my nose, curse me, threaten me, pull a gun on me. It made no difference. I kept those nerves as steady as a ticking clock. I had to. It was that, or die.

And this leads me on to my changed way of living.

I had to be a fighting man. I knew that the instinct was in me. Since I couldn't use my fists any more, except for one sock at a time, I began to pack a gun. Not that I was looking for trouble, but with my fighting stamina gone out of me, I felt scared and helpless. Packing the Colt made me feel better. And I used to ride out into the country districts and use that old cannon; I practiced pulling and pointing, when I was in my room. That revolver began to be a part of me.

In the meantime, the doctors had taken out the last of my dollars, and how was I to make any more? Well, with my hands and my face, not in the ring, but at a poker table. That face of mine was made of ice. It told nothing. If it was crooked work that the other fellows tried, my fingers got limber and educated enough to hold their own with most of the card mixers.

I began to rake in about a thousand a week. I was almost able to forget my sorrows, and then came the "bust" that kicked me off the face of Manhattan and landed me out in the cow country.

CHAPTER IV

End of a Poker Game

IT started in with a low-life rich man's son, by name of Steven Cole. He was the son of Parker Cole who had yachts in the East and mines and ranches in the West. Steve was the brother of that Betty Cole who was beginning to break into the society headlines. She was all right, too. You'll hear more about her, before I'm through.

This Steven Cole was sitting in at a poker game with me and Charley Newman, that red-headed crook, and Dick Stephani, and Lew Waddell. The Cole kid hands me the deck to cut on his deal, and I find a double crimp in it. I saw that the hound had run up the pack of us and I handed the boys the high sign.

Up to that, everything was easy and straight in that game, but when the kid tried to frame us, we trimmed him down to the oil. We just about put him out. At three o'clock that morning, he owed the game twenty-five thousand and a few extra hundreds. He looked a little sick, but he signed I O U's. My share was nine thousand; Stephani got twelve; Lew Waddell was only in for a few grand.

Stephani went to the door with Steve Cole and tapped him on the shoulder.

"You know, Steve," said he, "we'll take our money inside of a week. We give you that much grace."

Steve Cole looked over his shoulder at Stephani's dark features. Dick was the handsomest man that ever lived, bar none. And the blond kid got sicker and sicker in the face.

He came back inside the room and leaned against the wall; said that he didn't know how he could pay; wanted to pay, but he'd already overdrawn his allowance, and only the month before he'd got into a scrape and his father had come to his assistance for the last time, as he said. We stood around and listened to this line of talk, and Waddell pointed out that Cole would have been ready to win; therefore, he had to be ready to lose and pay. Then Newman stepped up with his jaw sticking out and said that a week was too long to wait.

"There's a safe in the cellar of your father's house," he went on. "You can get the combination to that safe. And we'll call on you in two days and clean the safe out."

Mind you, I heard the robbery proposed and I wasn't even shocked. It looked all right to me. The kid owed us the money, and he had to come through. Cole wrinkled up his face so that I thought he was going to burst into tears. But he finally said:

"I see where I am. I think maybe this job will turn me straight, from to-night on. You crooks!"

He looked bitterly at us out of his brown eyes. He was a sleepy, good-natured young fellow, a little sleek and soft. He was about my age—twenty-two, at that moment.

I said to him: "You started running up the cards. Don't call me a crook."

He was game enough. He lost his temper and came savagely over toward me.

"I've a mind to break your neck, Poker-face!" he said to me. "You can bluff some, but you can't bluff me."

I had my nerves in hand. I was thinking about that kangaroo heart of mine that I had to keep in order. There wasn't even a quiver in me, but when I saw him double up his fist, I said:

"If you lift your hand, I'll kill you!"

22

He started to sneer, changed his mind, and turned as white as a piece of cloth. He backed out of that room, watching me as though I were a ghost. At the door he turned and said:

"All right. Night after next. I'll be ready!"

He cleared out.

Waddell said to me: "It's all right, Jerry. He's gone, ain't he? What you looking like that for, now that you're bluff has worked?"

"Shut up," says Newman. "It wasn't a bluff. He meant it."

Dick Stephani was lighting a cigarette. He looked up at me through the smoke.

"You didn't really mean it, kid?" said he to me.

"I've lost my fists. You know that," said I. "I'll kill the first man that tries to beat me up. What else could I do?"

Stephani began to look thoughtful. So did the others. We all said good night, and arranged when and where we would meet to go after the Cole money the night after next.

Then I turned in. I felt pretty good about life at that time. And why not? I had been making, as I said, about a thousand a week and saving half of that, and here was a good tidy haul—ten weeks' work in one, very nearly. So I decided that I'd take a rest—go to Europe and see what the doctors there could do for me. I'd heard a lot about a great man in Vienna who could take a heart to pieces and put it together again.

I went to sleep on that idea, and I was happy as could be until the time came for us to go to the Cole house.

Newman was to be outside man, across the street. Stephani took the next corner. Waddell went in with me. I remember how loudly he breathed as we stood in the thick black of the hall. There was a smell of flowers in the air, and the hall was warm. I uncorked a lantern and spilled a few drops of light across the polished floors, that looked like water. The rays blinked across a mirror or two, slid and shimmered across a table top, before I saw Steve Cole.

He met us and told us that the safe door was open. It

23

was an easy cinch to go straight down into the cellar and help ourselves, only he hoped that we wouldn't take more than we needed to make up for the gambling debt. The kid was feeling bad. There seemed a moan in his voice even though it got no deeper in his throat than a whisper.

We told him, whispering, too, that we would have to clean out the whole thing, or else the job would look phony. I told him, for my part, that I would see that everything was returned except enough to cover the cash he owed us. He thanked me for that.

Just then a door closed with a faint booming sound, and slippers came padding down the stairs. Waddell and I backed up into a corner. Cole was left standing near the foot of the stairs, and someone fair banged into him, then called out.

I heard Cole gasp.

"It's you, Steve?" said a girl's voice.

"Yes, it's I," he answered.

"What are you doing down here in the dark?" she said. "What have you been whispering about? Who's here with you?"

She didn't whisper. She talked right out, not loudly, either. Her voice was soft and almost drawling. It was warm and deep the way a Negro's voice is, very often.

"Betty," said the youth, "quit it. You shut up and go back to bed."

"My goodness, Steve," said she, "you've grown up, all at once, haven't you? Ordering me about like this!"

"Betty, go back to bed," said he.

"I'm going back," said she. "I've no desire to spy on you. Only I had to come down and let you know that I guessed something was wrong. Now you go your own way, and get your hands and your heart just as dirty as you please. You know, Steve, the thing that makes me sick about you is that you're such a fool! Such a plain fool!"

She went running up the stairs again, and Steve came back to me.

"Will you quit this job for to-night, boys?" he asked. "You see my sister will suspect me."

"We're going to go through with it right now," growled Waddell.

He led the way. I followed. We got down into the cellar and found the safe. Its bright steel face was as easy to find as the moon in a clear, dark sky.

It was open, too, just as Cole had promised, and after we had pushed the door farther back, Waddell began to empty the contents of the drawers into a big felt bag that he had brought out from under his arm. He looked aside at me with an ugly expression.

"Do something!" said he. "Why just stand around and let somebody else do the dangerous work?"

"Show me what to do," said I. "Shall I hold your hat, you stiff?"

He looked at me again, with a twist and a lift of his upper lip. Just then, a little chamois bag that he was handling gaped open and a shower of diamonds fell on the floor.

"The devil!" breathed Waddell with delight.

Just as he spoke, I saw a shadow swing across the ceiling and I ducked my head. The weight of that blow whirred past my ear. I heard a man grunt right behind me. Two more were running from nowhere toward Waddell, and I heard him cry out like a bull terrier whining as he turned to face them and went down under their weight.

We had been trapped, d'you see? Instantly I suspected not the kid, not young Cole, so much, as Charley Newman and handsome Stephani, the black and the red of our gang!

I had my gun out as I turned. I fired and saw one of the three men whirl about and go down. I told myself that he was not killed; the bullet must have hit him high—in a shoulder, say. That was why the plunging weight of it whirled him about.

As he dropped, I stepped back through the door.

Two bullets split it from head to heel. There were the stairs in front of me, and I told myself that I didn't dare to run up them. Months and months of practice with sinking spells and collapses had taught me that the only way through a crisis was to go easily, smoothly, a step at a time. Still I feared the crash of my heart more than I did the bullets and the police. You see, the state of my heart was my professional preoccupation, so to speak.

Well, I got halfway up the steep flight of stairs before the door opened behind me. One man came charging through. One was flat with my bullet. The other was minding Waddell, you see. I turned around, but at the gleam of my gun, the detective gave a yelp, as though he had been kicked, and jumped for cover. I went on up the stairs and through the top door just as he opened fire.

But I didn't mind him so much; it was what might lie before me that troubled me.

When I came into the hallway, I could hear the hum and the roar of a big household waking up. In a corner of the hall I saw where Steve Cole had dropped into a chair. The girl was there beside him, shaking a finger at him and talking fast and hard. There was one light on. It made the hallways seem as big as a barn and as dreary. The high lights were like trembling ghosts on the watery floors and in the sheen of the mirrors.

"There's one now!" said the girl, spotting me. "If you've got the tenth part of a man in you, go for him, Steven Cole. Here's a gun. I'd rather see you dead than shamed!"

CHAPTER V

His Sister

ZINGO, but it was something to hear her talk! It would have taken a pretty confirmed coward to face that Cole girl, I tell you. Her brother, at least, didn't dare to stand up to her for a moment. He took the gun that she shoved into his hand and whirled about toward me.

I kept my own gun in my side pocket and my hand on top of it. I could feel my heart beginning to race. In another minute I would be sick with the strain. So, once again, the total call on me was to keep calm. Great Scott! Keep calm when every nerve in my legs was tingling to be off at full speed! But I had to keep that crazy pulsation in hand, and I did. I just walked on, while Steven Cole made a few running steps toward me.

I looked past him and saw his sister standing straight as a post. She looked like an Indian, her hair was so black, her skin so coppery, but there was more flame in her cheeks than there would be in the skin of an Indian. She was all lighted up now and if she feared for her brother, she didn't show it.

That fellow Cole charged at me, pulling the trigger twice. That didn't worry me so much, either, because I could see the crazy shaking of his hand as he shot. Then his gun clogged; he came straight on at me, swung up the Colt, and heaved it at my head. It barely missed, and as he rushed in, I heard the girl calling to him to fight like a man.

It was the effect of her voice on me that made me think twice. The first thought was that the Colt, of course, was what I had to use on the fool. The second thought was that there had been something rather fine, after all, in the way he had charged across that big hall at me. It made the killing of him murder. Murder of a real man, too, or of what might grow into a man!

Anyway, I used the second thought. I decided that for once I would do what the doctors said I never must—use my strength again. I brought out my hand with no gun in it and, as Steve Cole came in, I plugged him on the button with everything that I had. He went right on running by me, hit a wall, and flopped back on the floor, clean out.

That left the girl. And now I heard doors slamming and men's voices very loud in the front of the house. They had reserves coming in to swamp me, of course! But the girl hadn't moved from her place. I looked at her, a little bitterly.

That one wallop had seemed to tear me in two; the heart was pattering like rain, and noises roared in my ears. So I pulled out the gun and showed it to her. By thunder, she straightened, as though she expected me to shoot and didn't intend to run away. She would take the fire in front, like a man!

I only said: "I should have used this on him, but you saw that I didn't. Show me a back way, or a side way out of this place, will you?"

Watch the weight of the wind tip a bird on a branch— that's the way she hesitated for half an instant, and then she came up to me and said, "This way!"

She steered me through about twenty doors. That house was ten in one. And always we were hearing voices and footsteps, roaring and rushing. We came to a narrow, dark hallway. The light from a street lamp glimmered through a little pane of heavy glass, and beyond I could see the green of a garden.

Just there, I had to stop. My head was spinning, and

my breath wouldn't come. It was like the fourth round of the fight, and I felt myself going down—forever, this time!

So I put my hand against the wall and paused, and the girl came running back to me.

"Have you got a bullet in you? Did they shoot you, man?"

She shook my arm impatiently.

"Is it just a dead funk?" she exclaimed, stamping. I grinned at her like an idiot. I could feel the stretch of that grin as far back as my ears almost.

"Rotten heart," said I.

She shoved her hand inside my coat, then she shuddered.

"Will it pass?" she asked.

"Sure," said I.

"Lean on me," said the girl. "It isn't far to the garden. They won't search there. Put your weight on me. I'm strong."

She was, too. She braced herself and took the soggy, sagging bulk of me along with her down the corridor.

She began to pant. She said: "A fine one you, to be a robber! And you use your fists, too! You should have taken the gun to him. Shooting low, I mean!"

"All right," said I. "But I didn't."

We got to the door. She opened it and pushed me through. I staggered and nearly flopped.

But she had me under the armpits at once and supported me again to a bench in an arbor. I lay down flat. I was so far gone that she had to pick up my legs at the ankles and stretch me out. Then things got exceedingly dim, until cold water fell on my face.

I looked up and saw the girl, just an outline of blackness against the black pattern of the leaves behind and above her. She was kneeling beside me.

"How's it coming?" she asked.

"I'm all right," said I.

"Don't be a fool," she replied. "You're not all right."

She was taking my pulse.

29

"It's getting better," she said. "Try not to think about yourself. Give your rotten heart a chance."

"I'm not thinking about myself," I whispered.

"That's right; think about something else, will you? You're all right now. You're getting better. I'll see you out of this tangle. What mixed you up with a lot of crooks? No, don't tell me that, either. Don't excite yourself. I won't even ask for your name."

"My name's Jerry Ash," said I. "They call me Poker-face."

"What's the matter? Too sick to work for an honest living?"

I thought.

"No, I could have gone straight," said I. "But I took the easiest way out. Help me to sit up."

She did that. I was still pretty dizzy, but I could breathe a lot better, and my head was clearing at an astonishing rate. I slid my right arm over her strong shoulders, and she lifted most of the burden as I got to my feet.

"Steer me out," said I.

"You're not fit to go," said she.

"Steer me out. Don't argue."

She did as I told her to do, leading me to a little back gate of the garden. The lock screeched a little when she turned the key.

Then I turned my head so that my face was close to hers.

"Are you going to be a silly fool?" she asked me, though she didn't shrink away.

"I'm going straight," said I. "Will you try to believe that?"

"Never mind the future," said the girl. "To-day is enough for you to think about. How are you to get away from here?"

"On my feet," said I. "What's your front name?"

"Betty," said she.

"Well, Betty," I answered, "you're all out by yourself in front, and the rest are nowhere. Good-by."

"Good-by," said she, "and good luck."

I stepped back into the opening of the narrow gate and

30

paused there a moment to look her over and to let her soak in. Feature by feature, the shape of her head, the shoulders, her height and bulk, I worked them well back into my mind because I felt that I would be needing to remember what she looked like one of these days.

"Good-by again," said I, and went out into the street.

When I heard the creak of the gate being closed behind me, it made me feel pretty much alone, and in need of a doctor.

But I got on, stepping slowly.

I had my hands in my pockets as I came up to the next corner, and there a couple of flatties jumped out at me. I looked at them with a dull eye, and they split away to each side of me.

"Just a drunk," said one of them, but as I went on across the street, I couldn't help thinking how well the trap had been set around the house of Parker Cole. Young Steven must have been at the bottom of it, I decided, and that was enough for me.

Well, strange to say, the walking didn't knock me out, but straightened me up. The ripple and stagger of the heartbeats grew better. And then a cab came along, and I hailed it and went home.

I had the cab wait in the street, because I suspected that everything might not be right. If the others wanted to double-cross me, they had had plenty of time, and police might be waiting for me in the house at that moment.

When I unlocked the door of the rooming house, therefore, and pushed it open, I wasn't very much surprised to see two men waiting inside. They got up, pale faces under the light, and came for me. So I slammed the door and got back to the cab in time. They yelled and fired a couple of shots, but we got away.

I had not gotten very far, however, before trouble slugged me again. They wanted my hide and they wanted me badly. I was hunted from New York to Pittsburgh, down the Mississippi, on boats, on railroads, and they got wind of me in New Orleans and stuck a two-thousand-dollar reward on my head.

31

However, on that entire trip I never went faster than a walk and I put in eight hours' sleep each night. Because I knew that I had nearly died in the Cole house, from excitement and physical effort.

Things were getting pretty hot on my trail all over the East and the South, and that was why I slipped out West. I didn't have much idea what I could do, but I knew I had told the girl that I would go straight, and that was my goal. The job that I had in doing that is what comes next to relate. That brings me to Barney Peel, and Sid Maker, and Makerville; to Colonel Riggs and Piegan. In fact, this opens up everything—so many things that I hardly know where to start.

CHAPTER VI

The Holdup

THE reason that I headed for the town of Piegan was that it was young on the map and was also four days of hard staging from the nearest railroad. Those things appealed to me, because I knew that wherever I went easily, by boat or railroad, the police could go, also, and that they were not likely to let me alone for a long time to come. I needed to get back into the woods and the rough country, where I could get myself out of the first page of the police mind of the country, so to speak.

It's a funny thing how accidents get multiplied and enlarged, and trifles become important. There were still references in the newspapers to the "Cole robbery," the "Cole outrage," and the "great Cole burglary." But I've told you exactly how everything happened. Waddell was captured. One policeman was slightly wounded. Young Cole was knocked on the chin. That was all that had happened. But the police were furious because their perfect trap had failed to insnare the second thug. They could not guess how accident and the calm wits of Betty Cole had saved my neck.

However, since the price on my head had been boosted to three thousand dollars, I was glad to get onto the stage that started for the town of Piegan. Four days of staging, and in those four days I drove four decades, four lifetimes into the heart of the West. It seemed to me as though I had sped down a long chute into the very heart of a mystery.

It was a mystery to me—the look of the men who had gathered for the stage, the stage itself, like a finely modeled ship of the ancient days, and the six wild-eyed horses hitched in front of the craft that was to navigate that inland sea. I looked inside and saw a woman and three small children that had the look of tears. So I handed the driver an extra ten dollars, and he arranged that I should sit beside him. That was my post all through the journey, and on account of being in that seat, I met with a good deal of excitement and trouble, as you'll soon see.

My idea was to keep my mouth shut and watch other people, and so try to pick up the ways and customs of the community. But it wasn't a community or members of a community that I found on the stage. There was a Pittsburgher, and an Alabaman with a hat a yard across and a self-conscious air of gentility, a Chicagoan who was always gritting his teeth and looking at the future, and the woman with the three children who came from Maine.

She was going out to join a brother. We all used to pity that poor brother. But people from the State of Maine are like that. They follow duty to the bottom of the sea or clear up above timber line. There were a couple of others in the complement of that company, but I forget who they were. None of them was really out of the West,

33

but all of us would become good Westerners in the course of a few years, or else get our fingers burned and depart for the less strenuous East.

The most typical Westerner I ever knew was a Texan from Philadelphia. Westerners are made, they are not born. I've seen a man fit into the wildest West in three days, if he was the right sort. Or, again, he might not do it in thirty.

At this time railroads were pushing through the mountains rather blindly, thrusting out side lines and spur branches. Towns sprang up, disappeared into dust, or else became enduring cities. But for every one that succeeded, I think, there were two or three that failed. It was a period of wildcatting in town building. You picked out a patch of desert and paid ten dollars a square mile for it, and you tried to cut up that square mile and sell it in batches of building lots. The profits were practically limitless, if the deal went through and enough curious home makers and fortune seekers drifted that way.

Piegan, the goal of my journey, had just been put on the map and was the brain child of one Colonel Riggs, celebrated as a promoter of new cities. On the trip I heard a great deal of speculation as to the richness of the soil, the possibility of irrigation, the presence of valuable minerals in the hills around Piegan. But I was not much interested. What continued to occupy my mind was simply the fact that the place was four days from the railroad.

The first two days were hard ones on me. The road we traveled over was called a highway only by courtesy. It was a cattle trail, most of the distance, marked out with skeletons in gruesome style, a dotted chalk mark through the mountains. Only the matchless poise and spring of a Concord coach could have supported us over the rough spots with less than broken backs. The woman and all three of her children were seasick, those first two days, which didn't help the rest of us. And the pitching motion of the vehicle exhausted me so much that when we reached the sleeping quarters at night, I dropped in my tracks, without waiting for food.

However, by watching the way the driver handled himself, I learned the easiest ways of accommodating myself to the heavy laboring of the stage, and the third day I was feeling much better, when we changed drivers for a wild man, a regular fiend who loved to throw a chill into every one of his passengers.

He was a good hand with the reins. He knew how to use his brakes, too, which was an art in itself, and he understood every inch of that rough road. However, he was always forcing the team. Every time he came to a long up grade, he settled back with a growl of resignation; every time he saw the beginning of a down pitch, his eye gleamed, and he sent the team down in a mad rush while the people in the body of the coach hung on for dear life and the children screamed with fright.

I wondered why some of our rough-looking passengers didn't take a hand in the business and tell the driver what was what, but though the men grew more and more stark of expression, more and more grim of face, not a syllable was spoken directly to the driver. When he was overlooking the change of horses, I heard some pretty dire threats, but when he returned, nothing was said.

They all held back, I suppose, for the same reason that I myself said nothing. I was frankly afraid of that man. He was six feet and something, rawboned, but with a neck like a bull's. He carried a revolver with the air of one who knows how to use it, and his eye was as wild and as red as a heat-maddened steer's. He always looked as if he were about to break into a stampede, and like a stampede he drove the relays of horses.

He was to take the stage in the final two days of the trip. I knew that, so I locked my teeth and prepared to endure.

That third day my heart jumped up into my throat more than once, but still I managed to steady my nerves and got through with it fairly well. The fourth day was the worst of all.

We were climbing most of the time, and then the suffering horses were allowed to go along at a walk. When the down stretches came, however, they were frightfully steep, and that madman of a driver, with a yell and a slashing of the long whip, sent the horses racing at full speed. We whacked over rocks that threatened to smash our wheels. We skidded far out on curves and, heeling over, we could look dizzily down into great gorges.

I began to think that the driver was actually insane; perhaps he was, as a matter of fact.

I was almost glad when, as we reached the bottom of a hollow, lurched up the farther slope, and then came down to a walk, a rifle clanged from the brush ahead of us, and a masked man stepped out, the rifle still at his shoulder.

Two more voices, over on our left, yelled at the same moment for the stage to halt and the passengers to shove up their hands.

I did some split-second thinking. If we were robbed, a complete description of each of us would get into the papers. And that was what I did not want to have happen. I saw the driver throw on his brakes with a thrust of his foot and at the same time jerk up a sawed-off shotgun that leaned against the seat.

He never fired that gun. A rifle bullet cut through his arm as he raised the weapon and the riot gun dropped down to the road and went off with a roar.

In the meantime, the woman and the three youngsters were screeching like fiends, and it seemed to me that the noise was like a smoke screen that might cover me. As the driver dropped his shotgun, I got out my Colt and tried a snap shot at the fellow who was holding the horses.

He dropped in the road with a shout and started crawling for the brush, while the driver released the brakes and yelled to the horses. We swayed forward, the woman screaming that we must stop or we would all be murdered. But there was no stopping that big brute of a driver. He was standing up in the seat, letting the reins hang, his wounded arm dangling, the blood running down his side, but he had his Colt out, and held it poised, shoulder-high, cursing, swaying as the coach pitched, but always probing the bushes for the other bandits.

It seemed certain to me that they would open fire on us. But perhaps the heart went out of them when they realized that we were moving off and that, though they might murder some of us, they could hardly stop the rest.

We got to the pitch of the grade and went down the farther side. At the next hollow we stopped, and there the shirt of the driver was cut away and his wound was bathed and bandaged by two of the men. It was not a deep wound. But it stiffened his arm, and after that he went on more slowly, with such a blessed calm, in fact, that I wished the robbers had appeared the day before!

There was a good deal of talk, as a matter of course. The lot of us who had detested the driver before were now ready to call him a hero. In addition, we made up a purse among the lot of us, to reward him for his courage and to pay him for the time he would have to lay off from work. We gave him the purse, which amounted to two hundred dollars, just before we sighted Piegan from the top of the hills.

He made a speech, saying if it hadn't been for the dropping of the rifleman, we would all have been robbed of everything that we stood up in and he remarked that the pistol work I had done was worthy of an expert. He said quite a lot on that subject, and the rest of the passengers began to look on me with a great respect.

I was the only one who knew how lucky that snap shot had been!

CHAPTER VII

The Town of Piegan

PIEGAN lay out on a wide flat; that is to say, the upper surface was all about of a height, but the plateau was cut up with a lot of dry-bottomed draws and a few gorges cut by creeks. That bit of the flat was spotted with sagebrush. As I looked down on it for the first time that day, I saw a whirlwind pick up a cloud of dust and go swaying off with it to invisibility.

It wasn't the most cheerful prospect in the world. We could see the houses, the false fronts of the stores along the main street, and the shining raw wood which was being used for the frames and the boardings of the houses which were under construction.

I remember that the man from Chicago said, quietly, but with a grimness that made me listen: "Well, I might have guessed! It's just another——"

He didn't complete the sentence. He didn't have to. It was clear enough that he considered Piegan no good!

The rest of us seemed to feel the same way, but the driver, who had adopted a rather fatherly attitude to us since he became a hero, told us that the place was a lot better than it looked, that water could be put on that flat and make it bloom, and that some day a fortune would be ripped out of the mountains in the shape of gold and silver. He said that he had three lots in Piegan and that he intended to buy more.

This made us all feel a lot better, and we rolled on down into Piegan with more cheerful looks.

From the inside, the town looked bigger than from the hills. There were a few good stores and an ambitious hotel, which was all that Colonel Riggs had contributed to the town and all that he ever would contribute. There were some fairish houses, a lot of shacks and tents.

Riggs had put the place on the map for the moment but, of course, everything was very rough. The streets were staked out but they were not made. The wheels ripped and pounded them, and the wind cleaned out the ruts here and filled them in there. The stage went into that town like a small boat riding on big waves.

The last stop was the hotel. You could depend on Riggs to arrange that. His hotels were always the stage stations, as well.

He came out and turned himself into a reception committee. He was a tall man with shoulders so humped that his coat was pulled up above the seat of his trousers. He had a hollow chest, a large stomach, and long legs, a little bent in at the knees, like the legs of a stork. They gave him a look of possible agility, in spite of his size above the hips. He had a sallow face with the wrinkles that fit a smile well developed, and he had a sandy mustache, pretty well yellowed up with cigar stains and with a part nearly half an inch wide in the middle of his lip.

He looked kindly and simple, like somebody's grandpa, but the way he managed to shake hands with everybody at the same time and was particularly glad to see everybody told me something.

I got myself a fairish sort of room that looked out over the post office and the future location for the city hall, as the sign on the vacant lot informed me. The same sign declared that all of that land had been donated to the community free of charge by the liberality of Colonel Riggs. I had no doubt that the sign had been painted by order of Colonel Riggs, too. I stood in front of my window, reading the sign, listening to the wind hiss at me through the cracks in the wall, and wondering a good deal about my future.

It wasn't the police that crowded my mind, just then. The bigness of those mountains in the distance and the darkness of the forests that covered them told me that I had bored my way into the heart of the wilderness, where the law would not penetrate for a long time. I forgot that a single detective might have picked up my trail.

What bothered me most was that I was flat. My wanderings had cost me a good deal. A crook on the fly can't bargain or ask questions. He has to eat and pay on the run, and those prices are always the highest. I had dribbled a little streak of gold and silver right across the map, and all that was left to me of the stuff was sixty-two dollars.

Well, I had to do a good deal of thinking, when I considered how little that was. Just down the street I could see a restaurant with a menu in front of it. The names of the foods were written big, and the prices were written small, but I made out that steak cost a dollar and a half!

There was nothing for me but to locate work. Yet what work could I do?

Well, I could handle a pack of cards with the next one, but honest cards only pay when you carry a big bank roll, and my promise to Betty Cole barred crooked cards.

Dice, gambling of all kinds, in fact, had been ruled out in the same manner. And I wanted to curse myself for a fool. Besides, I had a sick feeling that I would break my promise before very long. I wanted to go straight, but in this part of the world men made money digging in mines, or with other kinds of manual labor. Outside of that— well, I might be a clerk in a store, or a cook in a restaurant, or wash dishes.

Why should I have turned up my nose?

I don't know. But I never had worked really, except in the gymnasium, training for a fight, and that's harder than other work, but different. Every time you poke the bag, you figure that you're soaking the other pug in the stomach, and it makes the day pass pretty quick.

Logically I saw that it was crooked work, manual labor, clerking, or starvation.

40

Crooked work I wouldn't do.

Manual labor I couldn't do.

Clerking I despised from the bottom of my soul, but it would have to be that or starving.

I should have gone searching for a job at once, but I decided that I would wait a while and see how fast the forelock of Opportunity grew in this neck of the woods.

Then I went down to the dining room of the hotel and laid in a good feed.

I had fried venison, corn bread, hominy, boiled cabbage, apple pie—dried apples—and coffee, for two dollars and a half, including the tip. That meal made my stock of coin seem much smaller.

I went out to the sidewalk. A blinding, stifling gust of wind and dust hit me and smothered me. I was ready to damn Piegan, all its ways and days.

There's nothing like a high wind to fray the nerves of a man, and mine were pretty badly worn, I can tell you. I was wiping the grit out of my eyes, my back turned to the wind, when a boy came out and tagged me on the arm and said that the colonel wanted to see me. He hooked a thumb toward the hotel.

I was in no mood to see the colonel, but I went in. At the door I stopped a minute and got myself in hand. A burst of bad temper was almost as bad, for my rickety heart, as a run uphill, I smoothed myself down and then followed the boy to the office of Colonel Riggs.

The door opened on him as if on a stage set. He was behind the biggest desk that I ever saw. There were stacks of papers on it. Some of the drawers were open and they were filled, too. He had maps on his walls of Piegan and of what it was going to be. He had filing cabinets in that office, too, and he looked to me like the busiest man in the world. He was writing in a rapid, flowing hand, and his head was cocked to one side, as he looked fondly down at the words he was making. I imagine that a poet must look very much like that when he's scribbling down some windy idea.

When he saw me, Colonel Riggs looked up, nodded, finished his sentence, then pulled the spectacles from his nose and came around from behind his desk to shake hands. His smile was perfect. It was stamped as in steel. It couldn't change.

"Your name is Gann, is it?" said he.

That was the moniker I had chosen, so I told him that he was right.

"I'm glad to know it," says the colonel. "But I wanted to tell you that there's another man in town who would be mighty interested in you if your name were Poker-face Jerry Ash."

I looked at the colonel and smiled. You know, I didn't feel like smiling, but I had had to practice control of emotions so long and so hard that it was difficult to give me a shock. What Riggs said went through me like a stiletto, a small flick of the wound almost deep enough to kill, but I managed to keep my smile steady enough.

"Glad to know anybody would be interested in Jerry Ash," said I. I looked at him, and he looked straight back at me. The grin faded from his face. He looked tired, old, and mighty serious.

"Step to the window there and look across the street to the opposite corner, just in front of the city hall sign," said Colonel Riggs.

I did what he suggested, and there I saw a bulldog of a man with a cigar clamped between his teeth and his hands locked behind his back.

"Is that the fellow who wants to see Poker-face Jerry Ash?" said I.

"I thought that you might recognize him," said the colonel.

I turned around sharp on him.

"Why did you tip his hand to me?" I asked.

"Tip his hand?" said the colonel blandly. "I didn't tip his hand. He simply asked a question of me, and I asked the same question of you. That's all."

"It's more than that," I assured him. "Did he tell you why he wanted me?"

Colonel Riggs put on his glasses, studied me, and took them off again, nodding as though the lenses had shown

42

him something of importance. He began to smile again on me.

"He told me," said the colonel, "that some of the finest detectives in the world had been on your trail, and that you had given them nothing but six thousand miles of trouble. They hadn't even laid a hand or a bullet on you. Is that right? No, don't answer. I can see in your face it's correct. And I'll tell you another thing. If that stage had been loaded with gold, it wouldn't have been so welcome to me and to Piegan!"

"Well, that's fine," said I. "But what am I to do for Piegan? Pave the streets?"

"Sit down," said the colonel.

"I'd rather stand over here," said I. "I can keep my eye on that flatty on the corner, from this place. Who's he got with him?"

"Ah," said the colonel, "you knew that no one man would ever be sent out after you. You knew that, my lad, of course!"

"Stuff," said I. "There are plenty who could handle me, easily enough. But they usually play safe. What does the side kicker of this dick look like?"

"He's a sad-appearing fellow," said the colonel. "He is a trifle bent and he has a thin blond mustache."

"Yeah, I've seen that ferret before," said I. "But that fellow on the corner, he's a new one. They must have picked him up along the way. He looks like business."

"He says that there is four thousand dollars' worth of business in you, Mr.—Gann," said the colonel.

"We'll drop the Gann business," I answered. "If I'm known at all, I might as well wear the correct moniker. Now, colonel, suppose you cut the corners and come right across and tell me what I'm to do for you, and you for me?"

"You could see at once that I liked you," said the colonel. "Of course you could see that and that I was not able to believe the cock-and-bull story that the detectives told me. I knew what police persecution can be!"

"What did they tell you?"

"They told me—oh, a great many things—about a retired prize fighter, a gunman, a gambler, and a safe cracker."

He paused and laughed.

"In the first place, you haven't the look," he said. "In the second place, you're too young to have done all of those things."

"The safe cracking—that's out," said I. "I might have the will, but I haven't the way. Now you tell me—what do we do for each other? You haven't called me in here just to pass the time of day, I suppose?"

He nodded. His smile went out. He looked older and grayer than ever, and his eye caught mine, held on it, and fixed it still and steady.

"You came to Piegan to stay here for a while?" he said.

"Yes. A while."

"And the first thing you want is to have that pair of dicks slipped off your trail?"

"That would be a help," I admitted.

"I'll have them out of town before three hours are over," declared the colonel.

I looked at him with new eyes.

"How'll you manage that?" I asked him.

"Life is full of struggles, Jerry," said that old crook, "and one cannot fight one's way through it without learning to use diplomacy, and diplomacy, and more diplomacy. You understand how it may be?"

"Yeah, I understand how it may be," said I.

"A touch of strategy," said he, "may be more powerful than the stroke of a sledge hammer, and there are certain ways and devices I may be able to use to persuade our two detective friends to leave the town for the time being —perhaps never to return to it again!"

"All right," said I, "you strategize as much as you want to. The idea pleases me pretty well."

"And now for the other side of the question," said he.

"Let's have the other side," I answered.

"You can make a good living in this town, Jerry," remarked the colonel. "I can open up certain safe avenues —I can show you where to play cards; you might even open up a saloon in a small way—"

I broke in: "Yes, and you might tell me which fellows have the safes that are worth cracking, and where the fattest rolls of bills are carried, but it wouldn't do me any good, Colonel Riggs."

"Why not?" he barked at me.

"Why not? Because I've turned straight."

"Ah!" murmured Riggs. "Is that so? Good lad! Good lad! I'm delighted to hear this. You've turned straight. I don't know, of course, that you've ever been very crooked, but one honest man is worth more to me than twenty crooks."

I shrugged my shoulders. I wondered what the old hypocrite was driving at. At any rate, he would be worth his weight in gold to me, if he could slip that pair of bulls off my trail.

"Go on, Colonel Riggs," I begged him. "Let me know how the deal might stand."

"Certainly," said he.

He was sitting on the edge of his desk and now he leaned forward and began to slap his right hand into his left palm, making point after point in little, short sentences. It was a sort of selling speech. He might have been out to collect votes with it.

"As sure as my name is Alfred Riggs, I've made this town.

"I found it a prairie and I've made it a town.

"I'll make it a city, if they'll leave me alone.

"But they won't leave me alone.

"I've invested capital, time, imagination, effort.

"I've advertised this place. I've written hundreds and even thousands of columns of copy that have appeared in the Eastern newspapers, and nearly every day I get letters which I answer—my bill for postage and correspondence paper alone is—but let that go! After what I've done, you'd think that the people might be generous enough to offer me gratitude, not to say congratulations?"

I nodded. There was no point in asking questions. He would say everything that was on his mind.

"But not they," he went on bitterly. "No gratitude.

"But envy!

"Suspicion!

"Malice!

"Actual hate—actual hate for one of the best-tempered men—if I say it myself!—that ever stepped upon the face of this earth!

"And further than that, what do you think?"

I told him that I could not guess; it seemed that he had said about all that a man could.

"I haven't mentioned the real danger to my life!" said he, lowering his voice and looking around cautiously at the window and then at the door. "But I live in such a danger, Jerry!"

"That's too bad," said I.

I sat down on the arm of a chair, guessing that this little yarn would not end right away.

"Men acquire a certain character, do they not?" said he.

"Yes," I answered.

"So do towns," he went on. "And the character of Makerville, our rival for county seat in this county, is that of a villain. As the town, so are the people in it. There are scores of Makerites who would pay thousands of dollars to see me dead! They would raid our honest town at any time of the night or the day. Their daily paper abuses us. The foulest language is piled upon my head, and I walk in daily danger of my life!"

He paused and drew a long breath. Then he looked rather wistfully at me.

"Go on," I remarked. "Say it, colonel."

He literally writhed in his chair, staring at me. He did not know how far he could go, and I was in no hurry to tell him, of course. I began to guess that the colonel was as thorough a rascal as one could find in a day's walk, outside of a jail. But there was something about him that amused me, too.

"Son," he said to me at last, when he had made up his mind to talk to the bottom of things, "I would pay a thousand dollars to see Sidney Maker of Makerville in this office—right in this office!"

I nodded.

"He's your big rival, is he?" said I.

46

"The scoundrel!" exclaimed Alfred Riggs. "He would murder me in a minute. And now that the election draws on, and the voting for the selection of a town for county seat is about to begin—why, Mr. Ash, there are no limits to which he wouldn't go. Bribery, corruption, every method of cramming the ballot boxes—nothing is beneath that—that—" The colonel had a large vocabulary, packed with just what he wanted, but for a moment, he hunted through the list vainly, trying to find the word proper to hitch to the name of Sidney Maker, of Makerville.

"You want me to do him in," said I, "but I won't. I'm not going crooked, colonel."

He drew in a great breath.

"Look!" said he.

He snatched open a drawer of his desk and threw a paper before me. There was a big scrawling handwriting that covered it. It ran:

DEAR COLONEL RIGGS:

I have just been offered twenty-five hundred dollars by Sidney Maker for putting you out of the way—or clear off the map.

What are your terms?

Yours as ever,

J. J.

"Why not hire J. J., colonel?" I asked, giving him back the paper.

"For three or four thousand, the villain?" exclaimed Riggs. "No, never! But to a man who is decently reliable, I would pay something like a thousand—"

"For Maker delivered into this office?" I asked him.

"Well, that's it." He nodded.

"What makes you think that I could turn such a trick?" I queried, looking curiously at him. "I'm no great hand. And I'm new to this country."

He shook his head.

"The driver told me all about the way you put the slug through that outlaw. He said that he never saw a cooler piece of business. Besides, there's something unmoved and calm about you that suggests that you can do what you wish to do!"

I could have laughed in his face, when I remember that it was my practice in schooling my nerves for the sake of my rotten, crumbling, shattered heart that had given me this calm exterior. But I merely said:

"Well, I wouldn't be any cheaper than J. J. I'll try the thing for twenty-five hundred."

"What?" he shouted. "Twenty-five hundred dollars? And after I've driven the bulls off your trail and—"

"Otherwise I'd want five thousand," said I.

He turned gray, literally, at the thought of spending so much money. He sprang up and stamped down his foot. Then he uttered a sigh that was almost a groan, and I knew that he was in my pocket.

CHAPTER VIII

The Road to Makerville

THAT evening, I sat up in my room and wrote a letter to Betty Cole in New York. It was the third I had sent to her since I left her there at the garden gate.

I told her everything that had happened, and I put my conscience to her like this:

What would you call it?

I'm going out to get a man, kidnap him, and bring him into this town of Piegan, if I can. It's illegal. But the same

48

fellow is trying to have my boss murdered. I'll be jailed, or worse, if I'm caught. But I don't feel that I'm going crooked. I don't think you would, either, if you knew the state this town is in. The people expect the Makerites to rush their place at any time and set fire to it, sweep it out of existence, and butcher the inhabitants. They're red-hot to become the county seat, which means that the county would spend a lot of money here putting up buildings. They're so hot to get the buildings erected that murder is in the air.

Well, I'm going to try to get Mr. Maker here until the county election is over. That will give my side the main and upper hand in stuffing the election boxes with ballots all over the county. When the thing is over, I'm going to try to get Maker safely away again. That I haven't told to Colonel Riggs.

Perhaps you'll say that I'm a black sheep. Perhaps I am. Anyway, I was tired of running. I don't know what other work I could do. So I'm tackling this.

This is a country you would like. It has a lot of raw edges, but it has size, and I gather that you'd like size. I'm not strong enough to do this country justice, but maybe you would!

When I finished writing that letter, I went downstairs to post it and asked the colonel if the coast was clear. He said that he had cleared it for me and that the detectives were both out of town traveling as hard as they could along a false scent with which he had provided them. Riggs seemed cheerful, but nervous, and he asked me when I wanted to make my move, and how many men and what equipment I would want to have. I asked the distance to Makerville, and when he said that it was only twenty miles, with a fairish sort of a road in between, I said that I would go that same night.

As for equipment, I wanted a good, fast team of horses, and another team to lead behind—they could draw the buggy on the trip back. I wanted a man to drive, and a man to look after the led horses. Both of them ought to be armed with rifles and revolvers. Otherwise, I wanted nothing.

Riggs seemed taken aback by the readiness with which I proposed to start and he asked me with a great deal of eagerness what plans I had made. I told him that I had made no plans at all, as yet, but that I wanted to see a plan of Makerville.

I mailed the letter, and then he took me back into his office and raked out a map of the rival city. It was a huge roll of paper that he hung on the wall. Most of the space was covered with red outlines. They were to represent the dreams of what the city ought to be. The actual facts about the buildings that already had been put up were delineated in black, and there was not more than a handful of black in the midst of that acre of red.

"Why, colonel," I said, "it seems to be a city on the same scale as Piegan, eh?"

He turned his head rather slowly from regarding the map and he eyed me steadily, with just a suspicion of a twinkle coming into his eyes.

"I don't know what you mean by that, Jerry," said he.

"I didn't think that you would," said I.

We both grinned openly. It made us feel a lot more at ease with one another.

Then we studied the map out with a lot of care. He showed me where Maker Creek cut through the center of town, and where the bridge spanned it, and the main stem of the place, and the house which Sid Maker himself lived in, a little out from the rest of the village.

"That's better," I said. "Not so many people in earshot —if there should be a fuss."

"Not so many people? He lives surrounded with people!" said Colonel Riggs. "Confound him, if it hadn't been for that—"

He stopped himself short and cleared his throat in a good deal of confusion. I could only infer that if Maker had not surrounded himself with a bodyguard of friends, Colonel Riggs would have cut him off long before this.

The game they played in that part of the world in those days was as hard as you please to think it.

Now that I had the town of Makerville firmly in mind, I sat down and drew off a sketch of it from memory, compared it with the original, saw the mistakes that I had made, drew it again, and then again. At last I was very nearly letter-perfect. I needed to be, because I would not only be working in a strange place, but also in the dark.

Before I finished, the colonel came back, looking very pleased with himself. He said that he had two men who were made to order for work like this. They would be at my disposal the moment I wanted them. He also had a good, strong buckboard; one of the two hired hands was greasing the wheels. And there would be four horses as tough as shoe leather. They would gallop all the way to Makerville and back, if need were.

In finishing, he pointed out that it was already after sundown!

Yes, he was as keen as a ferret that I should start the work at once, and I could hardly keep from laughing as I saw him striding about the office on his long, cranelike legs. However, there was plenty to crowd the laughter back in my throat, when I thought forward to the job that lay ahead.

Then the colonel took me out the back door of the hotel and across a vacant lot. There, waiting in a lane inches deep with dust, was the outfit—a two-seated buckboard, a span hitched to it, and another pair on a lead behind. The men who waited with the rig were humped over, looking no more human than shapeless sacks in that dim light.

Riggs made me acquainted with "Slim Jim" Earl, on the driver's seat, and Dan Loftus, handling the led horses. We shook hands all around. The colonel wanted to put in a big bottle of whisky, but I made him take it back with him. We said good-by, I stepped into the rig, and off we went, swishing through the dust. It was exactly nine o'clock.

Daylight had ended long ago, but every star was out in a pure sky, and the loom of the trail was distinct enough before us. One could always tell the difference in color between the dust of its surface and the darker ground around us. But we could not see well enough to dodge ruts and bumps.

I never had such a rough ride in my life. It fairly jolted and hammered the life out of me, especially during the first miles. For Slim Jim Earl wanted to distinguish himself immediately and show how careless he was and what a breakneck driver. Finally I had to tell him to pull up, and that he was the bravest driver in the world, but that I was not the bravest passenger.

He grunted when I said that, but he managed to control his disgust.

After that, we went along at a more moderate gait, but that road was the work of the devil. Rather, it was not work at all—it was simply an accident that happened to connect the two towns of Makerville and Piegan. It dipped into hollows, climbed to rises, staggered along bumpy levels, and swayed down again into abysmal depths which often had a cold, ominous glint of starlit water in them. Once we crossed running water so deep that it almost touched the body of the wagon.

No matter with what caution we navigated that road, the straining and the bumping began to tire me terribly. We went along, I should say, at about seven miles an hour; it would be after midnight before we arrived, even maintaining a steady pace. But I had to stop the buckboard twice and walk ahead of it. A pinch was coming in my side, threatening to double me up.

When we came in sight of the glimmer of lights in Makerville, I pulled up the buckboard again, wrapped up in a blanket, and lay down on the bottom of the wagon. They wanted to know what was the matter, and I said that we were too early for the execution of my plan. That was not true. I simply had to get the kinks out of me and stop the pattering downfall of my heartbeats. So I lay there and looked at the stars, and went to sleep.

When I wakened, it was more than an hour later—just one-thirty, to be exact—and I was cold and stiff. But the heart was behaving now, for the first time in hours, and I cared little about anything else.

My two companions were disgusted. They would hardly

answer when I spoke to them. They had sat up, shivering, all the time that I lay snug in the blanket. And it was a cold night. The wind was not strong, but it was nicely iced by the mountain snows over which it had blown.

They asked me what share they were to take in what was about to happen, and I told them that they were simply to wait where I wanted them. Where I wanted them was a good deal closer in. It was across the bridge, and bang up close to the house of the creator of Makerville.

"They may be watching that bridge," said Slim Jim, as we came closer to it.

But there was no light showing, and I thought that we might be able to chance it. So we drove straight onto it. The sound grew more and more hollow beneath the hoofs of the horses; the heavy planks that made the bridge surface began to rattle like castanets at the sides.

When we got to the top of the arch, I could see the glimmer of the water up and downstream, and two or three lights gleaming on it. A moment later, three men stepped out and covered us with double-barreled shotguns.

Yes, we put up our hands.

A man can take a chance with a revolver, and half a chance with a rifle. But shotguns are poison, at close range, and these were close. One fellow stood at the heads of the horses. The others were on each side of us.

"Where's Doc, with the lantern?" one of the trio asked, and another said that "Doc" was coming at once.

We could see him running toward us, his shadow swinging crazily between heaven and earth, with the lantern flashing beside him.

"This is an outrage," Slim Jim Earl was saying.

"Maybe it is, boys," said one of the three. "We ain't here to please ourselves, but to please Mr. Maker. It may be an outrage, but we ain't taking any chances. After all, it ain't a long cry from here to Makerville, is it?"

The lantern bearer came up and flashed the light in our faces.

"By thunder!" he cried out. "These are Piegan men! I recognize that one! He's Slim Jim Earl, one of Riggs's crooks!"

CHAPTER IX

Men of Makerville

AS you can tell electricity by the shock and the thrust of it, so you could tell by the sound of those fellows' growling that they meant trouble and big trouble for the three of us. I sat numbed and sick in my place, and my heart began to race like a stone bounding downhill, rattling and crashing. That was the thing that I had to think of first.

The four guards of the bridge had their guns under our noses. And Slim Jim Earl seemed to give up the fight, for he said:

"Well, I'm from Piegan, and that's a fact. What of it?"

One of the Makerites fairly shouted with rough laughter.

"He says what about it, but we'll show him what about it!" he declared. "We'll show him pronto. If they ain't ropes in Piegan, they maybe think that we ain't got 'em in Makerville. Who is these other two?"

The lantern was thrust in the face of Dan Loftus.

"I know that fellow, too," said one. "That's Loftus, and he's from Piegan, too. The whole three of 'em are from Piegan. Get them out of that rig. I dunno that we'll find a tree handier than the arch of this here bridge."

"D'you mean that you'll hang us for doing nothing but drive into your town?" roared Dan Loftus.

"Doing nothing?" said the lantern bearer, a big man,

who seemed to be the chief spirit among them all. "Living in Piegan is doing something. I'd rather see a man from the pen than from Piegan. A lot of worthless crooks you all are. And who's this one?"

He flashed the lantern on me, his face all viciously set to jeer. It wasn't an easy moment. I was walking on tiptoe, as you might say, along the edge of a cliff high enough to put the life out of all three of us. They meant murder, right enough.

Well, when I had the glare of the lantern in my face, I had to think fast and reach far for my words, and the only name or word or idea that came to me was what I blurted out:

"Maker! That's who I want to see."

The lantern bearer turned, like the brute and fool that he was, to one of his companions, with that same loud, bawling laugh.

"He wants to see Maker, he says. He'll see Maker, all right!"

"Yeah, we'll show him to Maker, and Maker to him," said another of the guards, and they laughed again, as though they were great wits.

I saw Slim Jim turn his head and look at me. His eyes rolled, and the whites of them were glistening. I never saw a man in greater fear.

"Look what you've brought us into!" he snapped at me, with a whine of high terror in his voice.

"You done the bringing, did you?" said the man of the lantern, jeering at me again. "We'll do the taking, though!"

"Is there any one here with half his wits about him?" I asked, looking around past their leader.

"Hey!" he shouted at me. "I don't suit you, eh?"

I still had my hands in the air and knew that I dared not lower them. But I was thinking of all sorts of chances —I might crash my fists down into his face and jump for the rail of the bridge and so dive over for the water beneath. Though probably the water was shallow enough to let me break my head on the bottom.

"You don't suit me," I said to him. "Or has Maker nothing but fools working for him? He talked sensibly enough when he told me to bring these two boys over from Piegan."

The man of the lantern was hot as a coal, when he heard me talk like this. He swung back his fist and seemed about to slam me with it, when something stopped him and kept him wavering for an instant, poised on the blow.

"He told you to bring them here?"

"Yes," said I.

"Sid Maker told you?"

I pretended to lose my temper.

"I've told you that before, you jackass," said I. "How many times do I have to repeat it? Why else should I be here with the pair of them if Maker hadn't promised me a good fat split, and pay for both the boys, if I brought them in?"

The man of the lantern lowered his fist. And at the same time I lowered my hands—but slowly. The guards hardly seemed to notice what I had done with my hands, they were so troubled by what I had just said to them.

Jim Earl looked at me again, but this time there was a wild hope mingled with the fear in his rolling eye. I was beginning to do a little hoping myself.

"What would he want you to bring them in for?" asked the leader of the guards, scowling at me.

"Go and ask him," I snapped back, sharp and quick. "You know most of his business, it seems, and so you might as well know that, too. Take us along to Sid Maker. He's the man that I have to see to-night—unless I'm hanged by fools on the way. Take us on to Sid Maker."

"What would Maker want men from Piegan for?" said the lantern bearer, growling out the words to one of the others.

"I dunno," said his companion. "I dunno what he would want with anybody out of Piegan."

"You know everything about Piegan, do you?" I broke in.

"I know enough about Piegan. I don't wanta know any more," said the fellow.

"Well," said I, "Sid Maker doesn't feel that way. He finds it hard to learn too much about Piegan. He wants to learn and to keep right on learning. That's his way. That's what he willing to pay hard cash for. Take us on to Maker, will you?"

"I dunno," said the lantern bearer. "I never thought of that. I never thought that they might be deserters, coming over to our side. I wouldn't blame anybody for leaving Piegan and coming over to our side."

"Scotch Malmsby came over last week, just this way," said another of the men.

That recollection seemed to make up their minds for them all.

The lantern bearer turned back on me and shrugged his shoulders.

"I dunno," said he, "but I guess that you're all right. I'd like to knock the loose jaw off of your face, and I guess that I'll do in for you, the next time that we meet—but you can go through, to-night."

"Come along with us," said I. "I want you to come along."

"Why do you want me to come along?" he asked.

"I want Sid Maker to see the sort of fools he has working for him," said I.

The man swelled like a pouter pigeon.

"I'm going to slam you right now. I ain't going to wait!" he snarled and made a step at me.

I let him come right up close and laughed in his face. I knew that he didn't have the nerve to hit what he thought was one of his boss's men. And I was right.

"Go on and slam me," said I. "Sid Maker won't believe what I've got to tell him, unless I've got your signature on me. But if I can show him that, he'll have your hide instead of pigskin and cover saddles with it. It's thick enough for that, I guess."

He went into another convulsion, but, stepping back, he ordered us to drive on. He said that he would fill us full of buckshot if we remained there another moment.

Well, I badgered him a little longer, and invited any of them to come with us, but they declined the job, with thanks. They had enough of our company, it seemed, and finally Slim Jim Earl started the mustangs up, and we went walking, and then jogging across the bridge.

When there was enough night and rumbling behind us to shut us completely away from the guards, Earl gave a little yell of triumph, and Dan Loftus joined him in cheering.

They seemed pretty pleased with the way that I had handled the thing, and I thought, myself, that I had been fairly smart about it. However, the truth was simply that a chance bluff had worked. Slim Jim wouldn't have it so. I couldn't tell him that his own words had popped into my mind the proper answer to the guards.

Slim Jim said that he was ready to follow on any trail in the world, no matter where it led. He said that he had been close to trouble before, but this night he had been so close to hanging that he could feel a kink in his neck.

And Dan Loftus said that he could agree to all that and that he had felt the scratching of the rope and the pressure of the knot under his ear.

I laughed a little as I heard them talking. It made me feel prouder, and I was warm all through to think of the way we had driven straight through that bridge guard.

But I didn't laugh very long. There were too many things before us and behind us now. For one thing, there was the necessity of getting back across that creek, if we were to return. And across the bridge we could not go. That was settled!

I thought the thing over and wished that I had made inquiries about the state of the creek's bank. We drove the buckboard down the side of the water until we found a place where the two shores were shelving and the water spread out so wide that it was almost sure to be a sound ford.

We would have to unhitch the horses from the rig and have them in readiness to use as riding mounts, on that return trip.

Both Slim Jim and Loftus groaned at the thought of this. Those mustangs were meant for driving, anyway. They were not intended to be riding horses, both of my companions said. So I had them unhitched, and bareback they rode the four.

I thanked my luck that only one of the four bucked, and even that mustang seemed to do it rather from excess of spirit than any real intention of getting its rider off.

Then I turned my mind straight toward the business of the evening.

CHAPTER X

Sidney Maker

SO I left the two Piegan men there with the horses and started off for the house of Sidney Maker. Now that I look back on it, I wonder at the folly of the thing—I mean, hitting off there through the dark like that, with no real plan, but just aiming blindly to get near to my man and then trust to luck. However, that was what I did.

Earl and Loftus, I remember, asked me what I had in my mind, and I told them, with a lofty air, that it would turn out all right and that talk would do no good.

That was true, because there were no ideas in my mind. Not a one. Well, I went on, and found the main road, and it wasn't hard, in the clearness of that starlight, to locate the lane that turned off to the Maker house. One could see it from a distance, bulking big and black against the glow of the white stars. Maker had picked out a large hill and crowned it with his house.

When I got up close to it, I found a large gate—two big stone pillars, rather, with the gates to be fitted in later on, I suppose. Inside of that there was a graveled drive, and I avoided that. There's nothing that makes such noises underfoot as gravel. So I skirted that, and when I came up under the house, I saw that it was a big two-story affair, with not a light in the front. The windows were as dark as the eyes in the skull of a death's-head.

That was not so very cheerful.

I went around to the side of the place. That was all black, too. I had brought along a dark lantern, and now I saw that I would have to get into the place and hunt from room to room, with a ray of light to pick out the sleeping face of Sid Maker.

Nothing to make one jolly, that idea!

However, I didn't shudder. You see, whatever I was doing, I had to keep telling myself that the most important thing was to keep my heart steady and quiet. Once it began rioting, I was done for, and might have to lie on the ground for an hour until it grew quiet once more. So I kept myself calm, and turned the corner to the back of the house.

There I saw a broad funnel of light striking out of a window and showing up a couple of patches of sagebrush and the dark of some trees beyond it. Sid Maker was apparently making a garden. I saw the winding of a couple of paths. The garden was chiefly blow sand and hope, but you could tell that it was a garden that he had in mind.

I tried to remember all the details that I had heard of him, but I stopped with the one sentence that everybody had repeated to me, without fail. He was like a bulldog. That was the main thing. A man who looked like a bulldog and *was* a bulldog. That was all. I couldn't fail to know him!

I tried to conjure up in my mind a picture of a bulldog's face, but I couldn't find anything essentially human in that. I had asked for a picture, but nobody had any photos of Sidney Maker.

I paused at the corner of the house, thinking this over,

and I was about to step toward the window from which the light came, when a smudge fell over my eyes. It was the dull shade cast by a great hulk of a man with a rifle in his hands. He had stepped out of some shrubs right into my path.

"Well?" he said.

The old heart gave a jump like a frightened antelope. I muzzled it down and choked it into submission. I told myself that this would be all right.

"Well?" said the big fellow sharply, his voice rising.

"Aw, shut up," said I. "Who d'you think I am? Riggs?"

"You might be," said he. "Just shove up your hands, will you, and let me have a look at you."

"I'm the other man that Sid hired," said I. "Don't be a fool."

"Yeah, maybe I'm a fool," said he, "but I'm going to have a look at you. I never heard nothing about another man, except Pete. And you ain't Pete. Shove up your hands, you!"

I shoved them up, with a Colt in my right hand, the barrel down, slipping into the cuff of my right arm. It's a simple trick. I had practiced it before, but never had used it. Dick Stephani taught me how to do it. A great old sleight-of-hand artist was Dick.

I held up my arms rigidly, as far as I could stick them.

"That's better," said the giant gruffly.

He was a giant, all right. He measured about seven feet six to my eyes, just then.

"Now turn in there and walk right into that shaft of light," said he.

As he spoke, he made a gesture with the rifle, and as he made the gesture, I socked him. Right alongside of the head I caught him with the heel of the gun. It seemed to sink in, and he wobbled and went down slowly, as though his will were fighting against the weakness in his legs.

By the way he fell, I knew that I hadn't really cracked his skull and I was mighty glad of that. He lay in a heap, all piled up, a mountain of a man. But I had some tie rope in my pockets, of course, and I lashed his hands and feet. He began to groan, so I shoved some cloth torn off his coat into his mouth and made a gag. Still he groaned, deep down in his throat—a sure proof that he could still breathe. After that, I got him under the armpits, and pulled him over into the brush, and when I had him there, I lashed his ankles to one trunk, and his wrists to another.

Then I leaned over and whispered in his ear.

"Listen, partner," said I, "I'm going to be busy around here for a while. If you make a noise, struggling, I'll come back and bash in your head."

He said nothing, of course, but I thought that I could see him try to nod his head in a convincing way. So I judged that he had understood.

I went off from him toward the light from the window, but the hammering of my heart told me that I would have to stop. I dropped to one knee and pressed one hand against the ground. It had taken something out of me, that brief struggle with the guard in the darkness. I could feel my lips grinning back hard, and the stretch of my nostrils as I breathed.

But I told myself that that was nothing and that I would be all right in another moment.

Well, it was true. The longer I lived with my disease, the more I came to know how the will power can control the body. And in a minute I was straight enough. I stood up, leaning on the rifle I had taken from the guard. I fumbled at the lock of it and saw that it was ready to use. Then I went on again.

When I came to the window, I saw that it was open, and voices rumbled out of it, as if out of a cave.

One fellow was saying: "I'll see that and raise you fifty."

"Not enough," said another. "Here's a hundred to fatten your winnings, Willie."

"And a hundred more, and another hundred on top of that," said another voice.

"Hey, who heard from you before, in this hand?" said one of the first speakers.

"Oh, I been in all the time," said the last fellow. "Only

I ain't been talking so much. I'm going to win this little old show."

I got up to the window. I could stand on tiptoe, I found, and look over the whole room, because the sill was low down to the ground. A bad idea, I've always thought, to have windows as low as all of that.

What I saw was the conventional layout—five men at a table, and one fellow off in a corner, pretending to read a paper, but really listening to the game. He'd been busted long before, I judged.

He was one of those long, dark, slim, sallow-faced men, who always look as though they have consumption. Of the five at the table, four hardly counted. One had huge ears that fanned out from his head, and bristling, whitish hair. "Swede," they called him. "Willie" was a fat fellow, with a lot of stomach in front of him, and a cheerful smile. But just opposite to the window sat the man I wanted. I mean, there was Sidney Maker.

Yes, I knew him at once. They had described him enough when they said that he was a bulldog, because the name fitted him all the way from head to foot. He had the thick shoulders, the width of neck, the muscular jowls, the disappearing nose, and the frowning forehead. He frowned, and yet he looked good-natured, too, if you know what I mean.

I judged him to be quite a man. Right then I wished that my luck had thrown me in with Sid Maker, instead of that knock-kneed crane of a man, Riggs.

Maker was the fellow who had just said that he had been staying all the time.

"Yeah, you'll win it, all right," said Willie. "You always win, when the pot gets big enough. Teach me how you talk to the cards, and you can keep the other things that you know."

"No, I've got no luck to-night," said Maker.

And he frowned harder, and tossed his head over his shoulder, like a dog biting at a fly.

"You got something on your mind," said one of the set.

"Here's a five-hundred raise on top of that," said one.

He was little, thin, sandy-haired, quiet. But I knew that

63

he was a man. At the first glance I couldn't tell which was more of a man—Maker or this small chap.

"Hey, Chuck," said one of them, "you're shooting the sky."

And right away they threw down their hands, all except Maker.

He hesitated. Then he said:

"Well, I won't let you hold a hand like that for nothing. I'll see you."

He shoved in his money. The table seemed to be covered with stacks of it.

"Thanks, Sid," said "Chuck" quietly. "This is what you're seeing."

He laid down a full house, queens high. I could see the starched faces of the ladies even from the window and at the angle from which I had to look. I could see the flash of them, if you like.

Well, with that betting, a full house, even queens up, was not so much, and I half expected Maker to put down four of a kind, but he only slipped his hand into the discard and muttered:

"Yeah, I knew it would be something like that."

"You've got your mind on something else," said Chuck. "You're not in the game, Sid."

He raked in the money as he spoke.

"That's all right, Chuck," said Maker. "I don't mind paying. But you're right. You're always right, Chuck. I've got something on my mind."

"What is it?" asked Chuck, gathering his cards as the next hand was dealt.

"That ringboned son of trouble, that McGinnis," said Maker. "I been waiting to hear from him."

"What about?" asked Swede.

"Oh, a job. A big job. I been waiting to hear from him. If I don't hear pretty soon, I gotta go downtown. And I don't want to pull out on you boys."

"Don't you do it," said Chuck. "Your luck will turn."

I liked the way Chuck said it. I could guess, somehow, that the winning or the losing of money did not mean a great deal to that fellow. He was all right. He was a man,

64

as I've said before. He sat sidewise to me, and he wore no suggestion of a gun, but I was sure that he was well heeled. Yes, he was a fighter; he was the real thing. I wouldn't have liked to get into trouble with that little man, I tell you. I knew it the first flash that I had of him, and everything that I had to do with him later proved that the first flash was right.

"McGinnis, he's got a head," said Swede.

"Yeah, he's got a head," admitted that bulldog, that Maker.

His tone admitted less than his words.

"McGinnis got a big job on hand?" asked the man in the corner, putting down his paper.

"Pretty big job," answered Maker, without turning his head.

"You know something, Sid," said Swede.

"Well?"

"I think about the way that you sit here, facing the window, and anybody could step up to that window and shoot you through the head."

"Have you tried the height of that sill above the ground?" asked Maker.

"Yeah, I've tried it," said the Swede, and he grinned, and had the grace to blush a little.

Everybody laughed, but it was rather hard laughter. I gathered that Swede was not the softest person in the world.

"McGinnis got a Riggs job on hand?" asked the man over in the corner.

"Always asking questions! Whatcha ask so many questions for, Bert?" demanded Sid Maker.

"Well, a man wants to know, don't he?" said Bert.

"Yeah, maybe."

They played that hand. I don't remember what happened in it. When they were dealing the next one, Chuck said:

"If you're worried about McGinnis, I'll go down and look him over. Only I don't like to pull out when I'm such a winner. I've picked a couple of thousand out of this little game already."

Maker laughed. His laughter sounded like a growl.

"Don't worry about money. None of you boys worry about money. We're going to roll in it, if we want to. I've got everything fixed."

"If you got the election fixed, it's all right," said Swede, jerking up his head.

"I'll have that fixed, too, by to-morrow," said Maker.

"Sure?" asked every voice in the room.

The chorus boomed on my ear.

"Yeah, by to-morrow."

"Then Riggs is licked," said Swede with a grin.

"I had him licked from the start," announced Maker. "I always had him licked. He's got nothing behind him!"

"He's got a pretty good pot of money," said Chuck, shaking his head in doubt.

"Money isn't men, always," said Maker. "I've got men. I've got you boys. I've got more in this room than Riggs has, with all of his brains and his planning. The trouble with Riggs is that he's got nobody that he can trust things to. That's the trouble with him."

He said this not with the air of boaster, but calmly, thoughtfully, cocking one eye up to the ceiling.

Then he added: "Blast that McGinnis. I ought to hear from him. I never should have trusted this job to him. He looked scared when I told him about it. I never should have trusted it to him. I should have given it to one of you boys. Chuck, maybe. Chuck never has fallen down."

"Chuck's so small that he can't fall very far," said Swede.

Chuck lifted his head and looked.

"I ain't so small as all that," he said softly.

"Oh, wait a minute, Chuck; you ain't so big, either," said Swede.

He grinned again. I hated his grin and the pale bristling of his hair. He looked like a bad one.

"Maybe I'm big enough, though—for the jobs that may be on hand," said Chuck, continuing to look straight at Swede.

"Are you?" said Swede, suddenly thrusting out his jaw.

"I think—maybe," said Chuck.

"Everything ain't cards," suggested Swede, glaring.

"No. There's guns, too," said Chuck.

He leaned forward, just an inch or two.

"I dunno that I'll take that, Chuck," said Swede.

"I don't care what you take," said Chuck, his voice gentler than ever.

"I say—I won't take it," said Swede, turning red and white in spots.

"Hey, shut up, all of you," broke in Maker angrily.

He banged his hand on the table. Slowly Swede shifted his eyes toward his boss, but Chuck never moved his glance from the face of the big man. There was no ferocity in his stare, but a calm, cold consideration. It scared me, somehow, just to stand there and look at this little fellow. There was poison in him, I knew.

"I don't want any more of this talk," said Maker. "You know me, all of you boys. I'm for everybody, until the gang begins to split, and then I'm against the ones that start the break. I'm against them with everything that I've got. Don't forget it. Swede, don't say a word, and you, Chuck, shut your face, will you?"

"I wasn't taking anything, that's all," said Swede. And he scowled down at his cards.

Little Chuck said nothing. He kept looking hungrily, thoughtfully, at Swede. I knew that one day that look of his would develop into something bad.

However, I had heard enough for the moment. I went around to the front of the house, thinking on the way. It was a hard lay, a hard deal. I didn't see how I could crack this layout. There was Maker, and he was a handful. There were five other men, and every one of them, by the look, was a hand-picked fighter. I never had done much work with guns, but I had had some experience with my fists, and I knew something about the look of men. These all had the right slant.

When I got to the front of the house, I banged a couple of times on the door.

I waited while the echo ran back through the house. After a time, I heard footfalls. The door was opened, and

67

a flash of light smeared across my face so fast that I jerked up my hands.

"Whatcha want?" said the voice of Bert.

"I want Maker," said I.

"What for? Starch?" said he.

"Yeah, starch," said I.

"Well," he said, "Maker is busy. Good night!"

He started to close the door. I wedged my foot in it.

"Take your foot out of that!" said Bert, his voice cold and small.

I snarled at him: "You thickhead, I said that I wanta see Maker. I mean it. Take me in to him."

"Who told you that he's here?" said Bert.

"McGinnis told me."

"Oh, McGinnis?"

"Yeah."

He paused for a moment.

"Well, come in then," said he.

I heard him step back, and I walked in through the door. Suddenly the cold muzzle of a revolver was tucked into the hollow of my throat.

"You lying skunk!" said Bert.

There was always that heart of mine to consider first. I told myself that I had to keep cool. No matter what happened, my heart had to be considered. No nerves. One touch of nerves and I was the worst kind of a failure, and a dead failure, at that.

"Oh, shut up," said I. "What sort of a play is this? Are you taking me to Maker, Bert?"

He grunted. "Who told you my name?" he asked.

"You think that nobody knows you, eh?" said I.

"Well, who told you?"

"Aw, Bert," said I, "take a tumble. You're not in the papers, but you're known. Take me in. Or better still, bring Maker out here. I want to talk to him. I've got to talk to him."

"McGinnis sent you, eh?" said Bert, considering.

"Yeah, McGinnis. Who else? Why else would I be here when I'd rather be in bed?"

68

He muttered something and then he said that perhaps I was all right.

"Oh, I don't care what you think about me," said I. "Not any of you. When I get rid of my message from McGinnis, I'll be glad to be shut of the whole works."

"Has something gone wrong?" asked Bert anxiously.

"Yeah, and damned wrong."

"McGinnis, I never put any faith in him," growled Bert. "Here, come along, you. No, you go first. Mind you, I'm watching you. There's no chances taken in this house."

"I'll take no chances when I get out of it," said I. "The farther from this town, the better I'll be pleased!"

"How come McGinnis to send *you?*" said Bert.

"I don't please you, eh?" I asked him.

"Oh, shut up," he answered.

But his voice had relief in it. This touch of heat on my part seemed to convince him more than anything that I had said before. So he steered me down a big hall and when we came to the door at the end of it, he called out:

"Hey, Sid!"

"Well?" growled a voice inside.

"Here's somebody that says he comes from McGinnis."

"Bring him in then," said Maker.

"Open the door, you," said Bert.

I opened the door, and walked into the lions' den.

CHAPTER XI

Bluff

NOW that I was in the room, I felt a good deal better.

It was like taking a dive—I might never come up, but at the least I was in the water.

The five of them looked calmly at me, like people who had seen a man before, even after midnight, if you understand my drift.

"You—McGinnis, he sent you?" said Maker.

"He sent me," said I. "He told me to get to you, Maker, if I had to tear the house down."

"That's a good way to tear a house down," said Maker, "banging on a front door in the middle of the morning."

He was mad and he showed it.

"You've got no neighbors," said I, "and it won't start any gossip, anyway."

Because it made me a little mad, too, to hear him talk like this. He flushed, turning a purplish red right up his forehead to the roots of his hair. He had a bull's temper all right.

"What does McGinnis want?" asked Maker.

"Something I'll tell you in private," said I.

"This is private. These are my partners," said he.

"They're not mine," I answered.

"Who the devil are you, anyway?" asked Maker.

Well, there was no use faking up a name. I told him straight.

"My name is Jerry Ash."

"Anything for short?"

"Poker-face. Is that short enough to suit you?"

"You're one of these chesty fellows, are you?" asked Maker.

It seemed time to get some action out of him. I couldn't afford to wait too long. I felt that I could manage my nerves for a short patch of time, but over a long rub, they'd wear thin.

"Are you going to come out and listen to me, or kick these fellows out and let me talk to you in here?" said I.

"You talk here in front of them. There's nothing between me and McGinnis," said Maker.

"Isn't there?" said I.

But I was stumped by that. Of course, I didn't know what had been going on between McGinnis and the boss. But I did know that there was trouble in the air. I was simply playing a bluff, and it seemed to be called.

Maker did not wait me out. He went on: "How do you know me, anyway? I never saw you before, Poker-face."

"I never saw you, either," said I, "but I heard you described."

"Can you recognize a man from a description, my bright boy?" said Maker.

I could see him leaning a little toward me and I knew that he was beginning to be more and more suspicious.

"I can recognize you," said I.

"You repeat the description that they gave you," said Maker. "There's something behind you, son!"

"They told me to pick out a fellow who looked like a bulldog."

Suddenly Maker laughed. And at that signal, the other five roared. They kept on roaring, when he had recovered a good deal from his own amusement, and I saw him pick them off with side glances.

Still he insisted that I should speak in front of them all.

"I'll whisper in your ear then," said I.

"You'll whisper what in my ear?" said Maker, half sneering.

Bluff again, for me! I hated it, but I had to go ahead. I slipped across the room and bent over him. Two men

71

pulled guns and covered me. But I whispered at the ear of Maker:

"Everything's a bust! McGinnis has his back against the wall."

"What do you mean that everything's a— Has he—"

He turned on the other five and bellowed:

"Get out of the room! What's keeping you in here, anyway? Get out and keep out!"

They went.

The last to go through the door was little Chuck, stepping as soft as a cat, and as he closed the door, he was still watching me in a way that sent prickles up and down my spine. There was trouble in Chuck; there was poison in him.

When the door closed, Maker jumped at me and grabbed me by the shoulders and shook me.

"Take your hands off me, or I'll crack your jaw for you!" said I.

He dropped his hands, cursing.

"What d'you mean, that McGinnis said everything was a bust?" demanded Maker. "How could be possibly—"

I laid the muzzle of my Colt right against his stomach.

"Whisper it, Sid," said I. "Somebody may be listening in from the hall."

He looked down at the gun and then looked back at me.

"You fool," he murmured. "You think that you can get away with it, Poker-face?"

"Turn around, Sid," said I. "Lift your arms carefully and see if you can touch the ceiling. Then lower those hands behind your shoulders. Steady does the trick—slow and steady."

He began to move as I ordered, but all the while he was arguing.

"You can't get away with murder like this," said he. "You know that I've got man-eaters all around me. They'll chaw up your bones, kid."

"I don't want to murder you, Sid," said I. "I don't think that I'll have to, either, because you have too much sense to make a quick move. I hate quick moves, Sid. I hate 'em like the devil! Move slow, and everything will be right."

"Kid," said Maker, gradually lowering his hands behind his back, as I had ordered, "you're making a great mistake. I could fix you for life. I don't care who you're working for, you could make more money working for me. That dirty snake, that wall-eyed imitation, that Colonel Riggs, he's nobody. He's no man, I tell you. You believe me, or not?"

"Perhaps you're right, Sid," said I, prodding the muzzle of the gun into his ribs, and with my free hand catching his left wrist in the running noose of a cord I had drawn from my pocket. "Perhaps you're absolutely right. But I've thrown in with Riggs, for the time being, and I suppose that I'll have to stay in with him. I hate to do this. I really hate to. But I'm going to keep on."

Then I threw a couple of hitches over the other wrist and had his hands good and fast. There's a lot of talk about people who can wriggle out of real rope ties, but I'd like to see one really manage it. Usually, somebody with a knife turns the trick for a friend.

When I had his hands secured, I went through his pockets. I got a plain little knife, a penknife, and then a pair of short-nosed revolvers. I might have guessed that Maker would prefer that kind of a gun. I got his wallet, too, and it was a good thick, hard-packed one. His upper lip twisted when he saw me take it out of his pocket, and he swore.

I had a balled-up handkerchief ready in my hand and, as he cursed, I shoved it between his teeth.

I thought that he would choke with his rage. He turned purple. His eyes started out of his face. His nostrils flared to twice their ordinary size. But there was no way he could work that gag out of his mouth except with hand power. There wasn't enough strength even in his tongue to push it past his teeth, because it was balled up into a knot, the way that Dick Stephani had showed me how to turn the trick. A handy partner was Stephani, I can tell you. He was full of tricks.

After I had Sid lightened, and tied and gagged, I asked

him to step through the window and be easy about it, because something told me that that little tiger of a man, that Chuck, was out there in the hall, listening as close to the door as he dared. I hadn't liked his parting glance a whit.

Maker hesitated one instant. I half thought that he would throw himself at me, tied as his hands were, and with the crash of the struggle that he made, bring in attention from the outside.

However, he thought better of it in the long run and made no foolish play like this.

I was more than half sorry for him, when he squirmed out over the sill of the window and slipped down to the ground, with me behind him. Of course, it meant a tremendous sacrifice of pride on his part, and pride in a fighting man like Maker is as great as pride in any emperor.

When he hit the ground, he stood up and looked hastily, eagerly around him.

"Too bad, Sid," I whispered at his ear, "but the big boy is asleep for a while. You'll have to come along with me."

He turned his head and gave me such a look as I never want to take again from any human. It was the exquisite perfection of boiled-down hatred and malice. Two looks like that would kill a man on the spot, I think.

But, after that single, silent glance, he went on obediently enough around the side of the house. I heard some one knocking inside the house.

"They're at the door of your room, Sid," said I. "But they'll be a little too late. You can break into a dogtrot, Sid. Head straight through those trees, if you don't mind."

He went on at a dogtrot, the way I had commanded him to do. And then, behind us, I heard the crash of a door flung suddenly open and after that the shouting of a fierce voice that was instantly answered by a chorus.

Such rage I'd never heard. It went through me even in the distance. There was a vibration in it, like the vibration of light. It made a red glow in my brain.

I could have guessed before what would happen if they

74

caught me. Now it was no matter of guessing. I knew. I knew that they were with Maker as a boss and as a friend. They were ready to die for him, like children for a father.

You can imagine that I felt as though I were stepping in a fire. We got to a fence, and I made Maker sidle between the bars of it, and then there was the roadway just beyond.

How I wanted to bolt down that road at full speed, but the curse was on me, and with my staggering, leaping heart, I could manage no more than a dogtrot again! So I forced Sid to go down the road at that gait.

It was a cruel thing to do, because he could not breathe through his mouth at all. But I didn't dare to risk him with the gag out, for a little while.

And, behind me, I began to hear the rattling of hoofs. Maker's trained man-eaters were beginning to scatter to hunt for their chief.

CHAPTER XII

The Pursuit

WE were about two hundred yards from the place where my two men and the horses were waiting, when I heard the beating of hoofs sweeping up fast behind. I dived with Maker for some tall grass and pitched myself into it, dragging him down.

Through the tops of the grasses I could see the riders come up and halt. The first was Chuck. I knew him by the smallness with which he loomed in the saddle, and even in the starlight. I could see how he had turned his head toward the spot where I was lying with my man.

"There's something in that grass," said Chuck.

"Chuck," said the voice of Bert, "are you crazy? I hear a horse running through the sand up there. Are you going to wait here and—"

"I hear something breathing," said Chuck, leaning a little from the saddle.

It was the whistling breath of my friend Maker, half-strangled, and pumping like a steam engine. But of course I didn't dare to take the gag out, as yet.

"It's a toad. Never hear 'em make that noise before? It's a toad, of course," said Bert furiously. "Come on, Chuck, or else stay here and go toad sticking by yourself. I'm hunting men, not vermin!"

He dashed off down the lane, and Chuck, shaking his head, finally lit out in pursuit.

After that happened, I sat up in the grass, took the gag from Maker's mouth, and stood up with him.

He was cursing, not loudly, but steadily.

"One fool can sink the biggest ship in the world!" said he. "That idiot of a Bert—"

"Look here," said I, "I'd hate to start shooting, but I love my own neck, and if they'd come this way, wouldn't both Bert and Chuck have gone out on the long trail?"

"Bert, maybe—and a small loss!" said Maker. "But you don't know that boy Chuck. No, you haven't even got an idea about him. No one man will ever kill that devil! He's a nine-footed wild cat, is what he is."

I was almost touched by this devotion of Maker to his chief lieutenant. But we had other things to think about now. I asked him to promise that he would not make a sound if I let him go without the gag, and I promised him a bullet through the head if he broke his word. He said that he'd as soon die by a bullet as to gag to death, and he declared that he would keep as still as a mouse.

So we jogged on, my heart fairly well in order again, until we came to the horses. My two men gave one look at Maker, and all at once they gasped:

"It's Maker! It's him! It's the big chief himself!"

"Boys," said Maker, "you've made a fine, brave play. But let me tell you that if you start to take me to your town, you're making the mistake of your lives, and you'll all be dead men before you get me there. Besides, I can offer you more than Riggs would ever——"

"Sid," said I, "you've talked a good deal already. Another stream of lingo like that and you've talked yourself out of court!"

He grunted something back at me, but he shut up.

Loftus and Earl had not been sitting still all of the time that I had been away. There were four strips of blankets cinched around the four horses, and with rope nooses they had even built stirrups.

I was mighty glad to see those stirrups, I can tell you!

We got Maker onto a horse, and the lead rope of that horse was tied to the cinch of Slim Jim Earl's mustang. Then we started out.

The devil was loose behind us, of course. I could hear horses racing through the darkness. I could hear men shouting, and then, out of the distance, came a fusillade of shots, and all of the beating of hoofs and the shouting swept away toward a far point of the horizon. They had started off on the trail of the wrong fox!

That was a ton's weight off me.

"By thunder," said Maker at this point, "I wouldn't have believed that it was possible. I still don't believe it. I don't think that it happened. I ain't here. I'm asleep back there at my house, in my chair. I'll wake up in a minute and find out that the whole business is a dream!"

"Maybe you will," I answered. "But here we have you with us. How about that ford of the river? Can we get across there?"

"Try it and see," said he.

By his violence in speaking, I guessed that we had blundered onto the right spot. Also, if it were the wrong one, he was pretty sure to let us know. A man whose hands are tied behind him is not likely to keep mum at a time like that.

"How did you manage it, Poker-face?" asked Slim Jim

77

Earl. "I can't believe what I'm seeing and hearing; that's all."

"I had some luck," said I.

As a matter of fact, I was feeling pretty high and happy, as though the work were all over and ended. But I talked small. It's easy, I notice, to talk small, when you're holding all the aces in the pack.

"You had some luck!" repeated Slim Jim Earl. "Yeah, and then something else, too! I never heard of such a play! You take him right out of his house?"

I didn't even answer, of course, and Maker breaks in:

"Poker-face, you tell me. Was there anything in that McGinnis business, at all?"

"Not a thing," said I honestly. "I never heard of him before to-night."

"Who talked about him to-night?"

"You did."

"I did? Not when you were there."

"I was behind you, Sid. I was outside the window, listening in."

He groaned and cursed, softly, steadily, for some minutes.

"It was a good play," he said. "I'll bet you play cards, Poker-face. I'll bet that's your special game!"

"I've given up cards," said I.

"Too hard on your nerves?" he asked.

"Yes," said I, and thought of Betty Cole, and the black, dropping shadows of that garden.

Maker was laughing ironically.

"And the big sap out there in the garden," said he. "What about him? Will you tell me that?"

"You know," said I, "I simply said that I was the other man you'd hired."

"Did that take the thickhead in?"

"No, he was suspicious, and had his gun on me, and stuck my hands up in the air."

"Did you use your feet on him?" asked Maker, with a hungry, almost a childish curiosity.

"No, I just socked him alongside the head with the heel of a Colt. I thought I'd killed him, at first."

"I wish you had!" said Maker. "I wish that you'd killed the whole bunch of four-flushing—"

He stopped himself.

"I'm talking like a fool," said he. "I've got the finest lot of boys in the world, barring one only. And you're the man that I mean, Poker-face. I want you! Chuck this yellow dog, this Colonel Riggs, and throw in with a real man and—"

"Quit it, will you?" I warned him.

"We might as well listen to what he has to say, chief," said Dan Loftus to me.

"Why not?" said Slim Jim Earl. "He's a man of his word, too!"

"You see, boys," said I to the pair of 'em, "you don't understand what this is all about. I don't want to see you losing your heads, but you, Maker, keep your face shut. I warned you before. Now if you begin to yap again, it'll be the last talking you'll ever do."

He grunted and growled, but he shut up, while my brain spun to think how close he had come to swinging that pair of lads over to his side of the business. A mighty smooth fellow was that Maker, as I could tell for myself.

At the same time, I was beginning to wonder if he were not worth a whole gross of Colonel Riggses? These two fellows ought to know what they were talking about, and both of them declared that he was a man of his word.

That's about as high a compliment as you can pay to a man on the verge of the frontier. If Maker was worth that praise, he was worth still more. Then, I had liked his way of playing cards. The manners of the loser mean something, and a great something, too.

Now we came down to the edge of the river, and I remember how the smooth water of the shallows darkened before us, as though the stars were throwing our shadows in front. Then Slim Jim Earl spurred is mustang in and towed Maker after him, and after Maker came Dan Loftus, and I, last of all.

Halfway out, I saw the leaders drop out of sight under water. They had blundered into a hole. Then Dan Loftus shouted, and pointed out something like a log, sliding

79

rapidly downstream. But it was not a log. For a log doesn't have motion in itself.

We floundered and smashed through the water till we came up with it, and the log turned out to be Maker himself!

That fellow had simply slipped out of the saddle and, his hands tied as they were, he was floating on his back and trusting to leg work alone to get him out of the tug of the mid-channel, and out of the shallows where he could stand up and walk.

A pretty desperate adventure, when you come to think of it. Desperate even to talk about in midday, before a cosy fire, but in the dark of the night, and with icy snow water to reënforce all of the terrors—why, it made the thing almost unimaginable to me!

We got Maker back to his horse and out of the river. By that time, every man jack of us was soaked to the skin, and half-frozen, but we did not dare to make a halt. Neither did we dare to push on straight for our home town, because we could guess that parties from Makerville would be rushing along that road, by this time, ready to do murder at a minute's notice.

To give ourselves distance from the danger point, we got behind the trees, and trekked four or five miles down the creek. Then we camped and built a fire, and I tell you what, the greatest relief that I ever had in my life was when that flame rose broad and high and the warmth of it soaked into me.

I was done for. I knew that if I made another stroke of effort, I would be fit to collapse. I had reached my uttermost limit of endurance, and so I ordered that we should camp there.

A glint of satisfaction appeared in the eyes of Maker when I said that. Well, I wouldn't trust him to the watchfulness of my two companions. So I got a length of young sapling and tied him to it with my own hands, and then I lay down and slept like a dead man.

CHAPTER XIII

The Teamster

ALTOGETHER, we slept for only about two hours. But that was enough to bring the dawn, and dawn was a sad thing for us, you can imagine! By this time, Makerites were scattered all the way between us and the town of Piegan, and they would mean business. They would be scattered across country, too. The longer I thought about it, the more hopeless it appeared to me.

I went out to the edge of the wood and looked across at the Piegan-Makerville road. I saw a couple of horsemen jogging down it, going past a wagon loaded with hay, that had six horses hitched on in front. A peaceful job, that farmer had. I wished that I were in his boots.

And the moment I thought of that, I decided that that was the best place for all of us.

The Makerites would probably expect me and my valuable captive anywhere rather than on the main trail. And they would be looking for horsemen, not portions of a load of hay.

So I got my fellows together, and we rode straight across the fields until we came up to the road at a bend, a good distance ahead of the hay wagon. Slim Jim Earl began to get excited, and he wanted to know if I had lost my head, and couldn't I understand that I was taking them straight up to the jumping-off place?

I didn't explain my plan. I was tired, groggy, and ready for bed. I just stuck out my jaw—as Maker was doing—and led the party up to the roadside. We dismounted, stripped the fixings from our horses, and turned them out to graze where they chose. Then we sat down by the road and watched the wagon coming up. The driver was a slouching lump of a man with a head that jutted out before him. This characteristic gave him something of the profile of Colonel Riggs—a caricature of the colonel, so to speak.

He stopped his team—six rugged mustangs—when he saw us.

"Hello, strangers," said he.

He gave us a grin and a wave of the hand. We all waved back, except Maker. His hands were still tied.

I asked the teamster where he was hauling his hay, and he said that he was hauling it seven miles down the road toward Piegan, and that he intended to put it in a barn he was building.

"What would you want," said I, "for hauling it all of the way into Piegan?"

"Sixteen miles?" said he. "What would I want to haul it there for?"

"For money," said I.

"You mean you know somebody that wants it?"

"I want it."

He looked at me and took off his hat and scratched his head for a time, with the most loutish look that I ever saw. However, he wound up by shrugging his shoulders. I gathered that it was not the first time that he had given up a problem before he came to the solution.

"Well, what would you pay?" he asked.

"How much is on that wagon?"

"Three tons."

"What did you pay for it?"

"Twelve dollars a ton. It's good hay, too."

"I'll pay you fifteen, and cartage. How much for that?"

"Well, lemme see. A dollar a day for each hoss is six dollars, and a dollar for me is seven. Then there's the return trip. That's fourteen dollars."

"You rate yourself for as much as a horse, but you won't pull as much," said I.

He seemed stumped by this.

"It's this way," said he. "I've got a pair of hands. They've only got hoofs."

He was only about two cuts above a half-wit. I began to be sorry for him.

"Fourteen dollars, and forty-five for the hay, that makes fifty-nine for the whole job," said I.

"I ain't added it up yet," said he.

He paused, cocked an eye at the sky, and began to work on his fingers. In five minutes or so he told me the right answer.

"How much for four passengers?" said I.

"You wanta ride?" said he.

"Yes, we want to ride on the load."

He hesitated.

"I wouldn't charge a man for a lift," said he.

"I want to pay, though," said I. "I want to pay for everything. And besides that, I want you to forget that you've seen the four of us. I want to pay you for forgetting. You understand?"

It took him a while to gather the meaning of this, but finally he nodded. Out of the wallet of Sid Maker, I had taken a hundred dollars in gold, and I passed that sum on to the teamster at once.

He weighted it in his hand, with his eyes staring. He lived in a country where money came easily enough, but it seemed as though he never had seen those familiar coins before.

"Why, that's a whole lot," said he, looking up in my face like a child, from his examination of the money.

It saddened me a good deal, to see his expression. I began to feel like a lucky fellow, heart or no heart, when I watched him.

"That's a hundred dollars," said I. "Fifty-nine for the hay and the hauling and your return trip, empty. And forty-one even for what you forget. We're going to climb up on that load of hay and disappear into it. Is that clear to you?"

83

After he had stared at me for a full minute, he began to nod, and then I waved the others on. They understood my plan, by listening to my bargaining, and they agreed that it was a good thing. We climbed into the load of hay and burrowed down into it. I put Maker in front of me a little, well buried. And I eased him by tying his hands in front of his face, so that he could rest with his head on his arms, if he had to. The other two were behind me. And then I saw the teamster looking up at the hay, and when he saw how we had disappeared, he began to laugh heartily.

I was glad of that laughter. It told me that the heart of the man was as right as his mind was simple.

He whooped to the mustangs, and off we went. I felt so secure that I prayed for one thing only—that we could get across the rocky draws on the way without a broken wheel or axle.

It was a rattling, crashing, hard ride, that journey to the town of Piegan.

We had just sixteen miles to go, and it took us twelve hours. We started not much more than an hour after sunrise. And the west was red when we pulled into the town.

Not once were we stopped!

That leaves out of the count five separate occasions when horsemen came up beside our driver and questioned him about what he had seen on the road, but he always said that he had seen nothing. Several times his ignorance and stupidity were cursed, but in every instance the riders went off. No one thought of that load of hay. It was too simple a place for such a valuable cargo as Sid Maker to be hidden, I suppose!

I was amused by Slim Jim Earl's talk, after we had gone through several of these close calls. He seemed to forget all about the success of this expedition, and he began to regret the good buckboard, and the four good mustangs that we had left behind us. I pointed out to him that the price of the horses and the buckboard would hardly matter to Colonel Riggs, so long as he had Maker in his hands. But still Earl kept on, speaking particularly of a chestnut gelding with all dark points, the best upstanding horse, he swore, that he had ever held the reins over.

It grew tiresome, but still I had to endure that chatter. I hated the English language, before the end of the journey. There were other things to make the trip unpleasant, such as the way the dust and the chaff from the hay began to work down the back of my neck and fly into my eyes and ears. And the sun was very strong, until well past the middle of the afternoon. It was true that the hay gave us shelter against the direct rays, but it also shut out the wind, and we fairly baked and steamed.

Twelve hours of almost constant going took us out of the last of the draws, and in the dying time of the day we pulled across the final stretch of soft sand that led on the widening of the trail to Piegan. At last we could afford to sit up on our load of hay, and I must say that the sight of the little scattering town was a blessing to my eyes. As for Slim and Dan Loftus, they yelled like Indians!

I begged them to keep still and finally managed to persuade them. So we drove up the main street, turned into an alley, and finally halted behind the hotel barn.

I got Maker out of the hay load and made the two guard him in a shed while I went into the hotel to make my report.

I was pretty well covered with dust and chaff. I paused to clean myself of this, and to roll a cigarette, and pull up my belt a couple of notches, for in over twenty-four hours, I had not tasted food of any kind, of course.

When I felt that I had made myself fairly presentable, and with the fumes of the cigarette comforting me, I went on into the hotel and asked for the proprietor.

The colonel was in his office, I was told, and must not be disturbed. He was in his office, discussing important business.

It was important, right enough. One could tell that by the stream of cursing that suddenly broke out into the air and was shut off again by the slamming of a door.

A man came hurrying out, ran down the steps, and flung himself into his saddle.

"This town can go to the devil, for all of me," he

shouted, shaking his fist at us, as representatives of the whole place. "Riggs has come to the end of his rope. I hope he rots!"

He dashed off down the street, and I rather wondered that two or three of the rough-looking bystanders did not unlimber their guns and take a shot at him. But they all seemed depressed. What they heard was as though they had heard it before, and more than half agreed with it.

Trouble was black as a cloud over the whole mind of Piegan!

I turned back to the clerk and saw him shaking his head.

"I've got to see the colonel," said I.

"You can't," he insisted. "Besides, it's too late for him to pay, to-night. The safe's locked, and everything."

"Go tell him that Ash has come back," said I. "See if that makes him open the door!"

He looked doubtful, but off he went at last, hesitating in his stride, from time to time, as though he knew that he was going on a fool's errand.

CHAPTER XIV

The Trump Card

THE clerk came back in a minute to say that I was wanted, and he looked at me with a queer interest as he said it. On the way down the hall he confided to me:

"I guess things are going smash, all right?"

I made no answer. It would not be surprising if things went smash, but I had no particular knowledge. I simply felt in my bones that the colonel was a rascal.

As we came closer to the office, the voices of the people inside it cut through the wall as a knife pokes through paper. I heard a man shouting that he had waited long enough and that he would wait no longer.

The colonel put in with a harassed, soothing murmur, which was cut short by the outright swearing of a second voice. I gathered that Riggs was getting it from two sides, and I cannot say that I was sorry for the oily old rascal. It amused me, and yet it was exciting to think that perhaps I was bringing the highest trump in the pack to this game.

When we got to the door, the dispute was at its loudest, and the clerk, after having his knock shouted down, so to speak, simply opened the door, and let out the full, flowing tide of the dispute.

I stepped inside and saw the colonel backed against his desk, a fellow in rough cow-puncher's garb planted before him, actually shaking his fist in the face of poor Riggs. But his voice was not as loud as that of a big black-browed man who stood with his arms folded, looking like a picture of murder in repose. He was bellowing:

"Talk is the cheapest way of striking coin, but it won't work all the time. Not when people get used to the loose-lipped gibbering of a—"

It made me pretty hot to see the poor colonel backed into a corner like this. It was plain that he was a man of language rather than a man of action, and I took pity on his sallow face and the frightened rolling of his eyes.

"Colonel," said I, "do you want these fellows thrown out?"

The clerk had been waiting behind me, to see how I was received, I suppose, or to spy for an instant on the scene inside, but when he heard this, he jerked away and slammed the door behind him with a noise like the report of a gun.

The attention of the three men inside the room was focused on me by that crash, and by what I had just said. I don't know why I made such a remark. Either of that pair looked able to eat me alive, but I was driven to say something by the look of Riggs. I suppose that one of the two would have started a gun play on the spot, but each of them seemed a little flabbergasted, and now Riggs called out to me:

"Not at all, Ash. Not at all. Just two friends of mine who have lost their tempers for the moment. We're all childish, now and again!"

That was rather a good remark, when you come to think of it. It had them backing up, at once.

Before they got their vocabularies unlimbered, the colonel asked me what I had to report.

At this the big man of the black brows bawled out: "Maybe he's got the election report!"

"No," I said, "I've only brought back a man."

"A man from where?" asked Riggs.

"From Makerville," said I.

"Who did you get?" asked the colonel, snapping his fingers nervously. "And why bring anybody but—"

"It's Maker," said I.

That seemed to split them apart. They all fell in different directions, so to speak, the colonel bringing up short against his desk and glaring at me. But he recovered himself a long time before the other two. The bigger of the pair had flopped heavily into a chair. The smaller man had spread out his legs as though bracing himself against another shock.

"You've got Maker, have you? And how many men has Maker with him?" he asked.

"Two," said I, "to see that he keeps his hands tied."

The second shock seemed almost greater than the first one. The colonel turned and looked out the window.

"Where—where is he?" he asked huskily.

"In the shed behind the barn," said I.

"I'll go get him," said the big man.

I stepped to the door.

"You'll stay here, friend," said I, for I had no mind to let my night's work be undone by the touch of a knife upon the rope that held Maker safe.

"Now who are you?" asked the tall fellow, striding slowly up to me so that he could look down on me.

"Shut up and back up, Hooker," said his friend. "If he has Maker out there, he *is* the devil."

Hooker took this hint as a chance to laugh. Then he spun around on Riggs and slapped him on the shoulder.

"I've talked too much, colonel," said he. "But how was I to know that you had cards like this up your sleeve?"

Riggs brushed the apology—if you could call it that—away.

He simply said: "I don't bear any hard feelings, boys. Only, remember that I've done something more than talk. You said that Piegan was not worth the blasting powder needed to blow it to pieces unless we won this election. And with Maker out of the way for two days, will you tell me how we're going to fail to win?"

He turned to the other man.

"Hooker's dumb with joy," said Riggs. "You tell me, Fernie."

Fernie was ready enough with an answer. He said:

"If we have Maker, we certainly have the county in our pockets, already."

"And town lots are good as gold payments to you boys?" asked the colonel, with a bit of a sneer.

Hooker used his loud laugh again. I didn't like that man from the first. I liked him less with the passage of every second. He said that town lots in Piegan would be kiting sky-high, as soon as the place was the official county seat. But first he wanted to have a look at Maker.

I saw the colonel parting his lips with a smile and about to say a thing that I couldn't stand for.

"That's too bad, Hooker," said I. "But you can't see him. The colonel and I can see him, and that's all."

"Hey!" shouted Hooker furiously, bridling at me like a hen, or a fool. "We're not to see him, eh? This little trick is just wind and words, too, eh?"

I wanted to kill him. I never wanted to kill a man more badly. So I looked hard and straight at Riggs, sort of asking his permission. The colonel looked baffled, blinking back at me, but he decided instantly on the line that he would take. He adopted the highest hand, at once.

"Look here, Hooker, and you, Fernie," he said. "I've taken more from the pair of you to-day than I've ever taken from human beings before. I took it because I know that you've been friends, and because I didn't want to let you talk yourselves out into the cold and the dark. I wanted to keep you on the inside, as from the first. But now I'm not going to take any more of this. You know that Maker is here. If you don't believe it, it's nothing to me. Jerry, we'll leave them here to try to find the light."

As he said this, he crossed the room, hooked his arm familiarly through mine, and went out into the hall with me.

He had carried off his exit in the finest possible shape. No actor could have done the thing better, but when I got him into the hall, I felt him stagger a little. He had been hard-pressed, and he was feeling his knees sag, I suppose.

He panted, like a man who had been running for his life uphill! "What do you mean, boy? Was it a bluff? Was it just a bluff to get me out? Of course it was just a bluff, but it was the best one that I ever heard used. It will get me out of this town with my neck whole, I suppose. You and I against the world, Jerry. You're a man after my heart. I'm glad I pulled the detectives off your trail. I knew that we could use one another!"

In a way, that was as bad a confession as you could ask a man to make. It showed that he was ready and willing to run for his life to get from Piegan before a crowd of angry investors lynched him. For I saw, now, that lynching was the very thing that was in the air.

However, I helped him out of the bottomless pit at once.

"I meant what I said," I answered. "I have Maker out there in the shed, unless those two fellows have let him slip away."

"Only two to guard him?" gasped the colonel. "Great heavens, man, that was rash. Only two! Maker is a snake. He could get through a solid stone wall! Only two to guard him. Let's hurry! Let's get there!"

He couldn't hurry very well, at first. He had to get his breath back, and we stumbled together through the dark across the empty yard and out to the shed behind the barn. When we came up to the barn, we could hear voices inside of it, and one of them was Slim Jim asking a question and the other was the deep rumble of Maker.

When he heard that, the colonel almost fell to the ground. He had to clutch my shoulder and support himself for a moment. His head was hanging down. He acted as though a bullet had ripped through his body.

"He's there! He's there!" he kept repeating, over and over again.

I heard him drawing deeper breaths, and then he raised his head and whispered: "Saved!"

I don't think that any one ever breathed out the word with more feeling than there was in Riggs's voice.

"How did you do it? How did you do it?" he murmured, but he wasn't wanting an answer. He was wanting to feast his eyes on the face of Maker.

We went into the thick shadows inside the shed, and Riggs straightened and found the trio with his eyes. Then he walked slowly up to Maker and said to him quietly:

"Maker, I'm sorry that we've had to be guilty of this outrage. We'll try to make you as comfortable as possible during your little stay with us!"

Maker merely snorted. He was no actor, like Riggs, and he merely blurted out:

"You big four-flusher!"

The colonel laughed gently, as though he had heard the most courteous rejoinder in the world.

"Don't take it too hard, Sidney," said he. "The fact is that *some* of your friends will believe that you were kidnaped by force, though I suppose that most of them will have to think that you ran away from your post!"

CHAPTER XV

The Wallet

WHEN it came to the rank and file of words, as you see, Maker was no match at all for the colonel. That last speech was my idea of a good, hard sock to the chin, but Maker only grunted something unintelligible.

Then the colonel wanted to know exactly what had happened, and I told him, putting in all the facts, and nothing else. It doesn't take long, when one is boiling everything down to the facts. I finished my story in about three minutes. Then I asked Slim Jim and Dan Loftus if I had left anything out or said anything wrong, and they both vowed that it was gospel, but that something had been left out. I felt the same way about it. I mean to say, it didn't seem possible that I had been able to produce the events of that entire night within the compass of two or three minutes of talk.

Even Maker said, with his usual grunt:

"The kid's modest, you know. Who handed you this one, Riggs? He ain't your kind of a man!"

Riggs said good night to Slim Jim and Dan Loftus. He praised them to the skies, and he told them that they were going to learn that gratitude can take a more practical form than mere words. In the meantime, he wanted to look around and see just what he could do for them. They thanked him. Jim wanted to know about the price of the four horses and the buckboard, and the colonel airily told him to come back in the morning, when they could talk everything over in more detail.

So we got rid of the pair of them. They shook hands specially with me, each in turn, and each in silence. That was a thrill for me. It made me feel that somehow I had passed the stage of initiation and had become a full-fledged Westerner.

Then with the colonel and Maker, I went into the hotel. I went first, to clear the way. Then Maker walked, and behind him was Riggs. According to his direction, we went up to the second story of the hotel, to a corner room with furnishings such as one doesn't expect to find in a hotel. I mean to say, the bed was bolted heavily to the wall, and the wall was reënforced with big six-by-six stanchions to accommodate the bolts. There was a chair, screwed to the floor, also; and there was an iron rod running across one side of the room, with a chain and a double pair of shackles hitched to it.

"We'll try to make you comfortable here, Sidney," said the colonel. "It's the best that I can do for you, at the moment."

He said this as he turned from lighting a lantern that was bracketed onto the wall of the room, and the falling glow of light etched his smile in white and black, and made him look like a very contented old devil.

Maker said: "This is all right, Riggs. When one end of the plank goes up, the other one has to go down. That's a law, I suppose."

He sat himself down in the chair and folded his hands. I've said before that I had tied his hands in front of him. The colonel noticed this and called it rash. However, after he had fitted the shackles on his guest and locked them, he seemed much more contented. In the meantime, he pointed out that he had hated to have a place like this in his hotel, but that there had to be something in lieu of a jail in a town like Piegan.

Maker only nodded, and yawned. He was as cool a fellow as I ever saw.

"Now, Sidney," said Riggs, "what can I do to make you comfortable?"

"Feed me," said Maker.

The colonel nodded, and pulled a bell rope that made a faint tingling in the distance.

"By the way," said I, "you owe Maker a hundred dollars."

"I do?" murmured the colonel, waiting for the point of the joke.

"I had to borrow a hundred dollars from him," said I. "I had to take it out of his wallet."

I pulled out the leather case as a sort of proof.

"By the jumping thunder!" said the colonel. "Is that Maker's wallet? Let me have it!"

I stared at him.

"I'm not a robber, colonel," said I. "I keep this until Maker goes free, and then he gets it back. I only want you to pass over the hundred to fill it up the way I found it."

"That's a good one, too." Maker sneered.

The colonel laughed. He was in the highest good humor, as a matter of course.

"Look here," he said, "I see a whole sheaf of papers in that wallet. I don't give a whack about the gold that's in it, but I'd like to look into the secret workings of Mr. Maker's mind. Let me have the wallet, Jerry. Don't you fear that I'll steal a penny from an old friend like Sid Maker."

He laughed again, holding out his hand, but I shoved the wallet back inside my coat.

"You don't understand," said I. "This belongs to Maker. It's not mine to give you."

By this time, Riggs was ready to gape.

"Say that again!" he commanded.

"I said," I repeated, "that I'm not a thief."

"Just a kidnaper, eh?" said Riggs, with his sneer, which was as ready as his smile.

I had to groan a little, when he called me a kidnaper, and I answered: "Well, colonel, you may call me that, I suppose. But this is a strange part of the world. You're all breaking the law, out here. When we got to the bridge over Maker Creek, we were almost lynched, all three of us. Heads are fitted on pretty loosely, it seems, in this neck of the world. And stealing Maker himself, why, that's in the game, as I see it. But stealing a penny out of Maker's pocket, that doesn't go."

In fact, that was the way that I saw the thing then, and to tell you the truth, that's the way I see it now. The whole set of them, on both sides, were ready to stuff ballot boxes, fight to the death, cut throats right and left. Grabbing Maker was simply in that game, it seemed to me. But Maker's wallet—well, that was different, and I had made a certain promise to Betty Cole.

No matter how clear the affair was to me, and my point of view, Riggs was staggered as if I had shot him through the head, and even Maker was agape as he stared at me.

"I know what you mean," said Riggs dryly. "Of course there's a value on that wallet. I know that you're not fool enough to give away your fortune, though I can't help telling you that if you resign your future into my hands, it will be all the better for you, my lad!"

The oily old hypocrite!

I looked in his face and smiled.

"Good for you, colonel," said I. "I know that you'll be generous. But the wallet stays with me till we turn Maker loose. It has to be that way because it's the only way that I can see. First I want something to eat. Then I want to sleep. And I'm going to do both inside of this room. Otherwise, we'll find that Maker has slipped out and taken to wings."

The colonel swayed back on his heels, as though he needed a little extra distance from which to look me over. And after a long moment of silence he muttered:

"Well, we'll let it go like that, just now! Only don't try to play both ends against the middle, my son!"

With that, he went stalking out of the room, in a cold fury!

I saw him go with no great concern. This was a pretty confused business, all right.

Presently they brought in a pair of heavy trays, and I set the hands of Maker free and shoved the table over where he could sit on the chair and eat in some comfort.

He said nothing to me, during all of that time, but just ate, and drank his coffee, and every now and then he lifted a scowling glance at me, and held it steadily on my face for a moment.

Finally he finished. I gave him the makings of a cigarette, and we smoked together, while I filled up the cups with the last of the coffee.

Then he said:

"You've got me beat. You've got me stopped, kid."

I shrugged my shoulders. There was really nothing that I could say to that, of course.

"What's the matter, Jerry—if that's your name," said he. "Why do you throw in with that long-legged frog eater, that crook of a Riggs?"

"I bumped into him first, and he's done me a good turn," said I.

He began to nod.

"You're right," said he. "It pays to remember a good friend. But I'm sorry for you. The pay will be slow, in your case, I'm afraid. But about that wallet. You meant what you said?"

"Yes. I meant it."

"Well, you've got me beat," said Maker.

He went on smoking, his scowl deepening, his eyes almost disappearing under his brows.

"Look here!" said he.

"Well?" said I.

"You know that Riggs will never stop till he has that wallet out of you? You know that he'll cut your throat to get at it? You know that what's in that wallet means more to him than I do?"

I listened, and could guess that he was right. When the colonel left the room, it was with the look of one who is coming back, before long.

"That's all right," said I. "A man has to take his chances."

"Well," muttered Maker, "I wish you luck. But you're going up against a tough one. Riggs, he looks good-natured. He is, too. He's free and easy, with the lives and

96

the money of other men. He never has used a gun in his life, but he's caused more killings than any ten men in the West!"

That I could more than half believe, too. And the more I thought about this picture into which I was fitting myself, the crazier and more dangerous it seemed. I finished my cigarette, stamped out the coal of it, and carried the trays outside the door, into the hall. Down the hall there were two shadows, leaning on things that were not walking sticks. I saw that my friend the colonel had blocked the hall with a pair of riflemen.

So I went back and locked the door behind me.

"Your chain is long enough to let you go to bed," said I to Maker. "I'll borrow one blanket off the bed and turn in on the floor. It won't make my bones ache. I could sleep through a hurricane, just now. But if you stir on the bed, or so much as lift your head, it will waken me. And the minute that you hear a noise, let me know, will you? If they try to break through that door or climb through that window, I'll stop them if I can."

CHAPTER XVI

The Celebration

I COULDN'T go to sleep at once, for all of that. Because suddenly Piegan woke up. The whole of that little town got up on its highest horse and came with tin pans and horns and lighted lanterns and flaming torches, and pranced and danced and raised the devil in front of the Riggs Hotel.

I said that the town seemed under a shadow when I rode into it that afternoon. But the shadow had lifted now. That was the sunniest little spot in the world, in spite of the dark of the night. A word and a rumor had gone around, and I could guess what that word and that rumor was, because when the crowd came yelling, they were singing the praises of Colonel Riggs, and cheering for Piegan, the county seat!

You can bet that they wanted to win that election. The winning meant that every man's investment was returned to him, multiplied by ten; the losing meant that the investment was wiped right off the books just the way that Piegan would be wiped off the map.

They yelled for the colonel; they demanded a speech.

I went to the window and saw a fellow get on the seat of a buckboard with a bottle of whisky in one hand and a revolver in the other. He would let off a sentence in praise of Riggs, and then fire a couple of shots out of his gun. And when he fired, the horses hitched to the buckboard would make a lurch and he would sway over and balance on one foot, like a performer on a tight wire.

When he rocked back to the level again, he would take a swig out of the bottle and resume his speech in the favor of Riggs, the maker, the creator, the savior of Piegan.

The crowd was greatly amused by this performance, and in the interims of the speech, they yelled and howled, and they called for the colonel over and over again.

Finally he came out and stood on the front of the porch, where I could just see him. How they yipped when they saw him. Some of them wanted to give him a ride on their shoulders. But he waved them away, and said it would be a shame to leave that spot, because he had just ordered a barrel of whisky to be tapped in the middle of the street.

After that, the crowd was pretty willing to linger right there!

Then everybody grew silent, and the colonel started in his speech.

He began it quietly, making a few jokes, and picking

out men here and there for a word or two, or a pleasant remark, and all heads turned, with a white flash, toward the people he was singling out. A neat way he had of making friends from the platform, that fellow Riggs. And one could see that he was a good fellow—in public!

Then he changed his topic a trifle, and he said that he feared it could not be a perfect evening for everybody in Piegan. He feared that there was one exception. He was afraid that there was a man in Piegan, that night, who was famous as a builder of towns. And he couldn't be sure that that man was really happy.

Of course the crowd appreciated this a lot. They howled and laughed, and then a couple who were already more than half drunk, began to yell that it was time to lynch Sid Maker, and that he had lived long enough, and that he was a treacherous snake, and not a man at all.

The colonel held up both his hands to command silence. It was quite grand and made a fine picture to see him stand there, with his long arms lifted, and the wind fanning the long tails of his coat—he had put on a claw hammer—and the torch light dancing and flaming against the silver of his flowing hair.

I admired him, and despised him, and laughed at him, and admired him again, all in a moment.

Then he told the crowd that it was far from him to wish to see any mob violence staining the pure record of Piegan. Some one burst out into a guffaw, at this, because it was known that at least half a dozen men had been murdered up to date in the young "pure" record of that city. The man who laughed was hit by about ten fists from ten different angles, and his laughter went out like a candle.

Yes, a nice, gentle crowd that was!

The colonel went on talking, after the interruption, and he said that he wouldn't countenance any harm done to Maker. He realized that he was only one voice in the growing city of Piegan, but that that one voice must always be raised against violence, and upon the side of right and law.

I thought that every one would break into a roar of laughter, at this nonsense, but the people simply nodded,

99

and murmured agreement. They had been ready to take off the colonel's hide, at sunset. They were ready to make him a hero, now, and a prophet, too.

He went on with some more balderdash, and finally he referred to "three brave young men who had endangered their lives for the sake of Piegan."

There was a long, loud howl, a cowboy yell, at that. And every hat went spinning up into the air, as though the thing had been rehearsed.

Then the colonel stretched out a long, skinny arm, and singled out a face.

"There's one of them now," said he, "as brave a lad as ever forked a horse!"

It was Slim Jim Earl, and the men near him had him on their shoulders, at once. He stood up in their arms and began to saw the air and make a speech. He had had too much of that free whisky, of course, and it had loosened his tongue clear to the roots. He declared that there had not been three. There had been only one, and two of them were just present, and that was all. He and Dan Loftus had worked on marching orders, and he wanted to tell them what Poker-face had done.

Believe me when I say that he told them. I never heard such a strong imagination at work. He knew a good deal of what had happened, and even that he embroidered with a margin of red and gold. And when he came to the missing chapter, my excursion to the house of Maker, he let his imagination run riot. He simply gave the boys red-hot shots, one after another. According to him, I seemed able to walk through walls, make myself invisible, out-shot five or six practiced gun fighters, and he wound up by having me run half a mile, carrying Sid Maker like a sack of potatoes on my shoulders, and turning, now and then, to shoot it out with the mounted Makerites.

I never had heard such rot. I heard the crowd grow silent. I waited, holding my breath, for the explosion of derisive laughter. But they didn't laugh! They exploded, right enough, but it was with cheers. They fairly split the sky with their noise, and made a flame jump in the center of my brain.

I turned back into the room.

"Slim Jim is the biggest natural liar that I ever listened to," I said to Maker.

He only laughed.

"We breed 'em the biggest of all kinds, in everything, out this far West," said he. "Don't be surprised, son!" And he laughed again. "Listen to 'em now!" said he.

They were cheering once more, organized cheering, and the person that they were cheering was Poker-face!

I have to be honest. It made me feel small. Something shrank inside me, but there was a core of burning joy that made me tremble. Then the speech of the colonel went on, but I had heard enough. I got my blanket, rolled up in it, and lay down in the exact center of the room.

"Maker," I said, "if anything happens, give me a call."

Then I went to sleep like falling off a log.

However, I wasn't due to sleep out the whole of that night. The colonel, confound him, had started that crowd to madness with his greasy, hypocritical talk. And it appeared that after I went to sleep, he talked right on, and gradually built for the people a pretty frightful picture of Sidney Maker, the man-killer, the destroyer who wanted to burn Piegan to the ground. And he particularly drew a bright picture of the guard posted on the Maker Creek bridge, with orders to hang any man from Piegan who attempted to cross it.

This thing went on for some time.

At last, through my sleep, I seemed to hear a sound of thunder. And next, a voice called:

"Jerry! Hey!"

I started up, with my heart hammering.

"They're coming for me, boy," said Maker.

That was it. The sound of thunder had been the roar of footfalls on the stairs. The noise was flowing down the upper hall now. It seemed to be right in the same room with me.

Outside, in the street, I could hear voices yelling: "We want Maker! We want Maker!"

Yes, that smooth devil of a Riggs had done his business thoroughly and started the bloodhounds after a helpless

101

prisoner. I saw the thing in a flash, and it made me sick at heart, I can tell you!

Maker was saying, as I ran to the window and looked out: "It's no use, son. They want me; and they're going to have me. I knew it would be this way, the moment I saw Riggs's face, when you refused him the wallet. He meant murder then. He's doing murder now. Keep out of the way and see that you don't get mixed in. I'll tell you this— you've been a white man. The only white man in the whole town of Piegan!"

Outside the door, the footfalls stopped. A hand beat heavily upon the door.

"Hey, Poker-face!"

"Yes?" I answered.

"Are you there, Poker-face?"

"Yes, I'm here."

"Is Maker in there with you?"

"No," said I. "He's in another room."

"He says that Maker is in another room," called the questioner.

There was a loud answer from the back of the crowd.

Then the hand beat on my door again.

"It won't do, Poker-face," said the speaker. "You're a good kid, a grand kid, and the pride of Piegan. But we want Maker, and we're goin' to have him. If you knew what he was, you wouldn't want to save him. Open the door, because we're goin' to come in."

I waited a moment. Then I sat down in the chair. I was sick. Icy sweat came out all over my body. It came out so thick that it began to run.

"D'you hear?" called the man at the door, beating on it again, and anger coming hotter in his voice.

His enunciation was a little thick. I guessed that he and two thirds of the rest were partly drunk. Just drunk enough for blind murder.

But something forced me ahead. I won't call it conscience, but a voice came up in me that found its own way through my lips, a thin, small, croaking voice that I didn't recognize.

"I'll shoot the first man through the door!" said that voice.

CHAPTER XVII

Gun Play

THERE was an uproar, in answer. I heard some of them saying that they would break my neck, and others yelling to the leaders to go on and break down the door.

Then some one put a big bullet through the lock of the door and smashed it open with a kick.

I was sitting in the chair telling myself that I must not faint. I knew that I was about as good as dead. For I had to interfere, and if I did, that mob would break me into pieces too small to find.

Well, as I sat there with the revolver hanging loosely out of my fingers, through the door charged the figure of a man I recognized, for it was that same Hooker who had been bullying Riggs in the office during the evening of that day. I tell you, I was positively glad to see that it was Hooker. If I had to shoot somebody, he was just the man for me.

When he saw me with the gun in my hand, he yelled out: "Murder! Come on, boys!"

Jerking up a short-barreled, heavy carbine that he was carrying, he let drive at me. The thing was a regular blunderbuss. The kick of it turned him half around, and as he turned, I fired.

I knew that my shot had gone home. Hooker sagged sidewise toward the door, for a step or two.

It seemed to me that there were ten people jammed in that doorway, but not a one of them made an attempt to break in on me after the shot I fired.

Hooker turned around toward them, with one hand held over the wound, and the other hand stretched out before him, as though he were groping for a light.

That big, roaring voice of his had become as quiet as the voice of a sick child, as he said:

"Boys, he shot me! Boys, he's killed me!"

He stumbled out into the hallway, and there I saw him collapsing, and hands grasping at him, and supporting him, and carrying him away.

Well, the whole crowd turned its attention to Hooker, and not a soul was left to charge me through that open door. I could hardly believe that the danger had come and gone like this. But there I sat, still master of the situation.

I was thankful that my heart was not rioting. I told myself that I would be hanged for this, in due course of time. But there was hardly any way for me to get out of the hotel, and in the meantime, I seemed dying of fatigue. So I gave my revolver to my prisoner, and told him to use it to stop any advance through the door, and to wake me up in the pinch.

"Boy," he said, "set me free from these irons, and you and I will break through ten walls of hellfire. Together, nothing in the world could stop me!"

I answered what I thought, for some reason. Perhaps I was too sick and tired to do any real thinking.

"I've started on this line, and I'm going to fight it out this way. I'll try to see that they don't double-cross you again, Maker."

He was too much of a man to argue. I wrapped myself in the blanket and lay down. For a time, I watched Maker, interested in the tireless way in which he sat up there on the bed, gun in hand, rigid, always ready for a fight. Then I began to wonder about the silence that had fallen over Piegan. It had been as noisy as a great battlefield, a short time before. Now it was as still as a graveyard. Only, from time to time, I thought that I heard whispering voices. In the midst of that wonder I fell asleep.

When I wakened, it was well past dawn, and along in the rose of the early morning. I got up and washed, and wished for a shave. I took some soap and water to Maker, and he looked me over with a grin.

"Not as neat as I've seen you, Poker-face," said he. "Give me the makings, will you?"

He made his smoke with his manacled hands, and I lighted it for him. He drew in a great breath of the smoke, and talked with the cloud issuing in a rush from mouth and nose, torn into fragments by his enunciation.

"That didn't mean anything to you, kid, I guess," said he.

"What? Last night?" said I.

"Yes, last night. You snored in your sleep. You've got enough brass in you to line all the boilers in the world."

"I was tired, Sid," said I, "but I was scared, too. I was terribly scared."

"Yeah, I'll bet you were scared," he drawled in unbelief.

"I was. I was scared to death."

"Quit it, Poker-face," said he. "I never saw a cooler thing in my life than the way you let that brute of a Hooker take a shot at you before you plastered him. That's drawing it pretty fine, boy, to let a man drive at you from that distance. You're cutting it pretty fine, Poker-face, and one of these days you may miss a trick. But I suppose that you've kidded with death so long and so often that you think she's a sweetheart, eh?"

"Listen to me, Sid," said I seriously. "You're getting an entirely wrong notion. My nerves are just as weak as the next fellow's. I didn't expect that Hooker would be brute enough to shoot at me before I'd lifted a hand against him. That's the only reason that I waited. Not because I wanted to give him the first chance. It makes me sick to have you wander around with the wrong impression of me, Sid. I'm just as common and ordinary in every way as any other man. There was once a time, but that's gone —that's gone!"

I stopped off short, for I was thinking about my palmy days, when I lived in the pink of condition, and ten hours slogging in the gymnasium were not too much for me. Those were the days when I was all India rubber and tool-proof steel. Those were the days when I could let the hefty socks bounce off my jaw, while I waded in with both hands, hunting for the knock-out.

But those days were all dead for me. And they wouldn't come back, either. I was a dead man. Half of me was dead, that is to say. The other half dragged on a miserable existence.

I recovered to hear Maker saying: "Once you were an artist, eh? Was that it? Now you're only the pet man-killer of Piegan. But you're doing pretty well in your line, kid. Don't you complain. You're making yourself a real head-liner."

I saw, all at once, that it was no use to argue. Maker was a level-headed fellow, but he had seen me under such circumstances that he insisted on making me out a prodigy.

I sat silently by the window and looked up and down the street. It was fairly empty. A man walked across toward the hotel with his coat collar turned up around his neck, and a derby hat on the back of his head, and his hands shoved down into his coat pockets. He looked dirty, unshaven, and whisky-sick.

I felt somewhat the same way, though I hadn't a drink in me.

How I yearned for a drink then! How I begged in my soul for one, but I knew that I didn't dare touch the stuff. Not with a crazy, shaking heart like mine.

"You better go to sleep, Maker," said I.

"I slept four or five hours last night," said Sid Maker. "I'm all right. I've had all the sleep that I can use. I want food, right now."

"Maybe they'll try to starve me out," I suggested.

Just then, down the hallway, came a light, long step, drawing rapidly near us.

"Hello, boys! Hello, Jerry," sang out the voice of that scoundrel, Colonel Riggs.

106

I took the revolver from Maker, shoved it into my coat, and went to the door. There I met the colonel.

"Well?" said I.

He tried to meet my eyes, but he couldn't.

Then he wanted to carry the thing off with a flow of words. He always had plenty of words, confound him.

"Things are swimming, positively swimming along," said he. "I've sent my agents all over the county. Makerville—you'll be sorry to hear this, Sidney—is buzzing like a hive of wasps, but the town has just learned that you're visiting over here, and they hardly know what to do. In fact, they're doing nothing, but letting Piegan step out and collect the honey!"

He laughed and rubbed his hands.

I let him come in and stood back against the wall, bracing my shoulders against it, studying him.

"The whole county will be swept," he said. "There's no doubt about the way that things are going. I won't deny, Sidney, that you had a great following, but you must understand how it is. People in this part of the world believe that a man is either on top of his luck or under it. They like to follow the man who's on top, and since they find me sitting in the saddle just now, they're following me. Several of your best men from Makerville have ridden over and offered to enlist with my forces, to-day."

"Have they?" snapped Maker, touched at last. "Bert?"

"No."

"Swede?"

"No, not that one."

"Chuck?"

"I haven't denied that a few of your men are faithful, Maker. I wouldn't expect them all to come away."

"If I have those three, I don't care about the rest," said Maker. "You're welcome to the lot. You hear?"

"I hear you, of course," said the colonel. "But, in addition, you must remember that the election is to-morrow. Forgotten that?"

Maker said nothing. He made his face a rather sullen blank and comforted himself with silence.

"Now then, boys," said the colonel, carrying on

smoothly, "I suppose that you have an appetite for breakfast. I've got some of the best ham you ever laid an eye on, and fresh eggs, too. And coffee—you can smell it from here! There's only a little trifle to ask of you first, my son." He turned to me.

"What is it, colonel?" said I.

"There are a lot of angry men in this town, boy. They want your life, but I'll stand between you and them, never fear. However, I think that you better intrust that wallet to me, in the first place. It would be safer, I should say."

I merely stared at him, my shoulders comfortably against the wall.

"Well?" he asked, somewhat impatiently. "What are you thinking of?"

"I'm thinking it's a strange thing," said I, "that nobody's killed you. Because I'm half of a mind to do that job myself, right now!"

CHAPTER XVIII

The Colonel Pays

IT was always amusing to see the line that the old rascal took when he was in a corner. He pretended to be very surprised now.

"Why, my dear boy, my dear boy! I'm offering you my personal guarantee of safety against mob violence in this rough young community. And in exchange, I'm merely suggesting that you should let—"

"Colonel," said I, "will you quit it?"

He dropped his manner at once.

"Quit what, Jerry?" said he.

"Quit this nonsense. Don't you suppose that I under-stand perfectly that you built up that crowd last night for the sake of seeing Sid Maker, here, smashed and torn to pieces?"

"I?" cried the colonel, lifting both hands in protest toward the ceiling.

Suddenly I began to laugh. I couldn't help it. The old boy was too perfect in his part and in his lines. I saw that he was a perfect rascal, and while I was laughing, I saw him looking toward me with a twinkle in his eyes.

When I could sober up, I said that I wanted a shave and breakfast for two.

"Come down with me," said Riggs, "unless you think that Maker may not be safe in your absence. Safe from the crowd, I mean."

"I've made him safe from the crowd," said I. And I nodded at Sid.

He lifted in his manacled hands the big, blue-barreled Colt that I had passed to him.

I thought that Riggs would faint. He actually made a step to get behind me.

"It's no use, colonel," said I. "That gun is a beauty. It would think nothing of shooting through a span of men at this distance."

"You've given Sid Maker a gun!" said Riggs.

"He was pretty lonely without it," said I.

"I never thought to see the day when Sid Maker would be in my hotel with a gun in his hand! Get out of this, boy. I want to talk with you. Come along with me!" ordered the colonel.

I tailed along behind him, and stopped at the door to say:

"I'd leave that wallet with you, Sid, but it would only get you murdered while I'm gone. I'll see that some break-fast is sent up to you, though."

He thanked me, and I went down the hall behind Riggs.

The rascal took me to his own room, which was furnished very comfortably, and he offered me a drink of whisky out of his own silver-mounted flask. Well, I stared at that drink which he had poured for nearly a minute, with my whole soul turning over from a desire for the shot, but finally I shook my head. I knew that even a single slug might put me in bed for twenty-four hours, if it happened to hit me in the wrong way.

But I took a bath and a shave, and left my clothes to be cleaned and brushed and pressed, while I wrapped up in one of the colonel's dressing gowns and had breakfast in his room—and what a breakfast it was. He was tormented by the sight of me eating, and as I put away steaks and eggs and ham and hot corn bread, and a lot of hot milk and coffee, Riggs walked up and down the room and made faces that looked like indigestion pains.

I ate and ate, and ate again. I stocked up for everything that I had missed. Supper of the night before had been merely a whet, so to speak.

In the meantime, while he stalked about the room, Riggs was telling me about his plans for sweeping the county. And I must say that he had thought up some good things.

He had a dozen men and women working in various places, quietly spreading rumors that boosted Piegan and dropped the stock of Makerville as a possibility for the county seat.

He had it out that Makerville was lying on loose gravel inclining toward the bed of Maker Creek, and that the first serious earthquake would spill the whole town down into the creek bed. Then, again, he had other people telling that the gravel on which Makerville stood would not uphold securely the foundations necessary for public buildings.

He had it rumored that Makerville was a fever hole, and that the place had always been avoided by the Indians, natural connoisseurs of healthful spots.

In a word, he was undermining Makerville from beneath and blasting it from above. And where these methods did not seem likely to succeed, he was rounding up all the floating "vote" of tramps and hoodlums and buying them for election day.

That was the way of it with Colonel Riggs, "maker of cities."

He got very enthusiastic, as he detailed his plans, and enlarged upon his schemes. And as he talked, he caught fire from fire, and new ideas came to him that made him jump for pencil and notebook. He said that I was a stimulating companion, and that it was easy to see that I got the best out of people by inspiring them. As a matter of fact, I had hardly said three words.

Finally, my clothes came back in neat order at the end of the meal, and I dressed. Then I suggested to Riggs that he might pay me for the work I had done.

"Come, come, my boy," says he, "you can't expect to keep the thing and make me pay for it?"

"Keep what?" I asked.

"You're keeping Maker in your hands," said Riggs.

"I'm keeping him from dirty murder, that's all," said I.

"He's no use to me," said Riggs.

"I'll turn him loose then," said I, "and you'll see how long it takes him to knock all of your fine election schemes into a cocked hat."

I started for the door.

"Hold on, Jerry," bawled the colonel, "you don't seem to understand that a man will talk in a heat, now and then, and exceed caution, a little. You must allow for a trifle of exaggeration. Of course I'm glad to have that rascal of a Maker here in quiet. Though it—"

"All right," said I. "You admit that he's worth a lot to you. But all I want is the twenty-five hundred that I bargained for. I want that and I want it now. I'm collecting, Riggs."

"But the bargain—" he protested.

"The bargain was that I should deliver him in Piegan. Here he is."

Riggs sighed. "I half expected," said he, "that you would take this line with me. But I'm too old a man to expect real justice from a young man. Well, well, my

111

friend, here is the money agreed upon. Take it, and good luck to you."

He held out to me a heavy little canvas bag. I took it.

"Now the hundred dollars to fill up Maker's wallet?" said I.

"Yes, I haven't forgotten that, either," said Riggs.

He smiled at me in the most genial fashion, and of course I knew at once that he was lying as fast as a clock can tick. However, I chose to grin at him.

He was in a good deal of a hurry now, and looked at his watch, and exclaimed that he had an appointment, and that he would have to run, as a matter of fact!

Well, I simply stood between him and the door and laughed some more.

"It's no good, Riggs," said I.

"What's no good?" said he, frowning.

"I'm going to count my money—so that I can give you a receipt in full."

He lost some of the pink in his hanging jowls.

"Tut, tut, Jerry," said he. "Between gentlemen—a receipt, indeed! Wouldn't dream of asking such a thing. I know that your word is as good as another man's bond. I have the most perfect trust in your integrity, my boy. The most perfect faith in the world."

He tried to push past me, saying that he would see me later but that now—

I caught him by the arm.

"Sit down, colonel!" said I.

He looked back at me, saw poison, I suppose, and submitted. He went over to the window and sat down in a chair, where a broad stream of sunshine poured in upon him. And his long, active fingers were drumming rapidly against the arm of the chair.

Then I opened the canvas bag and poured the money out on the table. The stack was big enough to contain twenty-five hundred dollars in gold, but as a matter of fact, a good part of it consisted of fine, fat, silver dollars!

I counted the sum over, calling to the colonel to watch me, and make sure that I didn't palm any of the coins.

He muttered something about perfect faith and trust

112

between gentlemen, but I paid no attention to that. I was stacking the coins in heaps of ten which made the counting easier, and that blackguard, I found, had put into the canvas sack, exactly one half of the sum he had promised. There were twelve hundred and fifty dollars!

"What did you put in here, Riggs?" I asked him.

"I? The sum agreed upon, of course," said he.

"That was twenty-five hundred?"

"Yes, certainly, and with the deductions—"

"What deductions?"

"Four horses and a buckboard—thrown quite away, my lad. You understand—"

"They were simply tools in the job. You knew that. What value did you put on them, though?"

"For the horses, I called it five hundred—"

"Five hundred?" I broke in. "You could buy a gross of ponies like that for forty dollars apiece, and you know it. But let it go. The rig?"

"For the rig, two hundred—"

"That second-hand affair is not worth a hundred."

"Come, come, my boy," said he, "business is business, you know."

"And robbery is robbery," said I. "But even checking it off at your rate, you take seven hundred from twenty-five hundred. No, from twenty-six hundred, and that leaves me with nineteen hundred coming."

"My dear lad, why should I pay for the hay load and hire? You receive a flat rate and you contract to deliver certain goods—Maker, in this case. Naturally, you may have certain incidental expenses along the way. Now you come to me and ask for repayment!"

"Granting you all that," said I, "you would owe me eighteen hundred. Now, you're exactly five hundred and fifty shy of that sum."

"My dear lad," said he, "you deliver Maker, but you keep a string on him. Turn him and his wallet freely over to me and—"

I sat back with a sigh.

"Colonel," said I, "think it over. I'm with you, if you want. I know that you can be crooked. You think the whole world is crooked. But I'm suggesting that you try to play straight with me. Think it over, and then tell me."

When I said that, he began to lean forward in his chair, and he kept on leaning as he stared at me, until I almost thought that he would fall. All the smiling was gone from his wicked old face. He was simply drilling away at me and trying to get at the secret that he seemed to think was hidden somewhere in my soul.

I looked back. And, as I looked, I wondered how many miles of muck he had waded through in his journey through the world. I felt suddenly clean, in comparison, even with my burglary charge, and all of that stacked up against me.

"You don't forget, my lad," said he, "that you're wanted by the police!" He slowly grated out the words at me.

"Haven't you forgotten it?" said I.

He hesitated through another long moment. He was working his brain so hard that I could see his forehead glistening with the heat of thought. At length he pushed himself out of his chair and got to his feet.

There was a heavy safe against the wall, in a corner of the room. He went to it, worked on the combination, opened the door, and reached inside.

Then he straightened and came back to me, with another sack in his hands.

"Here's the other half of what I owe you, boy," said he, and clinked it down upon the table. "And here's an extra thousand out of which you can take the hundred you borrowed from Maker's wallet."

I didn't count that new money. I knew that he had told me the truth, and I was so astonished I almost fell out of my chair. But I was doing some fast thinking on my own behalf, just then. I took up two piles of twenties.

"This will do me for the time," said I. "You keep the rest safe in your strong box for me, will you, colonel?"

And I went straight out of the room, leaving things that way.

CHAPTER XIX

A Youth's Pride

WHEN I walked downstairs, that day, I stepped into a new world that I had never seen before. It had changed, for me, overnight. I met no one till I got down to the office in the lobby. In the lobby there were three or four men sitting about, hard-looking cowpunchers, brown with wind and weather, and looking fit for anything. They were smoking, and when I came down the stairs, I saw that their hands stopped moving back and forth from their mouths. Every right hand was stationary, and from it the fumes of the smoke rose steadily upward. I knew I had stopped their talk, for the moment, at least.

I went over to the desk, and there I found the same clerk who had been on such a high horse a couple of evenings before. He had changed his tune now. He spoke to me and gave me a good morning, and he nodded so profoundly that it was almost a bow. Well, I listened to him chattering about weather, and saw him rubbing his hands together, and watched his foolish eyes go past me toward the others in the lobby. It occurred to me that the idiot thought he was talking to a really important person.

All I wanted to know was how Hooker was getting on, and the clerk said that the doctor thought he might live through the thing, though it was a bad wound, straight through the body. The clerk said that Hooker was a tough fellow, and that a lot of people had been able to guess that before, but that now they knew it!

I was glad to know that Hooker might recover. Tough as he was said to be, if he had lasted through the first night, I felt that it was better than an even break that he would entirely get well.

With that off my mind, I hunted for the writing room, which was one of the luxuries of the hotel of which Riggs was most proud. I found it empty, almost as a matter of course, and I sat down there and wrote my full report to Betty Cole. I put down all the facts in order, and I found that there were so many of them that I had filled six pages with the list, before the finish.

Then, after I had sealed and addressed the envelope, I sat and dreamed for a while, wondering how many days it would be before I could have an answer from her, and as I sat there, I seemed to be urging the trains faster and faster across the continent. A miserable long time seemed to lie ahead of me!

After a time I got up and went out on the front porch of the hotel, with the veranda stretching off to the left of it, the veranda which was a regular fixture with hotels in the West, and in towns of such a size as Piegan.

A dozen men were seated there, canting their chairs back against the wall of the building, and one of them was talking in a way that interested me so that I paused a minute. before stepping onto the porch. He was saying:

"He's one of those Eastern crooks. He's done a lot of time. That's why he doesn't show any emotion in his face. You take a man who's been most of his life behind the bars, he learns how to think one thing and to look another. That's the truth about Poker-face."

"Well, he's not so old," said another man.

"He's around thirty-two," said the first speaker.

That was adding ten years or so to my age, and it was quite a jolt to think that I really seemed that old to people. Yes, the last year must have put a lot in my face, for another man added:

"He's about that age."

116

The first fellow went on: "Probably been in the pen, off and on, ever since he was about eighteen, or so."

"Maybe," says another.

A nice picture they were making of me!

"He sits on that chair," said the first one, "and just lets the gun hang from his fingers, and then he lets drive at poor Hooker."

"I wouldn't pity Hooker so much," said another. "Hooker had a gun in his hands. They say that he fired first."

"That's a lie," said the first speaker loudly. "If he'd shot at Poker-face, he couldn't have missed, at that distance and—"

I pushed the door open softly and stepped out. I saw that the first and principal speaker was a youngster of nineteen or twenty. I felt pretty old, in comparison, as I looked at that smooth, brown face.

"I say," he went on, "that it's a pretty sad thing when the colonel has to call in Eastern crooks to help him run a town like Piegan, that oughta go straight, and I say—"

Just then he noticed that heads were turning away from him, and glancing down the line, he saw me. He gasped, and jumped to his feet.

I waited for a minute, staring at him. I had no desire for trouble. It seemed to me that I had been through so much in the last few weeks that a matter of personal opinion was nothing at all, even when that opinion turned on me.

So I walked over to the pillar at the side of the steps and leaned against it, and rolled a cigarette. Behind me, there was one brief murmur, and then a dead silence. I used that silence to tell my fool of a heart to behave, and it did, very fairly enough. For I was beginning to have it under my thumb, so to speak, and it dared not jump while its boss was watching.

I had lighted my cigarette, when I heard a quick step come down the veranda toward me, and then, close behind my shoulder, a harsh, high, strained voice barked:

"Hey, you!"

I turned around. It was the young fellow. He was

117

twitching all over; his face was white, and his eyes were crazy.

I heard somebody muttering: "Don't you go and be a fool, Harry!"

But Harry didn't look like a fool; he looked like a crazy man. Behind him, I could see men shifting rapidly out of the line that projected past me and the youngster. It was plain that they expected bullets to start flying. It was plain that Harry expected the same thing. For he had one hand behind him, clutching something at his hip.

I did not need to be a prophet to know that what he clutched was the handle of a Colt.

And I was wearing no gun! Upstairs sat Sid Maker, with my Colt!

I hoped it was a warm comfort to him, because it left me pretty chilly.

What was the matter with Harry, anyway?

I saw, a moment later, as he broke out: "I been saying some things about you, Ash. You heard 'em?"

His voice was higher and more cracked than ever.

"I heard some of them," said I.

"I only wanta tell you this," said he. "What I've said, I stick by it!"

Then I understood. He was half mad with fear, but his pride was stronger than his terror, by far. He had talked before a crowd, and he was not going to take water before a crowd. He would rather die. He was expecting to die, and at once.

Why?

Well, I could understand that, too. After the accidents and adventures of the last couple of days, the people of Piegan were beginning to think that I was one of those lightning artists with a gun. One of those dead-shot marvels who have appeared now and again, man-killers, apparently invincible, with a movement of the hand as fast as thought. Of course, that was rot. I never was a very good shot. And I never was above the average on the draw. There was no need of being above average, in a case like this. If I had had a gun, I could have pulled it out at my leisure and killed this fool of a kid.

118

However, I had no gun, and it was plain that he intended to fight the thing right through. He looked like a frenzied horse, that's ready to dash over a precipice.

What could I do? To say that I had no weapon would make me out a coward, in turn. No one would believe that. My hands were empty. All that I could do with them was to make them into fists.

"It's all right, Harry," I said. "Words don't hurt me. They're not bullets, and I don't carry grudges."

He blinked.

"You think that you can laugh at me?" he screamed. "Fill your hand, you—"

He began to curse me. He was shaking more than ever. His eyes were horrible to see. They were green, and rolling.

There was nothing for it. I had to lean once more on the old game and trust once more that there was something left in my right arm.

So I jerked the hand from below my hip and rose on my toes, and snapped the punch fairly home on the end of his chin.

He swayed back. A Colt swung out in his right hand, and I thought it was the end of me, but instead of shooting, he slumped to both knees and one hand. I leaned over and picked the gun from his nerveless fingers.

119

CHAPTER XX

A Friend

NOTHING that I know of was ever such a great comfort to me as that moment. I mean to say, to know that the old right arm still had some dynamite in it was more than a blessing. That Harry was a good, solid chunk of a fellow; I had been surprised by the weight of him against my fist. But there he was kneeling on the veranda ready to be counted out if ever a man was.

When I had his gun, I asked a couple of the bystanders to help him into a chair. Then I changed my mind and asked them to take him into the corner saloon which was also the property of the great Colonel Riggs.

In there, they put him into a chair. Everybody on the veranda had sidled in to see what might happen. As Harry was coming to, I gave him a slug of redeye, and he put it down, his eyes still rolling. The shock of it straightened him, all at once. He jumped up, saw me, and reached for his gun.

So I handed it to him, butt first, and he gaped as he took it. Then he felt the sore spot on his jaw. It was so childish and naïve, this action of his as he recovered his wits, that one of the fools looking on broke out into a guffaw. I turned and paid that fellow off with a glare that silenced him.

I felt no animosity towards Harry. In fact, I was simply

glad that I had had a target to shoot at with my fist, so to speak. I asked him if he were willing to shake hands and call everything quits, but he stared emptily at me, and so I turned around and went out of the place.

He worried me a good deal, so much, in fact, that I went down the street to the general-merchandise store. There I found a good gun counter and bought myself a pair of Colts. The storekeeper insisted that I should take the guns for nothing. He tried to compliment me by saying that as long as I was in town I saved him the cost of an insurance policy. But I made him take the money, and so I got out of the place and away down the street.

All this time I was thinking pretty hard and fast.

What had happened so far had made me, in the eyes of Piegan, a great man. That was all very well. It was pleasant to be a great man in the eyes of any community, large or small. But the better known I became, the more apt the law was to get on my traces.

Besides, it appeared from the actions of Harry that I was now celebrated as a gun-fighter. If not, he would not have made such a desperate scene with me. An ordinary fellow he would have allowed to pass. But if he let me go by, he would be said to have taken water.

That was bad for me, of course.

Beyond a doubt, there would be occasions when I would have to face armed men again, and on those occasions, every man would feel it his point of duty and of pride to take a fair crack at me with guns. All that was in my favor was this false reputation I had built up. I knew that there were fifty men in that one county who could shoot the eyes out of my head, who were far faster and surer in every way with a weapon of any kind. But the nerves of a good many of them would be upset by merely the reputation which was behind me, just as the nerves of young Harry had been broken for the moment, or strung to wire tension as he faced me.

You can see that matters were becoming rather complicated for me in Piegan, and I decided that as soon as the next few days had passed and the election was over, and Maker given his freedom, I would get out of that town

121

and leave it my blessing and a long back trail. For that purpose, I determined on studying the adjacent country thoroughly. In case I had to make a start, I must know where to travel, and how.

I had come, in my thoughts as I went back towards the hotel, to the conclusion that I would have to inure myself to horse and saddle, and build up endurance for the crisis which was almost sure to arrive, and just at this time I saw a form looming in my way and looked up to see Harry.

I could hardly recognize him. His face was no longer pinched and white. His eyes were no longer insane with determination and terror. Instead, he was just a big, heavy-shouldered kid, with the brownest, most handsome face you ever saw. I stopped short, but he stuck out a big hand towards me.

"I hope you'll take it, Mr. Ash," says he.

Of course I took it, and no one with a readier will. He almost smashed the metacarpal bones in my right hand. I have never met with such a terrible grip as he had!

I endured this for the long moment that it lasted, and then managed to keep on smiling back at him.

He said: "That was a hefty sock that you handed me, Mr. Ash. My head's still got an open roof on it. But that's all right. I'm glad you hit me with a fist instead of with a bullet. I'm glad to be still on earth. That was the first time that I ever pulled a gun on another man," said he, "and I wouldn't have done it to-day, only——"

He paused, and I finished off for him:

"That's all right. I understand about that. You thought it was a question of taking water or not taking it. I don't blame you a bit. Forget about it, Harry. We're friends, now."

"Forget about it?" says he, in a ringing voice. "I'll never forget about it! The boys tell me that what you did was the gamest thing ever——that I had my gun out before you moved. You ought to 'a' killed me, for a fool. But you didn't. You simply trusted to your fist. Well, I owe you my life, Mr. Ash, and I'll never forget *that!*"

You see how he took it! Somehow, I couldn't explain to

him that I had not had a gun on me. I knew that he would not have believed me.

"Drop that 'Mister,' Harry," said I. "My name is Jerry Ash. Or Poker-face, if you please. About the other thing, I'm going to forget it, even if you won't."

"It was like this—Jerry," said he, hesitating a little over the name. "Some of the boys had been talking you up, and I had heard you talked down, here and there, and I was saying what I had heard. Besides, I had had a few drinks under my belt, and I knew that that always makes a fool of me. I ain't asking your pardon. It's too deep for that. Only, the next time that there's trouble and you're near it, you see which side I'm on!"

A tremor came into his voice. So I shook hands with him again, and said that I believed him, and off he went, stalking.

He hurried across the street, and I went back to the hotel more thoughtfully than ever. It was occurring to me that that youngster had been blooded, on this day, and the next time that he pulled a gun, there might be a shake in his voice, but there would be none in his hand! Perhaps I had looked in on the making of a man!

When I got back to the hotel, Colonel Riggs was there sitting on the veranda, and he stood up and spread his legs in his manner when he was about to make a speech. Instead of making the speech, however, he took me by the arm and went slowly inside the hotel with me. He said, in a quiet voice, a voice that sounded new to me:

"I'm not surprised, Jerry. They've told me all about it. But I'm not surprised. Nobody else would have done it. But there aren't many like you, in this world. Don't forget it. There are not many like you in this world!"

This was too thick for me. I said: "Oh, rot. How's Hooker?"

"Hooker is going to pull through," said Riggs. "Never give him a thought. After this morning, nobody will ever hold last night against you. Nobody but me!"

He looked down at me with a whimsical smile and added: "You know why, Jerry?"

123

I stared back at him, and saw the trouble and the shadow behind his smile.

"I can guess, colonel," said I. "It's Maker."

"Ay, it's Maker," he admitted. "He'll never forgive me, as long as there's life in his body. And he'll never be satisfied until he's drawn out the last bood that's in my withered old veins. Well, well," he went on, with a sigh, "I'll have to stand for that danger, too. It's not the first time that I've been in danger, Jerry."

"And I hope," said I, "that it won't be the last time that you coin money out of it."

His grin was as sudden and bright as the grin of a boy.

"You're right," said he. "I'm going to coin money, now. And so are you. So are you!"

I left him on that note. It wasn't money that I cared about. It was only safety for my neck, and a chance to keep my internal heart quiet. Upstairs I went and found Maker, still heavily manacled, but perfectly cheerful, with a heavy growth of beard darkening his face, and making him look like a pirate. I set his hands free, and brought him hot water to shave with.

He whistled while he was lathering himself. He hummed while he was actually shaving.

"Your heart's up, Sid," said I.

"My heart's up," said he, "because my fortune's down, just now. But it won't stay down. It *can't* stay down. I know about that sort of thing. Life is a seesaw, my lad. Now down, and now up. Turn and turn about. Riggs is now in the air. Pretty soon he may touch bottom again!"

And he went on chattering, as cheerful as could be. He had had a good breakfast, he said, and every one treated him with courtesy. He needed no gun to guard him.

I asked him why not, and he said:

"Because they're too afraid of you, my lad. They'd a lot rather jump off a cliff than start you on their trail. And that goes from Riggs down the whole list of the black-guards! But one of these days I'm going to be out of this, Poker-face. And then I'll raise so much hell as they've never dreamed of in this country!"

I could believe that. He was cheerful because he was

124

seeing the future. I almost felt that it would be better for me to let the murderers into that room and finish Maker then and there. But I knew that I could never do that. I was pledged to him, without words spoken. He knew it, and I knew it. And we never spoke of the thing, for that reason; but his life was in my hands.

"They tell me," said Maker, "that you've done another pretty little trick this morning, and tapped one of the strong boys on the chin."

I shrugged my shoulders. The tale was too complicated for repetition.

"Tell me this, Jerry," said Maker. "Did you have a gun with you?"

I shook my head, and suddenly he scowled blackly, and began to nod.

"I understand," says he. "You left the gun with me!"

I jumped up and stamped both heels down hard on the floor.

"If *you* start making a hero out of me," said I, "I'll walk out of here and tell the boys to come in and cut your throat for you!"

CHAPTER XXI

The Election

THE days drifted on towards election. There was a grand whirl of excitement in the town, of course. The colonel was always away, riding or driving, with relays of horses that tore him across the length and the breadth of the county. Was it to be called Maker County, or Piegan County. Was it to be Makerville for the county seat, or Piegan? Well, the colonel was writing pamphlets, news articles, making speeches, talking to individuals, persuading this man and bribing the next. All means were good means, in the eyes of the colonel, so long as they helped him towards the accomplishment of his object.

They were not days of excitement for me, however. I spent most of the time playing two-handed poker with Sidney Maker, in his jail room. I asked him if he would give me his parole to stay put until election day, and he flatly refused. So I kept his ankles shackled, and was jailer to him. The people left him strictly alone, except that the colonel, whenever he was in town, was sure to look in, and say ten words. And Maker would look at him with bright, thoughtful eyes and never say a word in return.

If ever he met Riggs with free hands!

Then came the election day. The town was wild with excitement from the morning on. Rumors came sweeping up all the time. In the middle of the afternoon election returns began to come in, and the numbers from the voting districts were chalked up on a big blackboard in front of the hotel.

The first district to be counted and registered, of course, was Piegan itself, and it was pleasant to see the large zero that had voted for Makerville as county seat, and the scores who had voted unanimously for Piegan. That gave the colonel a good, fat lead, and he kept it until evening, though it diminished with every return. Finally, in came the Makerville report, and everybody held breath, expecting to see the colonel wiped out. But we were amazed when fifty-odd votes were cast for Piegan in Makerville, itself!

We were amazed, I say, all of us except the colonel.

"I paid highest of all, for those," he told me. "But they're worth it. They cost me hard cash, but they make the election a sort of a moral victory for me over Maker, no matter how the whole thing turns out."

The colonel's idea of a "moral victory" bought with

hard cash amused me a good deal, but I said nothing. There was no good in arguing with him. I was always afraid to unloose the large torrent of his vocabulary, you see.

As the evening wore on, there were only two precincts to be heard from, places which voted a good number at their mines, and where the voting had undoubtedly been done in the early morning, but fast riders, with relays of horses, could not get the news home to us any faster than this!

That was the sort of a county it was—spilled out all over the map, with Piegan about in the center.

It was ten in the morning when the first of the two missing returns came in, and the groans that went up from the town of Piegan fairly made the heart ache. Sid Maker, listening in his room, grinned like a child, with his pleasure.

"He's lost, the infernal old grafter!" said he.

I nodded.

"Ain't you glad of it, Poker-face?" asked Maker.

"No, I'm not."

"Why not?" he argued. "You know that he's a crook and a cheat, don't you?"

"Well," I said, "I'm not logical about it: I'm fond of him, in spite of everything. I don't want to see him with a broken heart! You, Sid, you have the kind of heart that won't break. Not hard, just tough."

"You have me beat, kid," said Maker. "You're a cross of everything that I don't expect to find in a man. I can't make you out."

I left him to puzzle out my character as well as he could, and down I went to find out how things had actually gone. All of the inhabitants of Piegan were gathered in the street or around the veranda, watching the blackboard. But they were as silent as a funeral. A good deal of free whisky was passing on the rounds, but it couldn't lighten the gloom.

Up to this point, there had been a lot of shooting off of rifles and revolvers, a lot of yelling and whooping, and impromptu speeches telling the world what a fine place Piegan was.

Now all of that was gone and ended. All that remained was a sickening depression. There was a single ray of light in Piegan, and the colonel furnished it.

He stirred about through the crowd and talked to every man and woman in it, and to the children, too. He remembered them by name. He said flattering things to them.

I drifted about in his wake and listened, and his talk ran like a brook, downhill.

The election returns, plainly posted in large chalkings, showed that Makerville was running exactly twenty-eight votes ahead of Piegan. Not a great deal, but enough to win the election, with hardly a doubt. For there was only one distant mining camp remaining to be heard from, a little place called Wayne Hollow. It seemed that the poor colonel had been to every other spot in the county, but not to Wayne Hollow, and therefore he could only reasonably see that the day had gone definitely against him. Maker would probably win by something like fifty or a hundred votes. Not much, but enough.

In the face of the certainty of defeat, the colonel kept up his cheer. I heard him say: "Mrs. Thompson, this is the fortune of war. We have the consolation of knowing that we fought to the last ditch, however."

That was not all.

He said to one of the men: "You know, partner, that a good fight is the best thing in life. We've made the fight together. I've lost, but it has made me rich. Rich in friendships!"

I admired him, I tell you, when I heard the old rascal going about like that. He might be rich in friendships, but it did not require a prophet to foretell that he would be broke in everything else. He had begged, borrowed, and stolen, in order to keep cash in his safe, and he had spent that cash like water in order to make the prospects of Piegan grow.

He had failed. Well, still he kept his head up, and did not let the crowd down.

Finally he saw me at the edge of the crowd, and came over to me, nodding, smiling, weaving his way through the crowd.

No one made any response to him. They did not seem to feel as he did about the virtues that lie in a "good hard fight, fought to a finish."

When he got to me, he said in passing: "Come in with me!"

I went into the office with him, and there he slumped into a chair and lay with his head far back, his eyes closed, his face looking like soap.

"Give me some whisky, Jerry," he whispered.

I got him some, and held his head while he sipped it. My heart ached with pity and with sorrow for him.

He swallowed the whisky and thanked me, in the same whisper.

"Don't leave me, Jerry!" he murmured.

He made a slight gesture with his hand, and I caught it and gave it a grip.

"I won't leave you, chief," said I.

"Chief?" said he, as faintly as ever. "Not your chief, Jerry. But never tell about this. Never tell a soul. Promise!"

He opened his sick eyes to watch me promising, and I swore that I wouldn't, and I haven't, until this moment that I write it down. He's where such writings as mine won't bother him a great deal, I dare say.

After a time, he could lift his head from the back of the chair, but it only slumped far forward, as though the spinal column were broken. Nevertheless, he could speak now, and his voice was perfectly steady, though small.

"You see how a small hole may sink a large ship, Jerry? Wayne Hollow! I was too confident. I shook my head when they told me that it was thirty rough miles farther up that trail. I turned back. If I had ridden on, that day, I might still be out there with the crowd, hoping. But now I'm lost, and so is poor Piegan!"

"You have a thousand better schemes than this in your pocket."

"This is my last deal," he replied calmly. "I'm too old. I've used up my enthusiasm, and enthusiasm is the chief stock of a booster like me, Jerry. It's gone, now. And my money's gone. Jerry, the money you gave me to keep for you, that's gone, too. In my safe there's a stack of papers, and nothing else. And that paper with worth nothing. Piegan will be blotted off the map."

"It's all right, colonel," said I.

"I spent your money," he said, meeting my eye with a strange, whimsical look, "but I gave you, in exchange, six of the best lots in the town. They would have made you a fairly wealthy man, Jerry. I gambled for you. I had no right, I know. But I did. Can you forgive me?"

"Of course I can," said I. "I've forgotten about it already. Don't have that on your mind."

"Ah, Jerry Ash," said he, "if I had taken the right road when I was your age, perhaps——" He paused.

"I must not be sentimental," said he, to himself. "Tut, tut, one must be a man. Jerry, help yourself to that whisky and pass it to me again."

I was pouring his second drink when there was a sudden yell from the crowd outside.

The colonel stood up, the whisky glass steady in his hand.

"I suppose the fools want to loot my place, now?" he suggested calmly.

I gloried in the calm of the desperate old rascal.

But then that yell from the crowd turned into a plain screech of whooping joy, a cowboy yell of triumph. You can bet that the colonel and I got out to that porch in a hurry, and there we found that the crowd was all milling around a rider on a sweating horse. His report was being chalked up in huge letters on the blackboard, and those letters announced that Wayne Hollow voted thirty-three for Piegan, and zero for Makerville.

By five votes Piegan was to remain upon the map; the colonel would be a millionaire; the whole camp was made. No wonder that the crowd went mad and tried to drown that messenger with whisky.

"Why, what would you expect?" said he, rather bewildered. "Wayne Hollow wouldn't vote for an earthquake trap like Makerville!"

130

The colonel leaned lightly on my shoulder, saying at my ear:

"You see, Jerry, that a good lie in the bush is better than a bird in the hand!"

CHAPTER XXII

Men with Shotguns

I LEFT the crowd yelling. Rather, I left them just beginning to yell, knowing that they would keep it up all the rest of the night, and I eased straight through that mob towards a little fellow on horseback, whom I had just spotted. He wore a good, long black beard, such as some of the old-timers away back in the mountains raise, just getting careless, at first, and afterwards sort of liking the grandfatherly look that it gives them.

But this rider with the black beard was not old. When he turned from one, the look of his shoulders was young, and there was something very trim about those shoulders, and the way the head was canted thoughtfully to one side that reminded me of a man who had sunk deep on my mind and my imagination.

I got to the side of this fellow and looked up into his face.

"Chuck," said I, "just slide off your horse and come in with me."

He sat motionless, wordless. I saw his right hand poised in the air near his hip, like a humming bird near a flower.

"It's all right, Chuck," said I. "Your chief needs you, and I'll show you a back way in."

Suddenly he nodded, and turned his horse away. I went through the crowd again, and on the way, I saw young Harry.

"Harry," said I, "will you do me a favor?"

"I'll give you my head—take it!" said Harry, with his grin that always made me feel old.

"Where can I get a pair of fast horses that are tough and will go?"

"I have 'em," said he.

"How much?"

"Nothing, to you."

"They're for a friend."

"A friend of yours?"

"Yes."

"Two hundred for the pair," said he.

I knew that a hundred dollars bought a very fair pony in that part of the world, but I could guess that this pair was outstanding, or Harry would not have asked so much. That was what I wanted—a pair of horses that could really travel.

"Get them," said I. "Here's the coin. Bring them around in back of the hotel, and tie them into that patch of poplars. Tie them right in the center of the thicket."

"All right," said he. "What's up?"

I took a long chance, but I did not want that youngster to think that I was working behind his back, and he might have strange thoughts when he learned what people had used his horseflesh.

"I'm getting Maker out of town to-night," said I.

I saw Harry start, but he was as game and steady as I ever have seen.

"Maker!" he said. Then he added hastily, as though he were being caught out: "All right. I'll have the horses there."

He looked grave and sober as a judge, in a moment.

And I went into the hotel just as a tide of celebration caught up the colonel, shoulder-high, and swept him into the saloon.

I was glad of that, for it began to look as though I could get Maker out of the hotel without real trouble. I wanted to manage the thing before the whisky turned sour in some of those wild brains and started them thinking of "revenge" in the midst of the triumph.

So I went to my room, got a pair of good files that I had ready for the emergency, and a can of oil. Then I stepped out the back way and spotted Chuck, at once.

He said: "I'm covering you from this pocket, Poker-face, if that's any comfort to you."

"All right, Chuck," said I. "But I happen to be playing this one straight."

So I walked in first, and he behind me, through the hall, up the back stairs, and so to Maker's room. When he saw us come in, he gave me a look and said:

"There was a whip snap at the finish, eh, Jerry?"

"About Makerville being an earthquake trap—the mountain boys didn't like that," I reported.

He grinned and nodded.

"All right," he said. "I'll have Makerville growing and going in spite of the colonel. But I've got to say that I never thought he could win this deal, even with me in a trap. I thought I had men who would handle my end of the job. By the way, who's your undertaker friend?"

"We were on the job, chief," said Chuck. "We worked day and night. We would have split this cheese of a town wide open to get you out, too, except that we agreed that they'd murder you the minute we attacked. I dunno how the luck happened to turn against us. We all five worked like the devil for you—and ourselves!"

"I should have known you would, Chuck," said Maker. "How do you happen to be here with that brush on your face?"

"It was all right, but Poker-face spotted me. He's a hawk. What's he to you, chief?"

"He's the reason that I'm not packed in clay and sealed for delivery," said Maker. "What's the game now, Jerry?"

But I was already at work with the files. I knew such things fairly well, having had some experience and the priceless advice of Stephani. But though the files worked

133

very well, that steel was as tough as could be, and I began to think over the possibility of picking the colonel's pocket for the key to the lock as the shortest way out.

We discussed that a little, but we finally decided that it was best to stick it out this way. We used plenty of oil, and after an hour and a half we could break the shackles off Maker's ankles.

He stood up and stretched himself. He looked to the gun which I had given him and which he had kept all of this time, and then he said, with a grin, that he was ready to start.

"There's just one thing," says Chuck, in that quiet, thoughtful voice of his, "and that's this: Suppose that Jerry, here, is walking you out into a trap that will swallow both you and me?"

Maker clapped him on the shoulder.

"You don't know Jerry as I do," said he.

"He's made a fool of me once," said Chuck. "I don't think that he'll make a fool of me twice."

"You see how Chuck is?" said Maker, half joking, half serious. "If you live to be a hundred, both of you, he'll never forgive you for that slick job of kidnaping. But you're wrong here, Chuck. Put the cold poison out of your mind. Jerry's all that's stood between me and murder every day that I've been here!"

Chuck turned to me again, and his eyes looked straight through to the root of my mind.

"What are you, anyway?" said he. "Are you in the air, the water, or walkin' on the dry land?"

"Wherever he is, he's right," said Maker. "Now let's start."

I went first out of the room, and down the hall. And when I came to the back stairs, I saw a group of four men huddled at the bottom of them. Every man was carrying a shotgun.

I stepped back and told in a whisper what I had seen.

"We all have guns," whispered Chuck.

But I shook my head. It froze my blood to see, in the dim light of the hall, the eagerness that was in Chuck's face. The man had no gentleness in his heart, when it

134

came to a time of action. Bloodshed meant nothing at all to him.

We went to the front stairs, and at the bottom of those stairs I saw not four, but five or six people gathered together. A horrible thought came to me that perhaps young Harry had given away the game!

Those fellows were all armed. They looked as though they were only waiting for a signal to climb the stairs and start business operations, and I had seen a whisky flask going around. If there's hell on earth, whisky is the stuff that makes it burn with the hottest flame.

I said: "Boys, they've blocked us here, too. But I'll tell you the best way for us. Chuck and I will go down first. You come behind us, and come close, Sid. You're short, and they won't see you very well. Keep your hat pulled down low. They'll probably think it's all right, if we walk down slowly. When we get to the foot of the stairs, we'll break through of a sudden when I give a yip as the signal. Then you two hoof it around the far corner of the building, and drive straight back for the poplars that stand off there. In the middle of the trees you'll find two strong, fast horses, saddled and ready. Hop them, and ride like the devil!"

Maker nodded at once. But Chuck gave me a long, careful look, and said not a word.

What I had suggested seemed the only way. Chuck and I walked deliberately and slowly down the stairs, and Chuck whistled a little song as we went. I've never forgotten the tune of it to this day.

Halfway down the stairs, I told myself that it wouldn't do.

That shotgun brigade was staring up at me.

"What's the matter, boys?" I asked.

One of them said: "Oh, it's Jerry Ash. What's on our minds wouldn't interest you a pile, Jerry. We're just doin' a little thinkin'."

He laughed. The others joined in with him, and while they were still laughing, we got to the bottom of the steps and walked straight through to the front door of the hotel.

Behind us, I heard the laughter die out, and then a

man said: "By thunder, boys, I almost thought that that last man looked like—"

Another shouted suddenly: "It's Sid Maker!"

"Run!" I gasped to my two companions.

I didn't need to advise them to do that. They were already through that front door like exploding shells.

I ran out and turned sharply to the right, and as I did so, about four shotguns roared at once, and the loads of buckshot screamed out into the night air.

Just across the street was the "post-office" sign. It was badly plastered. So badly that it was replaced the next day.

Those fellows followed their volley with a charge. They floundered out, and were lost in a moment's confusion. Then they rushed straight past me—they didn't seem to see my face—down the veranda.

Their yelling and the noise of the guns had the men in the saloon pouring out, by this time. Some of them hopped into saddles, and at the same time, they got their directions for the pursuit from the rear of the hotel.

For out of the darkness, from that direction, came two voices in a prolonged, wild, whooping, Indian yell of mockery and triumph.

So I knew, by that, that Chuck and Maker were on the wing.

I half wished that I were with them, because I could guess that times might become pretty hot for me, after this, in Piegan.

CHAPTER XXIII

Maker's Fortune

MURDER, surely, was in the mind of that shotgun brigade. But though the colonel, I have no doubt, had inspired the thoughts in them, directly or indirectly, the result of the affair was quite different from what I expected.

I thought that I would be the black sheep, the hated of the town for having thwarted that bloody plan, but instead, people instantly forgot about their first malice toward Maker, and Piegan as a whole seemed to take it for granted that the freeing of Sid Maker had been the act of the entire citizen body! I had been appointed, it seemed, to see that the man got off safely; and Piegan, the next morning, congratulated me as the agent, and itself as the employer of the agent!

I never saw such a town. I never saw such a lot of optimists. I don't know what other term to use for them.

The days went spinning by at a great rate, from this time forward.

The county was now Piegan County, and Piegan was the accepted county seat. The same election had voted funds for a courthouse, and other funds for the salaries of county officers. And suddenly we had a sheriff, and a lot of other people, put in at a special election.

That hardly mattered. For they were all Piegan men.

They would do what Colonel Riggs told them to do, and that was that!

The colonel had his hands full, of course.

One moment he was overlooking the digging for the foundation of the courthouse or the post office. The next he was hurrying off to receive a new batch of settlers in the place. Or else he was settling disputes of all sorts—he acted as an ex-officio judge and did it very well—or he was sitting in his office transacting business of a thousand kinds, writing articles for Eastern newspapers and magazines, or ordering supplies of one sort or another.

The cream of the week for him was Thursday afternoon, when he held an auction, and sold lots in the town. And the eloquence which he had been spilling during the rest of the week never prevented him from having an extra supply on tap when Thursday turned up. I loved to sit by and hear him spin his yarns, and paint the bright picture of what Piegan was going to be, and raise factories out of dust, and widen the streets, and fill up the outskirts with palatial residences.

A great liar—or poet—was the colonel!

My six lots, I hung on to. I could have sold them any Thursday, because the colonel, in a streak of strange generosity, had really given me some beauties. I had all four corners of a street crossing in the very center of things, and two more adjoining. As a matter of fact, I think Riggs had given them to me when he was in despair of really winning the election and pulling through. And now he used to advise me, seriously, at least once or twice a week to get rid of the things and take my profit. It was tempting, too, because the price of that stuff had gone up to fifteen hundred dollars a lot. I don't think that Riggs paid that much for the entire townsite, in the beginning.

Most of these prices were the result of sheer speculating, of course. Every inch the walls of the courthouse rose, the speculators had a new spasm of joy. And the prices leaped again.

It was while the first batches of new settlers, speculators, gamblers, et cetera, were coming into the town, and the stage service to the railroad had been trebled, that the colonel stopped me in the street, one day, and I saw that his face was very troubled.

He linked his arm through mine and walked along with me, pulling me in his direction.

"What's the matter, colonel?" said I. "You act as though Makerville had won the election—as though that election hadn't put thousands and thousands in your pocket—as though you were ready for the road, once more."

"The election has put a little money in my safe, I admit, Jerry," said he. "But the money I have is really, as you must know, held in trust for the entire community. Just now we are growing and prosperous, and if times should change, of course I will be here with my profits in readiness to throw into the breach."

"Yes, of course you will," said I. He looked askance at me, after a quick, shifty way he had.

"You're a pessimist, Jerry," he said, shaking his head sadly. "It darkens my mind and bothers me a great deal to see the tone you take, the attitude that you are assuming towards life. Nothing is built upon doubt except the castle of despair, my lad."

I only grinned.

"Save that for Thursday afternoon, colonel," I advised him. "Now tell me what's wrong. What's happened?"

"Makerville is permanently on the map, it seems," he said, bitterly.

"Has Makerville had another election on her own account?" I asked him.

He sighed.

"Copper!" said he.

"Copper what?" I asked him.

"Who would have suspected it?" he exclaimed, very irritated. "Silver or gold—yes, somewhere around. But copper! Who would have suspected copper!"

"They've struck copper near by, have they?" I asked.

"Near by?" he growled. "It's right in the town. Confound the luck. And all my fault, too!"

"How was it your fault?" said I, amazed at this.

"It shows you, Jerry," said Riggs, "that even the

139

enemies of a thinking man may profit by his thoughts. I never wish Sidney Maker well."

"I know that," said I.

"He's a ruffian," said the colonel. "The sort of fellow that we don't want in the West. A brutal type—a very brutal type!"

"I like him a lot," said I truthfully. "But go right on."

"You have the gullible and easy nature of youth, Jerry," said the colonel. "There is something charming in your naïve approach to life, Jerry—so open-hearted and believing in—"

"You had me a pessimist, a moment back," I broke in.

"Don't interrupt me, Jerry," said he. "You break straight into the center of my train of thought. You mustn't do that, I was about to say that I had warned the county about the loose gravels underlying the town of Makerville, rendering it an earthquake trap."

"Well, was there anything in what you made up about that?" I asked.

"The point is," said he, "that what I said troubled some of the citizens. They began dipping down to find out what manner of foundations were really under the town and now—the devil take the luck—they've found that Makerville is really sitting on top of a copper mine! Maker is a millionaire overnight, all of his cronies are rich, too, and a rush is starting that is likely to sweep my town right off the map."

"The rush can't sweep your town off the map," said I. "Not while you've got the courthouse here."

He writhed and groaned.

"Think of that ruffian Maker," he said, "sitting pretty with a fortune pouring into his lap like a fountain of diamonds, and here am I, working hard, a public servant, in fact, and only getting—"

"Just a few hundred thousand," said I.

"Don't interrupt me, Jerry," said he.

"All right, colonel. Go right on."

"The news is spreading through Piegan now. I tried to keep it back, but no use. The people are beginning to pack up and streak for the other place. They'll leave us as rats leave a sinking ship!"

He groaned aloud. The colonel was in a real agony, and I thought, for a moment, that he actually had an affection for his latest town aside from the money he hoped to make out of the town site.

Then he said: "Yesterday, I was planning the municipal park, and laying out the avenues of the better residential section. This morning, a thunderbolt comes from Makerville. Oh, Jerry, how I wish for a newspaper so that I could pour out some of my thoughts about that place!"

"You'll have a newspaper before long!" said I. "As for Makerville, I'm not sorry. I'm glad. We strong-armed Sid Maker, and in spite of that, he's winning his game."

Then Colonel Riggs gripped my arm harder and said a thing which I've never forgotten to this day. The words come again, striking home deep in my mind, for he said:

"The point is, Jerry, that this West is bigger than any man or men in it. None of us can measure its possibilities. It surpasses and overlies everything that we say about it. The harder I strain my imagination to strike at the truth, the more I fail. The reality is going to be greater than any man's dream of it, believe me! Where blow-sand is drifting to-day, orchards will be green to-morrow."

No wonder that I remember the words, because I've seen them come true. And they will be truer still, in the future which is coming. Where there is healthy space, there will one day be healthy men. And the finest fruits of the West are not gold, silver, oranges, cattle, wheat, none of these, but men, and men of a type.

But this is getting ahead of myself, by a good space. I must go back to the dusty street of Piegan, on this day, with Colonel Riggs gripping my arm, and his words vibrating in my ears.

And, just as he finished talking, the stage driver came hurrying up and called to me:

"Hey, Poker-face!"

I turned around, feeling rather black. I never liked that name. But all the people of Piegan were fond of calling me by that and by none other. They felt that it showed their familiarity with me. Having first erected me into a sort of man-devouring monster, they got a lot of comfort out of calling me by an insulting nickname. Every fool in the town felt at liberty to use that name on me, though I would rather have been struck with the lash of a black-snake.

"I've got a telegram for you," said he. "It come in at the other end of the line. It ain't so often that I have to carry telegrams, Poker-face. I hope that it brings you a lot of luck."

I ripped it open and read:

> DELIGHTED TO HEAR OF YOUR ADVENTURES STOP HAVE URGED STEVEN TO GO OUT WEST AND JOIN YOU STOP HE WILL ARRIVE THERE SHORTLY AFTER THIS STOP DO TAKE CARE OF HIM   BETTY

CHAPTER XXIV

The Detective

THERE was only one good thing in that wire—that was the signature. She might have used both her names for that, and I was mighty glad that she had signed with only one.

But the rest of the telegram was poison. Steven Cole! Why should I have that blighter on my hands? I wanted to bite through an inch plate of steel, and I felt I could.

Then I looked up, and saw by the far-away look in the

colonel's eyes that he had read that telegram over my shoulder. That was almost too much for me. If he had been twenty years younger, I would have plastered him on the spot. As it was, I swallowed hard and put the telegram back into my pocket.

"Nothing wrong, Poker-face?" said the stage driver.

I wanted to knock *him* down, too. But he didn't mean to be curious, or prying. He was simply showing a friendly, neighborly interest! They are like that in the West.

I told him that it was the best sort of news, and he looked relieved, and went off.

But the colonel said: "You can't deceive me, Jerry. And if the news is really bad, you always know that you can count on me."

"How did you know it was bad news?" I asked him point-blank. "Do you read minds, or just telegrams?"

That was a little too poisonous for him. He sheered off from me and gave me a parting bit of advice. He was full of advice, was the colonel, particularly on selling points!

"A fellow with your capabilities, Jerry," said he, "ought to mind his temper more strictly. However, I'm the most forgiving man in the world. Drop in and see me, one of these days, will you?"

He sauntered off down the street in the opposite direction, and I went on, very gloomy, very down on my luck. Steven Cole was a waster, a spender, and too wild for the length of his wings. I didn't want him. I had my hands full with my rickety heart, and my giddy, foolish position in that town.

So I went along in a brown study, and I had just passed the entrance of the general-merchandise store when a voice barked behind me:

"Hands up, Ash!"

I didn't put up my hands, but I turned around. And there I saw a bull in the middle of the sidewalk, his feet a good bit spread, his jaw set, his eyes narrowed for the kill. He had a pale face. He wore a derby hat. I knew in a flash that he didn't belong to this part of the world and that he had traveled a long distance for the pleasure of introducing himself to me.

143

"Stick up those hands, Ash!" he commanded. "Stick 'em up fast, or I'll drill you!"

He meant it. I never heard more honest meaning in any man's voice, and I gathered from it that the reward on me would be paid whether I were turned in dead or alive!

But still I failed to put up my hands. I just smiled at him, and kept my staggering heart in order and straightened it out again. I could afford to be calm, for in the doorway of the store, just behind the detective, appeared the big, capable body of Harry, with a pair of leveled Colts in his hands. I never saw a more handsome fellow, as it seemed to me, than Harry as he appeared at that moment.

He said: "Shall I blow his head off, Poker-face?"

"Don't hurt him, Harry," said I. "He doesn't know where he is."

That bull was game.

"You—behind me!" he snapped. "I'm Detective Charles Richardson, of New York City. I have a warrant for this man's arrest."

Said Harry: "I'm Harry Blossom, of Piegan, and you'll have to go to hell and back before you serve that warrant on Poker-face."

Richardson lifted his head a little, when he heard this. And, at the same time, three or four men slipped out from the store and stood close around him.

"I'm an officer of the law," said poor Richardson. "I've got a warrant for that man's arrest. What sort of a plant is this?"

"You may be an officer of the law," said a fellow I failed to recognize, "but you're a fool, too."

"Don't hurt him, boys," I begged them. "Just take his gun away."

There was not much of a struggle. Those fellows understood how to conduct the sort of an operation that I had asked for. They grabbed the arms of Charles Richardson in three or four places and took the short-nosed revolver out of his hand.

144

He spoke quietly. I saw by his quiet that he was a quiet man.

"Is there a sheriff in this town? I understand that there's a sheriff in the place, boys?"

"He wants to see the sheriff, Poker-face," said Harry to me. "What about it?"

"Well, why not?" said I.

They all laughed, tickled with the idea.

"That's good," said they. "He wants to see the sheriff. All right, we'll take him to the sheriff!"

And straight off they led him to the man he had asked for. I went along with him, and on the way I thanked Harry for what he had done.

"*He* ought to do the thanking," said Harry. "If the fool had pulled trigger, he would 'a' been burned alive."

"What sort of a town is this?" asked Richardson of me.

"This is Piegan," said I. "It's a town that's worth knowing."

He gave me a keen look, and said no more. And just then we arrived at the sheriff's place. It was simply a shack thrown up on a vacant lot. In due time, the sheriff would have his office in the courthouse, of course. This was an impromptu affair.

When we walked in, we found the sheriff tilted back in his chair with his spurred boots crossed on top of a table that was composed of a pair of planks set across a couple of sawbucks. He had his five-gallon hat on. The peak of it was all that we could see above the top of the newspaper that he was reading.

As he heard us coming in, he lowered the newspaper, and looked us over, and shifted the toothpick from one side of his face to the other. A better hand with horse, gun, or rope never forked a saddle than Sheriff Lew Dennis. He was an honest man, too. He never had cheated at cards, never had changed a brand, and his word was better than another man's bond. The whole range knew the truth of this.

Why did the colonel want him as sheriff of Piegan? Partly because Dennis would enforce law and order, and partly because his knowledge of law was strictly limited by his friendships and his enmities. The code of Dennis was the simplest in the world. It consisted of a profound conviction that his enemies could do no good, and his friends could do no harm.

Now, then, Piegan as a town was the sheriff's friend. Piegan had elevated him to a warm and easy job—a lazy hero was Dennis—Piegan had given him a brace of building lots, and Piegan did not work him overtime. As for the duty of picking up a few crooks, now and then, running a gambler out of town, or quelling a drunken gunman, Dennis hardly looked upon such things as work. They seasoned the day with pleasure and diversity.

In appearance, he was one of those leathery fellows whose necks are seamed and cross-seamed with crimson wrinkles, sharp-edged and deep, and about the eyes and the mouth there was a pattern of smaller wrinkles. He was big in the body and lean in the face, with a great nose, and the largest pair of ears I ever saw, except for those worn by Maker's lieutenant, Swede.

This was the fellow who lowered the newspaper and looked us over.

"Hello, everybody. Hello, Poker-face," said he. "Who's your friend?"

"I'm Detective Charles Richardson of New York City," said the bull. "If you're sheriff of this county, I appeal to you to arrest Jeremiah Ash, here present, on a warrant which I have in my possession."

Some of the boys looked a trifle worried, as they listened to this formal language. But the sheriff merely thrust out his lower jaw a little, so that the toothpick slowly rose to a sharp angle, while his expressionless eyes remained fastened upon the face of Richardson.

"That's all mighty interestin'," said he. "Lemme have a look at what you got. Leave go of him boys."

When Richardson was released, he drew out a wallet, and while he was taking the thing from his pocket, he looked narrowly into the faces of the men around him. He bore malice, did Richardson, and that's a bad thing to hold against a crowd.

146

Then the sheriff handled the warrant, and opened it, and looked it over.

"Looks mighty legal and right," he declared. "How does it look to you boys?"

He handed the paper to Harry. And Harry handed it to another. I could guess what would come of that warrant.

"Here's a photograph that lets on to be a picture of Jeremiah Ash," said the sheriff. "But I dunno that I recognize the face."

"It's a perfect likeness," said Richardson. "A blind man could feel the resemblance!"

His color was rising. Perhaps he began to guess what he was in for.

"Well, boys," said the sheriff, "what you think of this? Does it look like Poker-face, or don't it? I'd say don't, speakin' personal."

It was wonderful to see the way the boys kept their faces straight as they turned over from one to another that photograph and squinted at it, and raised it to the light, and shook their heads. It was a perfect likeness, as Richardson had said, but that made no difference to the crowd.

"What you got him charged with in that warrant?" said the sheriff, in a gentle drawl, putting his elbows on his plank table, and laying his red chin on one fist.

"Why, man," exclaimed the detective, "this is the Jerry Ash who committed the famous Cole robbery in New York City. We've combed the country for him. There's five thousand dollars on his head, right now! And I'd split the sum with you, sheriff," he added suddenly, as though feeling that the time had come for him to make some concessions.

The sheriff said nothing, for a moment, but looked calmly, blankly at Richardson.

"There's a chance of picking up twenty-five hundred dollars for ten minutes' work, Lew," said Harry, soberly.

"Yeah," said one of the other fellows, "twenty-five hundred would give you a pretty good start for that ranch you've always wanted."

And another added: "The money bein' a mite speckled with blood, that wouldn't matter. It would wash off, I reckon."

"Why, right you are, boys," said Lew Dennis, very soberly, nodding at them one by one. "I wouldn't mind twenty-five hundred dollars, either. But lemme see that photograph, again."

No one had it. Of course I had expected that. A dull red rose over the cheeks of poor Richardson. But he said nothing.

"Somebody dropped it?" asked Dennis plaintively.

"Maybe the wind blew it out a crack," said Harry.

"A man went through the door, just now, and you know it!" snapped Richardson.

"Who was it?" asked the sheriff.

"I didn't see nobody," said one of the fellows.

"Neither did I," said another.

"It's a dirty frame on me," said Richardson, snarling. "Gimme back the warrant, and I'll—"

"Who's got that warrant?" asked the sheriff.

No one answered.

Richardson began: "If that warrant has been destroyed, there'll be—"

"There'll be hell to pay!" declared the sheriff severely. "I'll be dog-goned if I'll stand for having a warrant destroyed around my office. You boys search one another and try to find it, will you?"

They went through the mockery under the eyes of Richardson, who was boiling with rage.

"This is a penitentiary offense, and if you don't know it, I'm telling you," he said to the sheriff. "You've allowed that warrant to fall into the hands of the man who left this room a minute ago—a man with a red and white bandana and the look of a man about—"

"I'd hate to go to jail for losing a warrant, mister," said the sheriff. "But the fact is that I didn't lose it. Somebody else done this. Boys, ain't I right?"

"I'll have you behind bars for this outrage, Dennis!" shouted Richardson, beginning to tremble like a fighting bull terrier.

148

"He'll have me behind the bars," said the sheriff, shaking his head with a pretense of sorrow. "I guess I'd better go out and try to find that fellow."

He stood up to his full height—some four or five inches over six feet.

"Mighty sorry about this, Richardson," he said. "Say, some of you boys try to entertain Richardson till I get back, will you?"

"Sure!" said the chorus.

"I'll go with you," said Richardson.

"No," said the sheriff. "It's mighty windy and dusty, outside. And the sun's pretty strong, too. So long, Richardson. Hope I'll be seein' you in a little while."

Richardson tried to go after him, but he was caught by a dozen strong hands and numbed by the grip of them. At the door, the sheriff turned, apparently oblivious of the curses of the prisoner.

"Say, Poker-face," said Dennis. "Might be that you could be a lot of help to me, searchin' for that warrant. You got a good pair of eyes, and you certainly oughta be able to recognize your own name on the paper!"

A hearty roar of laughter greeted this remark, and I waited on the threshold of the place until the noise had died down. Then I said:

"Boys, if Richardson should want to take a little ride out of town and see the country—"

"He's just been saying that that's what he wants to do," said Harry, grinning.

"You lie!" shouted Richardson.

"If you take him out," said I, "easy does the trick, partners. Remember that. Easy does the trick!"

CHAPTER XXV

Cole's Arrival

WHEN we were outside the sheriff's office, he said to me: "I reckon that you owe me a drink, Poker-face."

"I forgot about that," said I.

We marched across to Riggs's bar, where Dennis had whisky, and I sipped ginger ale and tried to like it.

I remember that he watched me with curious eyes.

"It's too bad, kid," he said at last.

"What's too bad?" I asked him.

"Too bad that you've got in so deep, at your age, too," he declared.

"You mean that Cole business?" said I. "I'll tell you about it. The fact is that—"

"Oh, not the Cole business," said he. "But all the rest." He waved his hand.

"I mean that you're in so deep that you don't dare to have a drink, even with a friend, not even in a town where a hundred guns would be out the minute trouble came your way. But still you can't trust to luck. You can't risk getting fog in your brain. You've got to have that shooting hand of yours always ready to do its best. I've seen 'em before, like you, but I never seen anybody get there so young."

And he shook his head, and sighed, and looked at me with an eye of sympathy, and a trace of awe.

Just then there was a great whooping and shouting, and we went to the swinging doors and peered over them in time to see Detective Richardson escorted at a gallop down the middle of the street by a screeching band of riders.

I grinned a little, I admit. And yet I was sorry for that fellow, too. I had an idea that he was made of the proper iron and that I would see him again, before very long. And I was right!

I have put in this incident in a good deal of detail because I wanted to give a picture of the peculiar conditions under which I lived in Piegan. To a degree, I was a marked man, but I was not marked in the way that the town thought. Between my odd adventures, and the care I had to take of my heart, and the coming of Richardson for my scalp, my reputation was built up like a tower which I expected to see crash, any moment.

I would have been rather glad if it had, no matter how high the dust flew. For it seemed that no matter what I did, it redounded to make me seem more and more of a desperado, a man-killer. The coming of Richardson was a sufficient proof, in the eyes of the town. It seemed to Piegan, after that, that the whole country wanted me, to put me in jail, and Piegan set its teeth and told the rest of the country where to go. That town felt that I was its pet gunman, and the bright, particular jewel of its crown.

Well, a couple of days after this, it developed that there was no fear of the population of Piegan slipping away to the copper claims at Makerville, because the townsmen of that place had staked out every inch of the territory around them, and the boys who had ridden over to take pot luck, came back without a thing to show for their journey.

Makerville settled down to being a copper-mining center; Piegan contented itself with being the county seat. Real estate was its treasure trove.

The colonel, however, was not one to allow a neighboring town to down him on any score without a protest. So he began to advertise Piegan, too, as a mining center. It was true that there were two gold mines in the mountains west of the town, and the old rascal had a little work done on the trails leading in those directions and he swore that he intended to build a road to each and so make Piegan one of the great mining centers in the country.

Well, that was the way that he talked, and the way that he worked. To the end he was always the same!

He came back this day from overseeing the work of a gang on one of those two roads, and when he got to the hotel he sent for me in a hurry. I came down and found him in the office, strutting up and down, on fire with excitement. His hair was rumpled. Still, as he talked, he was always thrusting his fingers into its long, flowing silver.

As I came into the office, he got hold of me and sort of dragged me into a chair.

Then he leaned over me and said in a hoarse whisper:

"Jerry—Jerry, listen. There's a railroad coming through!"

"Great Scott," said I. "Through Piegan?"

"No, no! Through Makerville. That is, they *think* that they're going to run the line through Makerville, but we're going to stop them. We're going to stop them, Jerry, do you hear me? You and I—somehow!"

I stared at him.

"Why d'you turn to me, colonel?" I asked him. "I haven't any influence with railroads, have I?"

He stretched out his long arm and glared down it towards me as though down a rifle barrel.

"Jerry," he said, "you're my luck. You saved me—and Piegan. Somehow or other, you and I—together—we'll break Sid Maker's heart for him again, and run that railroad through *Piegan!*"

He talked on some more. He was in a fury of heat and excitement, and he was desperate because, so far, he had not been able to think of a plan.

It amazed me, in a way, to see the furious jealousy of that man. He had brooded so long over the towns, and Maker, that he had come to hate Makerville as though it were a person. He said that he would see himself dead before he would let the railroad go through Makerville. They would have to build right across his dead body!

I listened to this rot for a few minutes, wondering when

152

he would come back to his senses, and finally he struck an attitude by his desk, and stiffened there, and seemed to grow taller, the crook coming out of his back. I saw that he was getting an idea of some sort, and I slipped out of the office just in time to meet the clerk.

He had a puzzled look, and said to me in a quiet way: "There's a man here who says that he wants to see you, Poker-face. I dunno. You wanta take a look at him before you meet him?"

"What does he call himself?" I asked.

"He says his name is Steven Cole," said the clerk.

That threw the spur into me. I went straight past the hotel man and in the lobby I saw Steven.

No wonder the clerk was in doubt about him. Steve looked as though he had just stepped out of a bandbox. He had pale-yellow gloves on his hands, and they were folded on top of a glistening walking stick, as thin as a whiplash. He wore sideburns, quite thick and long, and looked like a regular Apollo, but what the devil was the place for an Apollo? Not Piegan, I could lay my bet.

Well, I went up to him and shook hands. He was as cold as a stone.

He merely said: "Ash, I hate to trouble you. I'm here because I promised to come. I'll take myself off your hands almost at once."

CHAPTER XXVI

A Drive with Riggs

SEEING Steve Cole was no pleasure to me, and his speech was not a very good start towards better relations. I didn't like him, and it was hard to control myself, except when I remembered that he was the brother of Betty Cole.

"It's no burden to have you here," I told him. "Betty wired to me that you were coming, so I've been expecting you."

"Betty *wired* to you, did she?" he said, with a lift of his eyebrows.

It was plain that he thought she had demeaned herself by getting in touch with such a fellow as I. I swallowed that remark, also, and got him to sit down at a table in a corner of the lobby. Over across the room I saw Calkins and "Bud" Wentworth, and some of the other hardy lads of Piegan, and they were laughing with one another, and now and then sneaking glances at Cole. However, I stuck by my guns.

"She wired to me," I repeated. "And now that you're here, I want to do anything that I can for you. This hotel is the only place in Piegan. You can be pretty comfortable here, and I'll teach you the ropes."

"The ropes?" he said, with a sneering laugh. "Are there ropes to learn in Piegan? Ropes of a rig, maybe you mean?"

And he laughed again. The sound of that laughter was enough to turn heads toward him, there was such covert insolence in the tone of it.

I had to look down to the floor and tell myself, thrice over, that he was the brother of Betty Cole. Even that hardly enabled me to keep control of myself.

"What brought you out this far West?" I asked.

"It's about the jumping-off place," he answered. "But I was wanting a change of air, and Betty asked me to look you up. So here I am, as you see. She seems to take a sort of interest in you."

"That's mighty kind of her," said I. "All that I've heard from her has been a telegram. But I've written to her."

"So I understand," says he, sticking his chin up in the air, his eyes getting hard.

Plainly he thought she was disgraced by receiving letters from me. But I swallowed even this, the hardest of all, and explained:

"That seems like effrontery—an ex-pug and gambler like me—" I began.

"Is that all?" said he. "What about safe cracker, too, Ash?"

That was too much. I looked him straight in the eye.

"You know what made me become a robber, Cole," said I.

He shrugged his shoulders, and I wanted to slam him with the butt of my revolver. However, I gritted my teeth and managed to control myself.

"I would have been landed in the jail for that night's work," said I, "but Betty saved me."

"Yes, I know she did," said Cole. "I don't—"

At least, he had the grace to leave that sentence unfinished.

But now I opened up on him a little: "I've always wondered who got to you that night, Cole? What made you sell us out, after you'd asked us in?"

"Sell?" said he. "Sell you out? I don't know what you mean. Are you trying to insult me, my friend?"

Great Scott, what an arrogant rascal he was!

"Let that go," said I. "I want to forget about that night.

It nearly did me in. But I've been curious. Wasn't Stephani with you in the deal? Hadn't he planned it with you?"

He stared at me.

"I don't know what you're talking about," said he.

That made me more furious than ever. So I snarled out: "The fact is that the safe *was* robbed. You and Stephani planned the job. You would open the safe, split the profits between you, and then turn the blame on the fools of the party who were caught inside of the house! Isn't that the straight of it?"

"I've heard enough from you, Ash," said he, rising. "I knew you were a ruffian before. I've heard and seen enough of you here to prove that you're still a ruffian. Betty'll be interested when I let her know!"

I was on my feet, too, and the mention of her name made me insane. I laid a finger on his arm, lightly, I am sure, and I looked into his eyes and tried to find his soul there and destroy it with lightning. Because there was lightning in me, just then.

"If you try to corrupt her idea of me with lies, or your own ideas of what I am, I'll kill you, Steve. Remember it. Write it down inside your mind. Look at the writing every day, because it's true."

He made no answer. He just looked me up and down for a moment with a curling lip, and the greatest calm in the world, then he turned on his heel and went sauntering away from me.

I saw little Sam Harlow, the editor of the newspaper that the colonel was starting up, come into the lobby and stop the stranger, and ask questions, and I saw Steve Cole giving careless answers.

I leaned against the wall with one hand braced on it, very sick, trembling all over, afraid to leave before the tremor was gone. I saw that I had cooked the goose. That fellow had been sent out to Piegan by the express will of his sister. He was there because she wanted him to be there. And now I had cut off all relations with him.

No matter how he had tried me, I should have resisted and kept our talk smooth. Words should not have been able to irritate me. But they had been.

156

One of the fellows in the lobby—I think it was Jem Craig—came over and stood by me.

"What's the matter, Poker-face?" said he. "You look as though you wanted to tear him to pieces. Who *is* the dude, anyway?"

"He's a fool from the East," said I, shortly, because I was out of breath with the racing of my heart.

"I could see he was a fool," said Craig. "Maybe we'll be able to educate him a little, though!"

I hardly heard that; only afterwards I realized what he had said to me. If I had thought twice, I never would have gone off from Craig without making him promise to leave Steve Cole alone.

However, just then the colonel came rushing into the lobby, saw me, and hurried up and hooked his arm through mine.

I was glad to have him interrupt my thoughts. So I went along with him and listened to his chatter. He had a habit of getting me with him when he was thinking out loud. I rarely answered back. I gave him a placid audience that didn't make trouble, and he was fond of outlining his plans to me and the empty air, so to speak.

He hustled me into his buggy, this day, and drove at a spanking clip out of the town and up a road—trail, rather —to the top of some hills that rose to the south of Piegan. There he pulled up and stood on the seat and swept the plain with a pair of glasses. He drew the picture of the scene as it would be when the railroad went through. He showed me where it would come through the gap in the mountains, and how it would cut across the rolling ground, and then follow the easy plain straight to Piegan.

He said that it wasn't logical, wasn't possible for sane engineers to desire to run their line out of the way, and to Makerville.

"They'll get some heavy shipments of copper ore," I suggested.

At this he groaned.

"The confounded copper!" said he. "That's the root of all the trouble. I tell you, man, that Piegan cannot grow, cannot really flourish unless there is a railroad along which the blood of life can flow into her!"

"After a while," said I, "they might be persuaded to run a branch line—narrow gauge, or something like that—down here from Makerville."

"Piegan on a branch line from Makerville?" exploded the colonel.

I argued no longer, because it was pretty plain that argument was not what he wanted. Agreement was what he was looking for, like a man in love.

He took out some paper and a pencil, and sketched in the imaginary map of what the valley of Piegan would be like after the railroad came through. He put down some towns, on that mental map—some "tributary" towns, as he called them. And he expanded Piegan itself a good deal.

He worked for a long time, in this way. And he had the shining face of a bunco artist—or an empire builder!

After a while, he transferred some of his attention to the ground around us. He said that he had been a fool not to see the possibility lying in those hills. He could buy the land for a song, and then he would develop it as a sort of summer residential sector of the town.

I pointed out that this was only a couple of miles from the town and not near enough to be part of the place and not far enough and high enough to give a real change from the climate of Piegan. But he had his heart set on the picture, already, and he began to talk about "mansions shining on the height."

When he started on that line, I recognized the symptoms and the figures of speech and shut up.

But he went on ad lib. Then, driving back to survey the rest of the possibilities of the hills for their own sake, he ran into a ragged old fellow steering a burro down out of the hills, a gray and moldy prospector coming back to town with grubstake exhausted, but still with a fire of great hopes in his mind, and glimmering out at his eyes.

The colonel had a long talk with him about the back regions of the mountains—I must say that Riggs was as interested in the country as though he had made it—and when we finally straightened out for Piegan, the afternoon was nearly ended. A cold wind, I remember, was whipping across the hills and had us uncomfortably silent before we got back to Piegan.

And there the sky fell on my head.

I mean to say, it was there that I heard a newsboy crowing for the evening edition of that wretched sheet, in a tone as professional as any of his kind on the streets of New York. I heard two words of his song, and then bought a paper and read on the front page:

NEW YORKER JAILED FOR ATTEMPTED
MURDER

It was Steve Cole!

CHAPTER XXVII

The Palmed Ace

THE colonel asked me who Cole was, and if he was a friend of mine, but I just sat there and stared helplessly at the account of how that fool of a man had walked into a gambling place and raised a question about the turn of a card, and then pulled a gun to back up his opinion. His bullet had been high and to the right, however, and a chair had crackled over his head and shoulders the next moment. The sheriff had picked up the limp body and carried it to the "jail," which at present was the little room in back of Lew Dennis's office. I jumped

159

out of the buggy now, and the colonel called to me to stop, and wanted to know how he could help me. He said that Piegan would do anything I wanted. But I went on, without answering. I headed for the newspaper. It was operating in a tent—the press, the editorial chambers, and the reporting room. Sam Harlow was editor, advertising agent, reporter, and business manager. He always had ink on his fingers and a sleepless look in his red-rimmed eyes. Afterwards Sam went on to big things in the world of journalism. This was his bed-rock beginning.

I found Sam taking a moment off to eat and read over his latest edition. He was in his shirt sleeves, and the shirt was covered with inky finger marks. He was eating thick ham sandwiches, and had a pint tin cup of coffee standing on top of a cracker box beside him.

He looked up and gave me his professional smile.

"Any little bits of news, Poker-face?" said he. "You're a great mine of news for me, old son, but you don't give it out freely. Other imaginations have to work on you."

"You won't have to work hard to get news out of me to-day," said I.

"What is it?" he asked, forgetting his sandwiches, forgetting even his coffee.

"It's this," said I. "That you're a four-legged screech owl, and a wall-eyed liar, and your paper is a disgrace."

That was a beginning that I worked up pretty well, and Sam Harlow was staggered and gasping, before I got through.

"What have I done to you, Poker-face?" said he. "I wouldn't harm you for the world!"

"Cork up this whole edition," said I. "Call it in. And if you print another word in your rotten sheet about young Steve Cole, I'll come down here and wreck your joint for you!"

"If I dreamed that he was a friend of yours," says Harlow, "not a single word—"

"If you knew any of the news in the town, you might have known that!" said I. "Sam, get in those papers you've sold, will you?"

"I will," he said.

Then he groaned and struck his forehead.

"I can't! I can't!" he said. "They threw a scare into Cole and told him he'd never get out of jail for ten years, and he's sent a messenger all the way to the railroad to wire to New York for money. He wants to have enough to hire the best lawyer in town. Nobody told him that there isn't any 'best' lawyer here!"

He laughed as he said this, but seeing me glowering, he added:

"When I saw that messenger mounting—he's shooting through the hills day and night, using the stage relays—I just poked half a dozen copies of this edition into his saddle bag. I thought that the people on the outside might as well know, by now, that Piegan has a newspaper and can lift up a voice for itself in the world."

"You lift up your voice, and you knock the sky down," said I. "You're a poor excuse for an editor, Harlow. You're a poor excuse for a man, too!"

There was no help for it. I saw that in a few days the word of what young Cole had done would go across the continent, and it would be ice cream and cake for the big New York dailies when they had a chance to copy something like Harlow's headline on a member of the Cole family. The Coles were too exclusive. Those are the fellows that the reporters are trained to go after and pull down. The higher the family, the harder the fall, the more the dust and blood; and the Coles were due for a real bloodletting, this time. I could imagine Betty taking the blow with a white, set face, but never flinching. But what of her mother?

Well, I cursed Steven Cole as I went down the street. And I cursed the haste of Harlow who had sent out the news with such a rush.

I cursed the colonel, too, because except for him I would have been in town and could have stopped the whole affair.

I went down to the gambling place and found it crowding up, with the proprietor, "Lefty" Tom Gregg, at the faro table. I went over and talked to him.

"Socking this boy Cole," said I, "won't buy you a house and lot. Suppose you don't prosecute the case, Lefty?"

He looked me up and down, cool and steady.

"Is Cole a friend of yours?" he asked.

"I'd be best pleased to see him out of the trouble," I said.

"Well, I wouldn't," answered Lefty.

"Look here, man," said I, "don't talk so loud. Why not be friendly?"

He stared up at me, scowling. He had a jaw which shot out so far beyond the upper one that when he spoke he always seemed to be pouting, or eating dry crackers with small bites.

"This boy Cole, he comes in here and takes a slam at me," said Lefty. "That's not so good. That doesn't give me the kind of a happy, homy feeling the way that it used to do when I was a kid. Not when I hear the lead hissing and taste the burned powder in the air. I'd rather listen to bacon in the pan or taste it on the plate. Maybe you dunno what I mean?"

"I know, Lefty," said I, sympathetically. "But I wish that you would loosen up on this fellow. He's pretty young."

"He's older than you are," said Lefty, "and that's old enough to run most of Piegan. Only, you don't run me, boy!"

I saw that he was sour, and I was sorry that I hadn't taken a slower line with him. However, now I was in the hot water.

"I'm not trying to run you, Lefty," said I. "Why, not a bit of it."

"I know what you mean," he answered. "You're not trying to run me. You're just telling me what to do, eh? No, Poker-face, I'm sorry to hurt you, but I'm going to put that young fool behind the bars—I'll put him in the pen, if I can!"

"Well, I'm only asking you to think it over."

"Why should I try to please you, Ash?" he asked me, point-blank. "You never come down here. You never hang

162

around and chuck a few dollars away on faro. You never liven things up, and give the boys a steer."

"I don't gamble," said I. "That's why I keep away."

"Then I keep away from you, too," said he. "And we're both happy. Is that right?"

That called my hand, of course. I had to look him in the eye and wonder what was next.

"I'll cut you for the first ace on this deal," said I.

"Will you?" he asked me.

"Yes."

"What for?" said he.

"You mean, what do I put up?"

"That's it. Money talks here, Poker-face!"

He was as hard as steel. I saw that I had to put him down, or he would put me, one of these days. Besides, his voice had been large enough to draw a lot of attention. Some of the boys were edging near, pretending to notice nothing, really drinking up the trouble in the air.

I remember wondering if Lefty were a dope. He acted as unaccountably mean and nervous as though he were.

"I got some lots here," said I. "I'll put up one of those. Do you want it in writing?"

He met my eye coldly, but he shook his head.

"Your word is all right with me," he said.

Picking up a pack, he began to mix them, still looking at me, and saying something about the fracas of that day. It was very neat and smooth, but Stephani had taught me the trick, and when he shoved the pack across to me, I knew that he had an ace palmed, all ready for me.

We pulled two cards apiece, and then when I was afraid that he would flash his ace, I pulled my gun and laid the muzzle on the edge of the table.

"Turn your right hand palm up, Gregg!" I commanded.

He stared at me, not really afraid, but thoughtfully, and I knew what his thoughts were.

It wasn't the matter of prosecuting the case against Cole, but it was his own life in Piegan that mattered. He had spent quite a lot of money getting started and building up his crooked trade in the town, and if he were discovered cheating as openly as this, it would ruin his business at a stroke. Piegan would be too hot to hold him.

"What d'you think I am, Ash?" said he, and tried to jump the card up his coat sleeve.

But he missed, and the card slid over the edge of the table and fluttered down through the air.

An ace of hearts lay face up on the floor for every one to see.

That was the end of Mr. Gregg in Piegan. The growl of the spectators was like the rumble of thunder. It meant trouble, bad trouble, and lots of it—right away! The men came steadily in around Lefty, and he didn't move. He just stood there, staring at me, and seeing the black of the future rather than my face.

I knew that I had lined up another heartfelt enemy to fit in with Richardson, and the gunmen of Sid Maker.

However, the business was done, so I put up the old gun, and left the place.

When I got out onto the pavement, I stopped short suddenly, with an exclamation.

For in spite of the tenseness of that scene I had just gone through, my heart was bumping along as calmly and steadily as though it had never skipped a beat in the course of its existence. I didn't know what to make of that. But I had a wild hope that perhaps I was around the corner, and that the illness might leave me as it had come, suddenly, and make me a free man once more!

Well, the very happiness of that thought was enough to start it racing, hopping, jumping as badly as ever. So I shook my head and went sorrowfully up the street to the sheriff's office.

CHAPTER XXVIII

A Talk with Steve

DENNIS was in front, tightening the cinches of his horse and with a look of business in his eye. He said, grunting as he gave the straps a tug:

"What's up, Jerry?"

"I want a loan from you," said I.

"I've got three dollars and eighty-five cents," said he. "You can have that."

He reached for his pocket. He was serious about the offer.

"I want the man in your back room," said I.

"Which one?"

"Young Cole—if you have more than one."

"You can't have Cole," said the sheriff. "He's in for attempted murder, or something like that. He tried to plaster Lefty Gregg. Didn't you hear about that?"

"Yes, I heard. But Gregg is leaving town. He won't prosecute."

"How do you know?"

"I just saw him palm an ace. And a lot of the rest of the boys saw him, too."

The sheriff nodded a bit thoughtfully.

"That's bad," he said. "It gets the boys pretty irritated, when they see a thing like that. I dunno why. There ain't one gambler in twenty that's straight. But the punchers flock in and seem to think that the place *they've* selected is always straight. I do the same thing. That's what cleaned me out, last night. But what you want with this boy?"

"Give him to me on parole. Any way you say. Turn him out. No charge will be brought, you'll see."

"You can have him, and welcome," said the sheriff. "I don't want him. Come along in."

We went into his office. He disappeared into the back room with a bunch of keys and came back steering Cole in front of him, the irons still on the hands of Steven.

Big Lew Dennis sat down on the edge of his plank table and gave Steve a talk. Steve looked at me as though I had arranged the lecture. Said the sheriff:

"You've come out here, and tried to bust things loose. Is that right?"

"Lefty is a crooked gambler," said Steve.

"You tried to kill him," said the sheriff.

"He tried to cheat me," said Steve.

"If a man cheats you, do you try to kill him?" asked Dennis. "If you do, lemme tell you something. You won't last long. Not out here. If I was you, I'd cut out and run for the parts where you'll be at home. We don't want your kind of a man around out here. We got a lot of space, but we ain't got the room to put you up. You get out and you stay out."

"You've been telling him something about me, I suppose," said Steve, showing his teeth as he looked at me.

"I'm turning you loose because he asked for you, you puppy!" roared the sheriff, suddenly enraged. "Doggone if I know what he wants you for. I wouldn't have you for anything. But Poker-face wants you, and most generally he gets what he asks for, in this town. Because he's a white man. That's why he can have what he wants here. We're all solid behind a decent man. And if you can get up the hill and stand at the top, where Poker-face is, you'll find out what I mean. Now get out of here and don't let me see your face again. I'm tired of you!"

With that, he unlocked the handcuffs and turned Steve loose. I took him back to the hotel with me.

As we went down the street, he said, in a hard, constrained voice:

"Where are we driving, Jerry?"

"For the hotel," said I.

"I don't know that I want to be seen there," he said.

"You'll have to stay in town until there's no sign of a charge against you. You're out on parole with me."

"Suppose that I broke that parole?" said he, stopping short and staring at me.

The meanness of that idea almost sunk me.

"Yes, you could do that," I admitted.

He shrugged his shoulders suddenly, and walked on rapidly down the street, like a man with a new thought. He carried his head high, and it remained in the air when we walked up the steps of the hotel together.

As we did that, the loungers on the veranda were all silent. They sat up and stared at us, openly, and the looks they gave to Steve were not pleasant; they were darker than storm clouds. They looked at me, too, and shook their heads, because they could not make me out.

I stopped in the lobby and had the clerk give Steve a room next to mine. The face of that clerk was as cold as stone. He studied Steve with a sneer while he was signing his name, and then silently gave him the key to his room. I would show the way up.

When we got to the room, he went to the window and looked out, his arms folded high across his breast, his legs braced.

"You're not Napoleon on board the *Bellerophon*," I told him, pretty cruelly. "You're with a friend, Steve, though you don't know it."

He turned slowly around on me. He was looking at the floor, and his face was white. But it was a hard white. He was suffering, but not shrinking, and I saw that there was a lot more man in him than I had suspected.

"You can say what you want, I suppose," said he. "You've earned the right. Only, don't talk to me about friendship."

"Why not, Steve?" said I.

"You know what I've done to you. Or you've guessed.

167

What you guessed is right. I double-crossed you there in New York."

I nodded. It was sickening.

"That's something to forget, Steve," said I. "Thank God, we're not finally committed to every fool thing that we've done in the world. That was yesterday, and this is to-day."

"When Betty found out all the facts about what I'd done," said he, "she made me promise that I'd come out here and square myself with you, if I could. She drove me to it. That's why I came."

"Quit it, Steve," said I. "Take the whip off your back, will you?"

"My skin's gone already," he said. "I don't mind the flogging that I've got to take."

Then he said: "She would have gone to father and told him the whole deal. Everything that I'd done. You don't know my father, Jerry."

"No," said I.

"Well, if father thought that I had done a thing like that, he would jail me and hire the best lawyers in the country to get me a long sentence. That's the way he feels about justice—and clean hands. He's never liked me very much, anyway. Betty's the one. And she held him over my head until I finally swore that I'd come out here and put things right with you."

He paused, he was breathing hard.

"We'll talk it out another time," said I. "I've had enough now. So have you. Let's save something for another day. You're square with me. You don't have to worry about me. I've forgotten everything."

He looked up at me suddenly, and his glance was as straight as a ray of light, and as unwavering.

"You're sweating with shame for me, Jerry, aren't you?"

"Not a bit," I lied.

"Because of Betty, you've put up with a lot from me. You put up with a lot, and took it, and then came back and got me out of trouble! Out of jail, I mean, because I suppose that I'll be in trouble as long as I'm near this town!"

"Not a soul will hold a grudge against you, Steve," said I, "the minute that you begin to feel that the name of Cole is not a title, and that every man in town has as good a right to a place in the world as you have. That's putting it to you straight, but I have to say it."

He flushed a little, the first color that had been in his face for a long time.

"I want to murder you, when I hear you say that!" he told me, with a lot of quiet meaning in his voice. "But I'll take it. I know that there's no fool like a proud fool, and I've got to learn to take it."

"All right," said I. "I won't hit you again. I've said enough. The boys may hold off for one day. The second, they'll be with you."

"There won't be any second day," said he. "I'll be gone, by then."

"I wish you'd stay on and face down the music," said I.

He stared at me.

"You mean that you really wish it?"

"Yes," said I.

His eyes widened and yet they darkened with significant meaning, too.

He said slowly: "Betty made me swear that I would take marching orders from you." His voice went husky with shame and effort. "And I'm to do what you tell me —to make a man of myself!"

That was pretty hard on him. I could hear him breathing like the breathing of a tired horse. His nostrils were quivering. His whole soul was being burned up with shame.

"You'll get no orders from me, Steve," I told him, as gently as I could. "But I'll be glad if you'll stay on here and face the thing through with me. Will you do it for me?"

He groaned, suddenly.

"Ah, man," said he. "I know you hate and despise me. It's only for the sake of Betty—"

"No, no," I told him, and I was amazed to find that I meant what I said.

I hurried across the room and stood close to him.

169

"You've got the real stuff in you," I told him. "You're as good a man as Betty is a woman. I know it. I gamble on it."

He closed his eyes.

Then he opened them again and drew himself up.

"There's one other thing that I've got to tell you," said he. "Betty gave me a letter which I was to deliver to you. I opened it and read it. I thought you were not good enough to get a letter from a daughter of the Cole family. I read the letter and I tore it up—"

I was silent. This hit me hard.

He went on, forcing out every word with terrible pain:

"In the letter, she said that she—was fond of you. She said—that—she never had met more of a man—than you!"

CHAPTER XXIX

"The Luck of Piegan"

THE hardest shock in my life had been the fourth round of my last fight in the ring. The greatest joy was that moment when young Steve Cole admitted to me what his sister had said in the letter. I couldn't speak. I was numbed by pleasure.

He went on to say that she believed in me, and that she knew that I would go straight from then on. And he told me a good many other things that I drank in like a man dying of thirst. I wanted to hear him talk on forever. But a knock came at the door, and then the voice of the clerk saying that the colonel wanted to see me at once. I told the clerk that the colonel could wait, but the fellow said that Riggs wanted desperately to see me now, just for a moment.

So down I went to the office of the old fraud, and found him in a heat of excitement. He had a letter in his hand, and when he talked to me he flourished the sheets in the air so that they rattled loudly.

"Now, my lad," said he, "our backs are against the wall. Piegan has the gun held under her nose. Shall she throw up her hands, or shall she fight back?"

"Ask Piegan," said I. "I can't read her mind for you."

"Oh, Poker-face," said he, coming over and dropping a hand on my shoulder in the most affectionate way, "the truth is that you and I compose the majority of Piegan. The head and the hands of it, so to speak."

"You can be the head, colonel," said I, "but I'm not the hands. My skin is not thick enough to handle the jobs."

He laughed a little.

Then, growing serious and dramatic, he pointed a finger at my head like a gun.

"Do you know what is about to happen?" he asked.

"No idea," I answered.

"To-morrow morning, Sidney Maker, of Makerville, Piegan County, is sending a special stage to meet a train on the Q. & O. line. On that train will be two important engineers, and President Tracy Dixon! Think of that! Dixon himself!"

"President of what?" I asked.

"President of what? Why, every man and child in the country knows that he's the president and almost the majority stockholder of the Q. & O. He's a captain of industry, my lad. He's made of money. That's the man that I'm talking about."

"Does he want a stage ride to Makerville?" said I.

The colonel paused, breathing hard, and looking out at me from beneath lowering brows.

"Jerry," he said gloomily, "there are times when I think that you'll never live up to your promise. But I—"

He paused again and cleared his throat.

"I have faith in you, Jerry," he went on. "You will understand in due season, Sid Maker, of course, wants to take the president of the road to Makerville, and there bulldoze him into building the branch line on toward that starved, worthless town!"

"If Tracy Dixon is such a big man," said I, "he'll see through Makerville if it's really such a bad bet."

"See through?" cried the colonel. "Great heavens, my lad, how can I explain to you that all any of us see is words, even a Tracy Dixon? Sometimes, when I think of the folly of human nature, I have tears in my eyes, my lad. Actually, I have tears in my eyes! It's a sad thing. We don't see rivers or mountains, even. We only see the words that have been spoken to us about them. I have seen a forest turned into a desert, and a desert into an alfalfa field by the power of words. I have done it myself! And when Sidney Maker gets Dixon into his hands, he'll never stop until he has convinced him!"

"What's wrong with that?" said I.

"What's wrong with it?" shouted the colonel. "Are we to sit here with our hands in our pockets and see the chance of a lifetime, the lifetime of a growing city, thrown away to the dogs? That's what it means if the railroad goes to Makerville. We'll be dwarfed and done for in the eyes of the world. I'll be a laughingstock—so will all of Piegan."

He steamed up a good deal while he was talking like this, and I felt a stir of excitement, I must say.

I was about to say something about the ease with which a branch line could be run down to us from Makerville, but then I remembered how the colonel had greeted that remark earlier in the day. So I said nothing at all, but shrugged my shoulders.

"Something must be done! Something must be done!" Riggs kept repeating as he stalked up and down the room.

"There's nothing to do, though," said I. "That's obvious."

"The world would stand still if everybody felt as you do!" he shouted at me. "It's people who attempt the impossible that make for progress in this world, and you ought to know it! You *do* know it, if you stop to think."

I shrugged my shoulders again. After all, there was nothing much to answer to such an attitude of mind.

"Push on, push on," said the colonel, getting poetic. "Excelsior! That's the idea, and that's the word for it. Push on, hew to the line as far as the line runs, and then keep on striking in the dark. Illumine your way with the sparks you knock out of existence."

He would have gone on like this almost endlessly, but another thought struck him, and he paused with a groan.

"One day of grace!" he said. "If only I had a chance to think, to devise—but there's only one day of grace!"

He flung himself into a chair and buried his face in his hands. I almost expected to hear him sobbing. But at length he looked up with a corrugated face.

"Say something!" he commanded.

"What?" said I like a fool.

"Anything!" he roared.

"Maker's a tough one," said I, speaking the thought in my heart.

"Tough. Too tough to break. But I'll bend him. I've bent him before, and I'll bend him again!" declared the colonel. "If only I had a little more time! But no," he went on, arguing aloud with himself. "That's the attitude of a dastard and a dolt. My back is against the wall. Vast odds to face. But still there may be some Napoleonic stroke. Tracy Dixon is coming. Coming where? To Maker-ville. That's the curse! He must not go to Makerville! He must come here instead! It must be arranged!"

"You show me what chance there is," said I, "unless you make him think that *you're* Sid Maker, and go in his place!"

He began to make a hasty answer, but then checked himself, and remained for a moment with parted lips, staring at me, his eyes blank with distant thoughts.

He murmured at last: "Have I struck out and raised a spark that will show me my way through the darkness? Has it happened? Do I see the light?"

He got slowly out of his chair, pushing himself gingerly

up with his hands, and then tiptoed across the room with a hand stretched out before him, like a boy trying to catch a butterfly.

"If I could stop Maker and get there myself!" he whispered hoarsely.

Then he whirled about on me.

"*You* will stop Maker. *I* will go on and meet the train at the end of the line!"

I laughed in his face.

"Listen to me, colonel," said I. "You're talking through your hat. I've tackled Sid Maker once, and I'll tackle him no more. That's flat. He's too hot for my fingers to hold him. That's all there is to it."

The colonel struck his hands together. "Where shall I find lieutenants, daring men, fearless, devoted men, men after my own heart?" he cried.

He stalked up and down the room, shaking his head, and getting no apparent answer to his question. Certainly I would not be fool enough to volunteer!

No, I understood my luck when I found it, and, having managed to come off fairly well in my first encounter with Maker, I wanted no more trouble with that bulldog. I still shuddered with relief to think that I had given his wallet back to him, just as I found it, before I turned him loose.

Part of my thoughts seemed to react upon the colonel, for he broke out: "If only I'd had my hands on that wallet of his, I would have found letters, plans, correspondence. I could have pushed something through. But your infernal stubbornness, Jerry Ash, is now endangering the whole future of my city!"

This complaint was so childish that I merely smiled at it, and my smile infuriated him. He glared at me, started to speak, changed his mind, and, planting himself in front of me, he said solemnly:

"Jerry, you're my luck, and the luck of Piegan. Outside of you, where is our good fortune? Nowhere! You are our man, the man of the hour. And now, Jerry, you turn your back on us. I'm surprised. It saddens me to think of this.

174

I'm not prepared for it. Any other man, yes—but not you!"

I could see perfectly, of course, that the old deceiver was flattering me; but, still, what he said was mildly amusing and pleasant to hear. It lulled me in an odd way. It put me at ease. It made me feel stronger. Sidney Maker, for one thing, no longer seemed such a whale of a man.

"Colonel," said I, "I'm not going to have a thing to do with it. That's flat. And you can see for yourself that there's no way short of murder of stopping Maker. And even murder wouldn't stop the rest of the people of his town from showing Tracy their city and its prospects. Copper ore is something that he probably knows a bit about."

"Who talks of murder?" said the colonel angrily. "I talk of delay, not of murder. I talk of delay—putting brakes on that stage which goes to meet the train—way-laying the vehicle in the pass, and there—I don't know what—running off with the horses, perhaps, and—"

"Look, my lad, and try to see," he continued, suddenly running at me and clutching me. "They could get through the journey in one day, but they won't try to. They'll take their time, because they'll want to have their animals fresh in order to give Dixon a decent journey back the day after. Isn't it clear to you? That night, when they camp in the hills, you slip in on them, sweep away their horses, leave them stranded—and the next morning it is Colonel Riggs, sir, who meets Tracy Dixon and conducts him to Piegan, the queen of this valley, and convinces him—"

I hardly heard what else he was saying. A vicious excitement had hold of me, and I began to conceive of that scene as he had painted it. I wanted nothing to do with it, but still I felt with a sinking heart that I was entrapped.

CHAPTER XXX

The Final Plans

WELL, of course, the colonel had his way with me. The moment he saw that I was giving in to his idea somewhat, he renewed the pressure, and in no time I was beginning to enter into the spirit of his plan.

It was not so impossible, either. That is to say, *my* part of the plan was not so impossible. It looked as though it might be very humanly feasible to stop the cortege from Makerville and tie it up long enough to make it late in arriving to meet Tracy Dixon, the great.

After that, how the colonel was to succeed in persuading Mr. Dixon, no matter how smooth and oily his tongue, I could not see. That was his share of the affair.

But you know that the greater the difficulty, the more intriguing is the problem, always, and so it was on this day. In a few moments I was poring with the colonel over maps of the trail—our trail toward the advancing railroad, and the trail from Makerville toward it.

It was not the line from which I had staged in. As a matter of fact, that line was never likely to push up through the mountain passes as far as our valley. But the Q. & O. line had been working for some time to the north. It was driving for new territory, and Tracy Dixon was laying down hundreds of miles of track at a venture. The time was to come when his name was no longer one to conjure with, and when he was to be tottering in his high, imperial position as a railroad magnate. But before the end of his career he saw himself vindicated. The West vindicated him. It made the desert blossom where he had dared to lay down his tracks. It ripped open the mountains and found rich ores to ship on his lines. And along the course of his roads it turned crossroads into villages, villages into towns, towns into bright, flourishing cities.

However, all of this was in the future, and what mattered now was that the Q. & O. was king where Piegan and Makerville stood. We wanted the Q. & O. And the colonel had his idiotic plan for getting it.

"Colonel," I said finally, "it may be that I'll have the luck to stop Maker and his men, because I dare say that they won't be expecting us on their trail this time. But I don't want to be present when you tell your flock of lies to Tracy Dixon and try to persuade him that you're Sid Maker from Makerville, and then that Piegan is better than Makerville, anyway!"

The colonel laughed.

"It would make you sweat and blush a good deal to be around while I was talking to him like that, wouldn't it?" said he.

"It would," said I.

"Ah, Jerry," said he, "you're one of the men of action. You don't understand that conversation, also, has its Waterloos, and its Austerlitzes, too. But one of these days you'll learn—you'll learn, if you watch me closely enough, and listen to me."

He grinned at me in a peculiar way, and then he added quietly: "It's just about half of this battle to have persuaded you to come into this with me."

"Let that go," said I. "Let's make the final plans. I don't suppose that you want me to tackle this scheme alone, do you?"

"You can take all the men you want," said he.

"And what about the cost of horses, and such?" said I, smiling at him.

"Come, come," snorted Riggs. "Why go back so far into our early history? I know you now, my lad, and every-

177

thing that you want is yours long before you ask for it. You know that!"

Well, I didn't entirely believe him—but almost.·

He tried to throw a spur into me again.

"If that railroad comes through the town, you know what you get, Jerry?"

"Make it good, colonel," said I.

"Tut, tut," said he. "I understand perfectly well what a risk you're taking in this business, bearding the man-eaters of Makerville. But it will be worth your while. It will make an independent man of you, I say! You have six lots, among the best in town. I'll tell you what I'll do. I'll make it sixteen lots. Ten more for you. And right clustering around your first holdings. Those lots are going to skyrocket in value when people guess that the railroad intends to tap our city. You're going to be able to get rid of those big, wide, deep, central lots for anywhere from five to twenty-five thousand dollars apiece!"

"Twenty-five thousand apiece?" said I. "Come, come, colonel. You don't ask me to believe that sort of talk, do you?"

"I tell you seriously that I mean it," said he. "You've never seen town fever at work, but I tell you that it drives men just as mad as the gold fever. I've seen thousands of dollars bid into tens and twenties of thousands for a patch of land where not a stick of timber had yet been put up— a dream city, pure and simple!"

I made a quick calculation. The price would not have to be twenty-five thousand apiece. Six or seven apiece would do for me.

As I thought about that possibility of picking up a fortune—with clean hands—my mind went back to Betty Cole. What would she think of such a deal? Would she consider that my hands were clean?

Only the danger of the thing had stopped me before this, but now I said to the colonel: "What about it, Colonel Riggs? What will be thought of me if I stop Maker and his men? Won't I be put down as the worst sort of a border ruffian?"

"Ha!" cried the colonel. "You? Put down as a border

178

ruffian? I should like to hear that term applied to you in Piegan! I should only like to hear it dreamed of by any fool in this town. He would be torn to bits!"

"That's not the point," said I. "I've been rough enough in my day, but—"

"Ah, lad," said the colonel, "don't dwell on your past. Forget it. You're not asked about your past out here. You're only asked about your future! I know that you've had your ups and downs in earlier times. But we'll wash you clean of any stains—"

"Oh, quit it, colonel, will you?" said I.

"What's the matter, my boy?" said he.

"Drop that salvation manner, please," I answered. "I'm only wondering what law-abiding people will think of such a job—even if I manage to work it through. If I'm killed—that will serve me right. If I win through, then I'm simply a successful ruffian."

"Whatever happens," said the colonel, "to Piegan you're a flawless hero."

"It may seem strange to you," said I, "but just for the moment I'm not thinking of Piegan."

He actually smiled. His sense of humor was generally fairly near the surface, I must admit.

"Look here, Jerry," he said. "I'll tell you the straight of it. If you win, you'll be Piegan's idol. You're that already. If you lose, you'll still be the idol here. To the world outside, for the young men, you'll be a hero, too— a fellow they envy and admire. For the older men and women you'll be a plain nuisance, worthy of a penitentiary sentence—or worse! But the point that counts is the girls, I take it. Am I right, my lad?"

I said nothing, but stared at him. Perhaps my color mounted a little, for I remember that the width of his grin increased.

He said: "As for the girls, they'll shake their heads and gasp over you, Jerry. They'll smell fire and brimstone, and see sparks around you. But American girls don't marry haloes, my boy. Never forget that. They like to have their hands full. Remember that!"

Suddenly what he said lifted a weight from my mind.

I shrugged my shoulders and asked him what was next. What men could I have?

"Anything you want," said he.

I thought it over.

"Slim Jim Earl and Dan Loftus rode with me before. They're good lads, and they have a certain amount of faith in me. Then I want a good trailer and a practiced horse thief. There's only one people in the world who are perfect horse thieves, and they're the Indians, I understand. Well, I've seen a long, lean half-breed around the town. Can I put any trust in him?"

"You can trust a half-breed just half as far as you can a full breed," said the colonel sententiously. "I know the man you mean. It's Charlie Butcher. Charlie *the* Butcher, they call him. He has a pretty black reputation, son."

"I don't particularly want a white reputation for horse stealing," said I.

"That's true," said the colonel. "Although I generally feel that I want good men even for bad jobs! Well, well, well! We are moving on. That's three men for you. Who else?"

I had a sudden thought.

Poor young Steven Cole had to stay near me for a time in Piegan. He had to redeem himself in the eyes of the town if he could, and therefore he would never have a much better opportunity than this of riding in the company which was advancing for the forlorn hope of the town.

I named him.

"That young man from the East—the dude?" snapped the colonel.

"He's more than a dude," said I. "I have hopes of him."

"You're wrong," thundered the colonel, smashing his hand down on the table. "I make a prophecy right here. I swear that if you include that young puppy you will ruin the expedition—you will ruin everything."

Well, I simply pulled myself up and stared.

"I'm going to take him. I've made up my mind," said I.

"Then I wash my hands of the job!" shouted the colonel.

"All right," said I, "we've just wasted a lot of time and imagination for nothing."

As I got to the door he overtook me.

"Tell me," he said. "Do you really mean it? You really want to take that worthless fellow along?"

"I've got to take him," I said.

"Take him, then, and confound you!" said the colonel furiously. "Go and round up your party. Better make it seven or eight in all. There may be fighting. There's almost sure to be fighting. So get yourself some men who know how to use a rifle!"

CHAPTER XXXI

The Half-breed

WHEN I found myself squarely embarked upon one of the colonel's missions again I swore a good deal, and wondered how in the world he had managed to turn the trick with me. However, the thing had been done, and there I was in the trap. So I went out to make all the preparations I could.

I found Slim Jim Earl and Dan Loftus together. Since their Makerville exploit, they had always been together, and I'm sure that they never had been able to spend a cent in the town. For them, drinks were free at every bar, and food and room cost them nothing in the hotel. Besides, they were pointed out and admired a good deal. When I found them, I thought they looked pretty seedy.

"Look here, boys," said I. "Do we ride together again on a little job?"

"What kind of a job?" asked Dan.

"Any job is better than Piegan," said Slim Jim, making a face.

"You're whisky-soaked," said Dan. "But I'm not. I could use another week of the stuff."

However, they both agreed that they would go with me. They asked no questions, either. Only, when I said that there would be a hundred dollars apiece for their time for two days, Dan pulled up his belt a couple of notches.

"There's going to be hell popping again, is there?" said he.

But that question answered itself. Who gets fifty dollars a day for anything inside the law? At least, what puncher on the range gets it?

Then I looked up Harry. That young fellow was as clean as a whistle. The town was treating him pretty well, too, since he had pulled down on the detective, Richardson, in such handsome style. The youngster was considered one of our rising citizens, you might say. But he let that all go, and paid no attention to it. He simply laughed at Piegan and at its drinks. A good, steady job was what he wanted, with a dash of fun thrown in. That was what he told me on this day.

Well, I told him that I could offer the fun and a hundred dollars for two days.

"How many men do I have to kill?" said he.

"Nobody," said I. Then I added: "Nobody, I hope." He nodded at me.

"You know, old son," said he, "I told you before, and I meant it: You can have everything that I've got, because except for you being a white man, I'd be pushing daisies by now."

"I don't want you to look at it that way," I told him. "That's all forgotten. We're friends, and that's enough for that other. Make up your mind all fresh."

"Do you need me?" said he.

"I'd like to have you, yes."

"Then I'm with you," said he.

Well, he was old enough to make up his own mind, even if he wasn't old enough to vote. And I was mighty glad to have a kid like that along, all wool and a yard wide with a horse or a gun or working out a trail. He was born to the business.

That left the breed for me to tackle. And he was a different proposition.

I found him, after a good deal of inquiry, in a corner of the Thomson Brothers Saloon. He was sitting on a bench, sagging, his hat pulled down over his long, cadaverous face.

"Is he drunk?" said I to Jud Thomson.

"No. He's only waiting for a drink," said Jud.

I went over to him and asked him to have a drink with me. He got up, pushed back his hat until his hair came in a black shower over his greasy forehead, looked at me out of his popping, red-rimmed, puckering eyes, and came over to the bar with me.

He took about four fingers and jumped it down his throat, and held out his glass for more. Jud looked at me, I nodded, and the breed got his second shot.

"You don't want to drink with me," he said. "You drink ginger ale. You want me, but you don't want me to drink with you."

"I want to drink with you," said I. "But I can't go the whisky."

"Neither can I," said he. "But the whisky can go me. What dirty work have you got for me to do?"

I frowned at him. And he saw me frowning and didn't care. I had a good deal of a reputation—entirely a sham, as you've been able to see—as a fighting man. But the breed didn't care. I saw suddenly that he didn't care about anything. And I understood why.

"It's not dirty, but it's dangerous," said I.

"How much?" said he.

"Fifty dollars a day for two days."

"A hundred a day," said he.

"You're crazy, Charlie."

"A hundred a day," said he.

"I don't want you, then."

"All right," said he, and slouched to his corner again. I realized then how badly I wanted him. And I looked at Jud Thomson.

Jud merely shook his head and said: "I'll tell you what, you'll never be able to do anything with him now. He's got his mean streak on."

I called after him: "You don't even know what the job is, Charlie. You're acting like a fool."

He was already in his slouching position, and now he lifted his head slowly.

"Don't call me a fool, Poker-face," said he. "Some of the boys around here are afraid of you. But I'm not like that."

"Quit that, Charlie!" shouted Jud Thomson. "I told you that you could sit in here if you kept your mean tongue still. You know that I told you that!"

"Yes, you told me that," admitted the breed. "Well, I'm not hunting trouble. Only, I won't be called a fool."

He got up and came back and stood before me, very tall, sick to death, drooping, but never surrendering.

"I've taken your whisky," he said. "I ought to listen to you—for a hundred a day."

"I'll pay you fifty," said I. "You never made so much in your life."

"Yes, I made more than that," said he, "and I served eight years in the pen for it. However, I've made more than fifty a day. But what's your idea, Poker-face?"

"You ride with me for two days. You do what I tell you on the way. That's all."

"You tell me to jump off a cliff, and I do it, eh?"

"Yes—if that's the sort of a boss you think that I'll make. Look here, Charlie. You have more sense than this. You know that I'm offering you a good thing, so why don't you take it?"

"Maybe we shoot a lot?" said he.

"Maybe. And maybe we get shot a lot. I don't know. We take our chances. How does it sound to you?"

"How many men?" he asked sourly.

"Four besides the pair of us."

184

"Two days?" said he.

"Come on, Charlie," said I. "You need something to take your mind off yourself."

"You want me a lot, eh?" said he.

"I want you," said I. "Yes, that's true. Otherwise I wouldn't be arguing with you."

"I know why you want me," said Charlie Butcher. "It's dangerous work. Somebody's apt to drop. Why not the half-breed? Who would care if the breed tumbled? Why, not a soul. Tell me—would you care?"

I looked back into his sneering eyes.

"No more than *you* would care, Charlie," said I.

He appeared startled. He even forgot his settled sneer.

"What do you mean by that?" said he.

"You're only around the corner from it, Charlie," said I. "And you won't care much when that corner is turned. I don't know what's the matter with you, but I guess that there's not much more time left for you."

That was a brutal speech, but he had fairly pulled it out of me. Now I saw, with horror, that I had been talking to a sensitive man. He straightened a little; his face grew pale and glistening as he watched me.

"Very well," he said. "I've deserved that. And I'll ride along with you, Poker-face, whenever you say!"

I told him to get his best pair of horses. I told him where to meet us, and then I went for the hotel once more and found poor Steve Cole sitting in the dusk by the window, with his head fallen back against the top of the chair he was sitting in. At first the moveless, solid outline of him shocked me, but then I saw the stir of his breast, and knew that he was breathing.

"Steve," said I, "can you ride?"

"I've ridden all my life," said he, "cross country and that sort of thing. But I'm no champion."

"Can you shoot?"

"Yes. I've done a lot of hunting."

"I don't mean shotguns."

"Rifles? Yes. Revolvers, too, rather recently. I've practiced a lot."

"Did Stephani teach you?"

185

"As a matter of fact, he did. How did you guess that?"

"I don't know. But he's a great teacher. I know that much. Listen to me."

"I'm listening like a convert, Jerry."

"Get up, jump into old clothes and riding boots, and then jam a hat on your head and get ready for two days of rough riding."

He got up without a word and began to peel off his clothes.

"What's up?" he asked finally.

"Horses, guns, and all that sort of thing," I told him.

"That's all right," said he softly.

I knew that he meant it: On that little ride which I was planning there would be one beside Charlie who cared not a whit whether he lived or died.

But I had my hands full now. I wanted to get out of the town shortly after sunset—as soon as the countryside was good and black. Then my plan was to ride briskly along that night, and get up in the Cash Hills by the dawn at the latest. That would give our horses and ourselves a whole day of rest—or nearly an entire day—before the Makerville party came through. We could scatter, watch the three possible trails that the stage might be following, and then, when it was seen, we could signal to one another.

That was the plan to commence with. And with that part we went straight through.

CHAPTER XXXII

The Makerville Party

THIS grows a little complicated, so I have to explain the tactics and the strategy. The strategy was this: I marched for the Cash Hills—so called by an early prospector who did *not* find gold in them—and hunted till I.found Maker. After stopping him if I could, I was to push on and try to get to the end of the Q. & O. branch line in time to join the colonel as a guard of honor, so to speak, on his return trip. Also, *if* Maker and his men got under way and suspected our plans, they might cut across our line of retreat and give us a hot reception.

The colonel, in the meantime, was to get the reserve stage which was always kept at Piegan in case the regular one was broken up. He was to get six fast horses on it, and a good driver, and with a few of the most respectable citizens, he was to go across to the end of the branch line, leaving Piegan about dawn.

That was the plan of campaign. The main battle would be, probably, between my gang and the Makerites. Everything depended on that, for a beginning. And in the ending, it would be the persuasive tongue of the colonel that would tell the story with Tracy Dixon.

I saw the colonel for farewell instructions, and he had little to say. He was nervous, of course, but cheerful. He swore that he would make me a rich man if this deal

187

went through, and he vowed eternal friendship and confidence whether it went through or not. So I pulled out of Piegan on time, and we jogged our horses steadily through the night.

If I doubted the value of the half-breed on such a trip as this, the doubt disappeared before we were an hour out of the town. That fellow took the lead at once, and he had eyes like a cat in the dark of the night. He got us across two bad places where freshets had washed out the trail, and throughout the night he kept the lead.

I kept to my place at the tail end of the party most of the time, because in that position I could favor myself as much as possible, and the others could not see so well my various odd positions in the saddle. For I had to do everything I knew in order to make the ride less fatiguing. Even so, I could not make the ride without a long halt, and after we had gone, according to the breed, about two thirds of the way, I had the party pull up, and we made a fire and rested for at least an hour.

I wrapped myself in a blanket and lay flat. After a moment, while the other boys were chattering together and seemed in high spirits, along came a shadow and sat down beside me, and the husky voice of the breed said:

"You, also, Poker-face."

"Also what?" said I, working to keep the weariness out of my voice.

"You will not last long, either," said he. "I saw it in your face when you saw it in mine. And that is why I came for this little ride. But you are very tired. You had better stay here, and I'll go on with the rest and do the work. Tell me what the work is to be."

"No," said I. "That's fine of you, Charlie. But I'll have to stay along with the others. I'm better than you think. But I have to take things by easy stages. That's all."

He grunted. I could not make out the words.

"Tell me, Charlie," said I, so softly that the others could not hear, "where you were educated."

"In college. No good telling you where. I'm no credit to it," said he.

"You're credit enough," said I. "I wouldn't have any man in the world in your place in this party."

"That's only because I don't care what happens," he suggested.

"No, it's because you've got a head on your shoulders."

"What good does it do to have a brain?" said he. "For an Indian, yes. For a white man, yes. But I'm only a breed."

He went on trying to persuade me that I should stay behind and let him take over the direction of the party. I was amazed. I would never have dreamed that there was so much generous kindness in the make-up of that fellow. I don't think that another soul in the world ever guessed it at the time.

When he saw that he could not move me, he grunted again, and went off by himself.

I waited there until the thumping of my weary heart was smoothed out and flowing along on a fairly steady level. Then I propped myself up, and we took to the saddles again.

I must say that the halt seemed to work out well for the horses, and we kept up a good, steady pace right through the night, and reached the Cash Hills just when the dawn was beginning to stretch a pink band around the sky line.

There we hobbled the horses and turned them out to graze, cooked a good breakfast, and then I had everybody turn in for a sleep. Perhaps it would have been wiser to post a guard, but I was confident that we were too far off any beaten track to be taken by surprise.

For my part, I had the shadow of a big boulder to shield my face, and I slept straight through until noon. I might have slept still longer, but the noise of voices wakened me, and I got up to find that I was the last of the party to be stirring.

We still had plenty of time; the Makerites could hardly be expected before the middle of the afternoon. So we cooked another meal, finished it off with coffee, and then I posted my lookouts. Before I sent them out, I explained the whole plan in detail—that is, I explained the part

189

about stopping the Makerites. As for the scheme of the colonel, or what this deal might mean to Piegan, I said nothing. I was afraid that the thing would seem to the rest of them as foolish as it now seemed to me. For, after sleeping on it, I confess that it looked the most ridiculous thing in the world. The only reason that I kept on was because I had put my hand to the job and thoroughly committed myself.

As for my gang, they listened carefully to what I had to say. The business of stopping a party of Makerites seemed perfectly logical to all of the boys except young Steve Cole. And, of course, he was not asking questions!

As for the rest, they were willing, if I said the word, to open on any body of Makerites and shoot to kill! That I didn't want, and I insisted over and over that not a bullet should be fired until I gave the word. And that word I fully intended never to give.

However, to get on to the event of the day.

I had three lookouts on three ridges, each of them able to signal to the others. The moment the stage was sighted, we could draw to a head and focus on it. As a matter of fact, we had to wait all through the afternoon, and it was almost too dark to see the signal before Slim Jim called us to him on the double.

The whole gang of us slipped over to his ridge, riding hard, and when we pulled up and sneaked over the crest among the boulders, we lay down flat and peered, and saw the picture for which we had been waiting.

Only, it was more of a picture than we had gambled on.

You've seen that Colonel Riggs and the Piegan men were willing to take a lot of chances, and do things in a big way, and spend money liberally. But the Makerites were just as ready, or even more so. I saw a specially big stage, all bright with gilding, and drawn by eight horses. And those horses had white and red plumes on their harness, and bells that jingled and tinkled and made a very sweet and far-away music, coming up through the still air of that ravine.

That was not all.

No, it was hardly more than a beginning, because before that stage, and behind it, and riding on both sides, were twenty men from Makerville, and I did not need to have second sight in order to guess that they were the keenest and bravest and hardiest men in that keen and hardy town. Through the rosy haze of the sunset light I could see that the lot of them were armed to the teeth— all the more to impress Tracy Dixon, I suppose, but, incidentally, very tough for us!

Dan Loftus was lying on his elbows close beside me, and he turned and made a long, sour face at me, muttering:

"There's our pie. I'll cut it, Mr. Ash, if you'll eat a piece."

"Yeah. I'll eat a piece, I guess," said I.

But I hardly meant it!

Suddenly and mightily I hoped that they would not camp in the hills, as the colonel imagined that they would.

It was only a matter of a dozen miles to the end of the branch line, according to our calculations, and they might push through.

However, when I saw the gilding on that resplendent coach, I could not help shaking my head and thinking that the colonel's guess would be the right one. They would not take rough chances with such a land ship as that!

We went along our side of the ridge, keeping pace with the caravan in the darkening ravine, and presently, as they came over the divide of the Cash Hills, they stopped. They had completed the long pull up the grade, and now there was before them an almost equally long grade swerving in gradual curves down to the end of the Q. & O. line.

There they halted. The grade was not much, but they blocked the wheels of the stage thoroughly with stones, and stripped off the splendid harness of the horses, and piled it inside the vehicle. Then that gang of men pitched camp, and they did it fast and in good style. They built up a ripping fire, and cooked on the edges of it, and it seemed to me that I could smell the coffee steaming.

We, six cold, miserably depressed fellows, waited on

191

the backbone of the ridge and looked gloomily down at the numbers of those men, and at the extent of their preparations.

They ate their meal. We could hear the stir of their voices, sounding even farther away than the fact, and then we saw them settling down for the night. They hobbled their horses and turned them out as I had done with ours the preceding evening. But they posted an armed man to guard the great stage. The rest lay down in the brush on both sides of the road, and near to the stage.

My heart began to rise. I called Charlie aside, and I said to him: "Charlie, I'm not an expert horse thief, but it seems to me that some of us can easily drift our horses down one of these side gullies and walk along beside them among the horses of Makerville and cut those hobbles. And when that's done, is anything easier than to send the whole herd whooping down the valley toward the end of the line?"

"Nothing is easier," said Charlie Butcher. "But the others can attend to that. You and I, partner, have something better to fill our hands."

I looked at him with amazement.

"What else is there to do, Charlie?" I asked.

"I have an idea," said he. "Come with me."

"You may take me to the devil, Charlie," said I.

"What do you care, Poker-face?" said he. "You are a man without fear."

Suddenly I said: "No, Charlie. The boys are entirely wrong about me. They've given me a great reputation that I don't deserve. My nerves are in a worse state right now than those of any man in the party."

I heard him laughing.

"They'll be in a lot worse state before you're through following me," said he.

"I won't follow you, Charlie," said I.

"You will, though," said he, "because you won't be able to fight off your curiosity. You won't be able to help that!"

"What do you plan to do?" I asked.

"I'll show you as we go along," said he.

"I'll not budge a step with you," said I.

"You will, though," he insisted with an odd surety.

It angered me a little, it excited me a good deal more, to think that he had some secret plan of importance on hand. Finally he said:

"Well, you give your orders. Those boys down there are having their first sleep and their hardest one. Tell the men to start working toward the horses."

I got the men around me, and I told them how to drift their horses down the gully, and, walking beside their horses, work in among the horses of the Makerites, cut their hobbles, and be prepared to rush the entire herd down the valley.

"It's a cinch," said Harry. "This here is goin' to be one of those easy things that folks talk about afterward. They'll make us out a lot of big heroes. And it ain't nothing at all. When shall we start the rush?"

"We'll fire a gun to let you know," said the breed, suddenly speaking up.

"Ain't you goin' to be with us?" snapped Slim Jim.

"The chief and I," said the breed, "will be down there in the middle of the camp."

"You'll be what?" shouted Dan Loftus.

"What?" groaned Steve Cole.

"The chief hates to get this close to Sid Maker without leaving his card for him," said Charlie.

The whole gang of boys looked at us. I could have cursed the breed, but somehow shame kept me from speaking. If he really had conceived such a crazy plan— but no, I felt sure that not even a dying man, careless of his life, would dare so far as to go among the armed men of that camp.

But there I was, hand-tied as it were, and placed in the hands of a man who, I rather felt, was more than half insane.

Shame kept me still.

Steve Cole came up to me and said:

"It's not true, Jerry. You won't go down there like a madman. What on earth for? Do these barbarians take scalps?"

But that was the way the thing was managed. We even left our horses behind us, at the dictates of that rascal of a Charlie. And the other men were to bring the nags along with them.

"Charlie," I said as we started down into the gully, and the others of my gang slipped on beside their walking horses, "how can we possibly get away without horses?"

"I'll show you an idea," said Charlie, "that's worth ten of the best horses."

"If you mean to run," said I, "you may be able to manage it. But I couldn't sprint a hundred yards without falling dead. That's a fact."

"I don't mean to run a step," said Charlie.

"What *do* you mean to do?" asked I.

"You will see," said he, and began to chuckle.

I stopped short. This sounded more and more like madness.

"I won't go," said I.

"Good-bye, then," said he.

He walked straight on.

Then I hurried after him and caught his arm.

"Charlie," said I, "have you got your wits about you?"

"Never clearer in my life, such as they are," said he.

I went on beside him, muttering, cursing.

"That's right," said Charlie. "Keep on swearing, but keep on coming. That's the best way for it!"

He laughed again.

"The more a man swears, the lighter his heart will be," went on Charlie.

Somehow I felt, suddenly, that there was no madness, except that of extreme daring, about my companion. I looked back, however, toward the dark outlines of my gang and their horses coming down the gully well behind us. Every one of those men, beyond a doubt, thought that I was the leader in this foolhardy excursion. Every man of them was holding his breath. Most of them, no doubt, were wondering where I could get such colossal nerve. Not a single man would dream how weak and shaking were my knees!

Well, I decided that it was foolish to look back, or to

think of anything except the way of putting my feet forward upon the ground in the most silent fashion. So we went steadily down that gully and then turned out among the boulders and the brush of the floor of the big ravine.

It was a comfort to me to see the size of the obstacles.

For, when I had looked down on them from the ridge above, the rocks and the bushes had seemed very tiny indeed, but now I found that they gave the most excellent cover. With the advantage of this we forged on until, as we neared the trail, I saw the stage looming before us on the crest of the rise.

"That's what we want," said Charlie, touching my arm and pointing.

"What?" said I, unable to believe my ears.

"The stage," said he.

"The stage?" I exclaimed. "What are you talking about, man?"

"I'm talking sense."

"What'll we do? Pull it along by hand?"

"We'll manage to take it," said Charlie, nodding his long head.

"Man, man," I exclaimed, "we've no horses along with us."

"We won't need horses, either," said Charlie, and began to laugh softly.

"Will you explain?" said I.

"Seeing will be quicker than hearing," said the breed, and walked on.

I wanted to stop and protest, argue, ask questions—anything to kill time. But he was as relentless in his forward movement as a boulder rolling downhill. I went after him. I never felt so like the useless tail to a kite.

When I caught up with him, I whispered: "There's a guard posted in that stage!"

"Of course there is," said he. "But only one!"

The significance of that gave me a distinct and vital chill. However, I was almost out of breath with excitement, fear, and the effort of keeping up with his long steps. I could not talk any more. My heart was thundering in the hollow of my throat.

195

In the meantime, the breed began to stalk, no longer walking erect, but bending well over, and moving like a cat from one bit of cover to the next. Smooth and fast work it was, and soundless. For my part, I shamelessly walked behind him and tried to put my feet exactly down where he had stepped. Even so, it was impossible for me to avoid making a few noises as pebbles rolled under my tread.

However, that devil of a Charlie would not stop, but went weaving on until the stage was like a house almost beside us, and I dared not look to the side, where I knew that many men were lying in their blankets. I could hear the snoring of them beside me, behind me. We were now well inside the trap.

And was it not a trap?

Suppose that Charlie the breed had decided that he would make more than fifty dollars a day—he could make several thousand, no doubt, by betraying me in the midst of the camp of the Makerites!

You can believe that this thought did not soothe my nerves particularly!

Then I saw the breed make a gesture and sink to the ground. I did the same.

We were in an almost open space close beside the stage. There were only a few small stones, some little bushes, between us and it. An eye, looking in our direction, was sure to spot us, even in the dimness of the starlight.

But would we pass for sleeping forms, the fellows of the rest? That seemed the only hope if any one were up and stirring, or if the guard looked out from the stage.

And some one *was* up and stirring.

I saw a dark form rise and move toward the stage. I heard him say:

"All right, Ed."

"Is that you, Will?" growled the voice from the stage.

"Yeah. It's me."

A man opened the door of the vehicle and stepped to the ground.

"It's cold in there," he said.

"Shut up. Don't wake up the boys."

"I'm not waking anybody up. Listen to Doc snorin'. He's got a special tune that he plays, and he always winds it up with a whistle. I recollect once I was up in Carson with him, and—"

"Sid is pretty happy, ain't he?" broke in the other.

"Yeah, and why not? This puts Makerville on the map."

"The copper put it on the map," said Will.

"The lies of Riggs, they put us on the map. His lies about Makerville standin' on gravel, ready to slide into the gulch!"

"Yeah. That's true, too. I'll bet he's gnawin' his thumbs when he thinks of that."

"Him and that Poker-face, too."

It was odd the thrill I had when I heard them refer to me.

"Poker-face, he don't care none. He's in the game for the cash and the excitement. I like his nerve, that devil!"

"They're goin' to put up a statue to him in Piegan, I've heard."

"Well, I'm goin' to turn in. I wish that Poker-face could see our layout."

"Maybe he's seeing it now!"

"Oh, shut up."

And Ed went off to find his blankets.

CHAPTER XXXIII

Stealing the Stage

WILL walked up and down for a time beside the coach. I saw him yawn, and the shadow of his arms against the stars. I saw him push back his big-brimmed hat and scratch his head. Then he worried at something—a plug of tobacco, I dare say, for presently I heard him spit.

He began to hum as he walked back and forth, and, pausing very near me, he put back his head and stared long and hard at the stars. As he did so, another shadow arose to the side a little and behind him. It was the breed, moving with such dreadful caution that to this day I see the breathless and hanging deliberation of his attitudes. But at length he was straightened, and moved softly forward.

At the last moment, something troubled Will, the guard, and he whirled rapidly around, a gun gleaming in his hand.

The sight of that got me to my feet. Distinctly I heard the clank of the blow of the long barrel of the revolver as it glanced off the hardy skull of my friend, the breed. He had been in the very act of springing in, one arm outstretched to hook the fork of it about the throat of Will. In that moment the latter had wheeled and struck, moving all in an insant, with a wonderful adroitness and readiness.

He did not fire, did not shout, but stood for a moment with poised revolver, watching Charlie Butcher go through all of the steps of a drunken reel. Any other man in the world surely would have fallen, brained by that stroke, but Charlie's head was apparently of gun metal itself.

Then I heard Will muttering: "What drunken fool are you, anyway?"

I understood, as I came up behind in my turn. Will took it for granted that the other was a member of the Maker party. He could not conceive of an enemy having walked in upon them; such a conception was too much like madness, to be sure.

But just then I laid the muzzle of my own Colt against the small of Will's back.

He did not turn, but I felt the shuddering of his body from my hand to my shoulder. I whispered in his ear:

"It's all right. Be a mouse. Don't even mutter; don't even step hard, or I'll have to part this backbone of yours."

He nodded. I reached a hand in front of him, and he silently put his revolver into the fingers I presented. So with two guns touching his body, I held him until Charlie came up. He had recovered as by magic from the terrible effects of that blow.

Charlie said, in the most hushed of voices: "Now we're all comfortable again. Slog him on the head and put him away, or sink a knife between his ribs, Poker-face."

"It's Poker-face!" I heard Will murmur.

His knees sagged as he said the word. What a lot of nonsense was believed about me, at that time, in Makerville!

"I'll not murder him or slug him, either," said I in an answering whisper.

"The devil you won't," said Charlie Butcher. "Then herd him inside of that stage and sit there with him with a gun at his head."

"Inside the stage?" I repeated.

He already had turned his back and was stepping to the vehicle.

Certainly this was no place to pause for argument. I was still as blank as ever as to the intentions of Charlie.

So I pushed little by little ahead with Will, the prisoner, and got him into the stage, on top of the piles of harness, which almost filled the interior. For that harness was harness, so to speak. There were pads and silver-gilt back pieces, and the leather was so rich and heavy and strong that it bent hardly more easily than wood.

In the meantime, I heard things grating under the wheels of the stage, but I could not make out, still, what was in the mind of Charlie. Yet I submitted blindly to whatever might be in his mind. It shows how the ready and quick-witted man will take charge of a situation. No private in an army could obey a major general more humbly than I obeyed that iron-nerved breed.

Then a voice spoke up, not very far away, and said: "What are all you boys doing there?"

I recognized the voice of Maker himself, and it nearly paralyzed my brain. I nudged Will in the ribs with the muzzle of my gun and told him to speak up, and he drawled:

"Nothin', Sid."

"Whatcha mean, nothin'?" said Maker angrily. "There's three of you scrapin' around and makin' enough noise to rouse an army. We ain't an army, but I'm going to show you—Hold on there, and tell me what the—"

He stopped. My own heart almost stopped at the same instant, for suddenly the stage had begun to move, and now in a stroke I half understood what had been in the mind of Charlie. He wanted to steal the stage itself right out of the midst of the camp, and for that purpose, he would try to run it down the grade away from the Maker-ites. Without horses, how would he steer the big, lumbering vehicle?

Well, that was another problem for Charlie, and I would not attempt to solve it.

What he had been doing was simply to pull the stones from under the wheels, and now we were getting under way down the slope, which continued for I could not tell how many miles!

At the same instant, the explanation seemed to come to the mind of Maker, for his voice rose into a yell that brought every man in his party up from the ground. They stood like so many prairie dogs which had suddenly popped up out of as many different holes, and just as prairie dogs bark, that crowd started to make a racket.

I looked over the edge of the coach and saw Maker leveling a rifle, and ahead, I could see the breed pulling at the tongue of the stage, giving it needed momentum.

Then the rifle spoke from the hands of Maker, but the breed did not go down. Instead, he leaped back and got on the crosstress at the base of the wagon pole. That tongue, you must understand, was propped up high into the air, held by a natural stiffness in the joint that crossed the doubletree. Otherwise, I don't know what kept it there in the air.

And now we were going forward at a walk, at a dog-trot, at a run.

I heard Maker yelling to his men to stop us, capture us, murder us, and suddenly twenty guns unlimbered. Or so it seemed to me. The roar of those guns will never be quite out of my mind, and I heard a number of the bullets crash through the woodwork of the coach.

"Don't spoil the wagon. Stop it!" screeched Maker.

And he set the example of sprinting toward us.

Others started with him, and gained upon him, because he was a short-legged man. It seemed to me that the infernal rolling coach was simply crawling over the surface of the road, but by the slowness with which the runners overtook us, we must have been traveling already at a good clip when the runner in the lead leaped up on the side of the coach, on my right. He had to catch on with both hands to keep from falling. In one hand he had a revolver clutched, but for the instant in his struggle to maintain his place, he was helpless. I used that instant to jerk a sharp elbow into his face. He threw up his hands, dropped his revolver, and fell with a loud shout into the road.

Another fellow landed on the opposite side of the coach, just then, with a gun ready leveled at me, and perhaps I would have been a goner, but the stage happened to hit a good-sized rock, just then, and heeled sharply over. The

Makerite fired into the air blindly, and then fell back, reaching at thin air to hold himself up.

By that time we were roaring along down the hillside, and at the same moment, I heard loud yelling up the left-hand slope of the valley. I hardly needed to look there, for I knew. And now I saw that the boys had done their work, for the whole herd of Makerite horses was being stampeded in our direction. I could hear the lads yelling, whooping at the top of their lungs. Above all, I heard them laughing with half-hysterical joy.

And after them some of the robbed people were running foolishly, shooting as they ran. But whoever heard of targets being struck by excited men who were on the run?

These fellows, at the least, hit nothing. We learned that later, and now our coach was leaping like a broncho down the rough mountain trail, bounding from hummock and rock.

It was the roughest ride. There was no question about keeping a gun ready for my prisoner. He had his hands full, hanging on, and so did I. It needed a good grip or we would both have been flung out onto the road. If I fell, and the Makerites found me, there was no question in my mind about what would happen to me. No matter under what obligation I had put Maker himself, his whole party would be maddened, and it was lynching or nothing, for me!

Then I forgot all about Maker and the bullets which still whined through the air around us, for our whole attention was given to the mad course of that stage.

It veered and wheeled like a crazy thing. I heard Charlie calling, and in answer to his yells, I climbed over the front of the jumping, bouncing wagon and got down beside the breed.

He was steering that coach by the pole, pitching his weight first to one side and then to the other, and I helped him, imitating as exactly as I could every move of his. I dared not look ahead, because my nerve was completely gone. We were rushing into blackness. Whole mountains loomed before us. We were going like a train, and there were no smooth tracks ahead of us. The stars blurred above my head. I was waiting for the last shock, and then mercifully brief death. I only prayed for that, not to have to linger too long.

Then I heard a screeching. I saw Charlie reaching up and pulling down the long lever of the brake. The grip of it seemed to affect our progress not at all, for a long moment, but gradually we came under control. We hit a small stream, dashing the water with stinging force up where it drove against our faces. And on the farther slope of the stream, we came to a halt, the brake groaning loudly.

Well behind us, far outdistanced by our headlong speed, we saw the dim forms of the horsemen driving the stampede toward us. Up the valley to the rear there was no sight of man, no sound of gun, and suddenly I knew that we had won, and far more than I had ever dreamed of winning!

CHAPTER XXXIV

The Words of the Breed

WHEN we climbed down from the doubletrees, we could hardly stand. I looked back into the body of the stage and saw that our captured Makerite, Will, was lying extended in a complete faint, and I blamed him not at all. My own head was so dizzy that the bright stars turned into circular lines and haze spinning through the central portions of the sky.

The boys came up with the horses. Two of them went ahead to keep the captured herd in hand. The other two rounded in a few of the horses and onto these we huddled harness.

I say "we," but I mean that they did all the work. For my own part, my heart was hammering so that I could barely speak a word. I wanted to kill the men who came up and hammered me on the back, and said it was the greatest thing that had ever been done on the range, but I told them that Charlie had thought of everything, and managed everything.

They would have smitten Charlie on the shoulder, too, but he was too known a man; they would sooner have taken liberties with a rattlesnake!

Well, we got eight mustangs hitched into that splendid harness, so gilded that it shone even under the starlight, and I, still exhausted, tremulous, thankful that the night might cover the whiteness of my cold face, climbed into the coach, and we drove off up the valley, heading toward our goal.

I told Slim Jim, who had an eye for horse, to try to keep the stampeded herd as quiet as possible, so that when the dawn commenced, we could try to pick out the best of the lot to serve for harness work, for already it was dawning on me that Piegan never could furnish a team equal to the splendid turnout which the Makerites had sent for Tracy Dixon, the Great!

At first, I was too sick, too suffering from shock, to fix my mind upon anything. But gradually the effect of much straight living, in that magic air of the West, exerted its effect upon me, and I recovered. It always amazed me, in those days, to see how my strength was gaining, how much more I could do one week than I had been able to do the week before. A vague hope was rising in me that perhaps, before many years, I could lead almost a normal life.

Then, as my brain cleared, I could look further into the future and see that the colonel, after all, might be able to erect this wild night adventure into a great thing for Piegan. But such idiotic and piratic freaks of the fancy he was always building up his own fortune and that of the town!

We had enough time before us now.

Those fellows behind us were all on foot. Their splendor of costume would have to be dragged on weary foot over the rough mountain miles until they came to the end of the branch road, and long before they got there, I hoped that the train would have arrived and we would be carting the deluded Tracy Dixon not toward his right destination, but on the trail toward Piegan.

And Sid Maker?

I really shuddered when I tried to conceive the fury that would be in the soul of that fellow. And all his companions, too, would be madmen. It seemed to me that I had recognized through the dimness of the night the second man to leap at the stage and fire in the air, unbalanced by the heeling of the vehicle. I thought that it was Chuck, the gunman. And if that were the case, and he learned of my presence there in the coach, I knew that the man would never rest until he had murdered me.

Well, that hardly mattered. I curled up in that coach, begged mad Charlie Butcher to drive on slowly, and slept soundly all the rest of the night, in spite of the infernal slamming and banging of the coach over that rough trail. But I needed more sleep, and I got it, and wakened with the coach standing still, and the boys rounding up the entire horse herd quietly around me.

Slim Jim had found the best of the lot to make carriage horses of them. We spanned in eight, and away we went again, slowly and steadily.

Dan Loftus I sent back with a good pair of field glasses to scan the country behind us, and he declared that there was no sign for many miles of the Makerites coming along on foot. For that matter, we all agreed that since those fellows had lived most of their lives in the saddle, they would be apt to sit about for a long time and commiserate, before they started hobbling in any direction in their narrow-soled, pinching riding boots.

No, we had plenty of time before us.

Well on in the morning, we came in sight of the distant

gleam of the railroad tracks, and when we got down to them, we turned out and polished up the stage, rubbed the scratches, whipped off the dust, and made all ship-shape. From the harness we worked away the salty incrustations of the sweat, and we dressed down the horses, to their great surprise. Mustangs are not used to such attentions.

It was something after the prime of the day when the colonel pulled in.

He had the regular relief stage that was kept in the barn at Piegan, just as he had planned, and he had picked out six good horses to draw it. When he took off his duster, he revealed his most genteel costume, and he had made a concession to the West by buckling great golden spurs on the heels of riding boots. He looked a cross between a pirate and a college professor, more professor than pirate, perhaps.

And when he saw our splendid equipage, the boys who were with him told me afterward that he almost fainted.

"Poor Jerry Ash has failed at last!" he said to them. "I gave him more than a man could perform."

Then he realized, at the last, that the Makerites actually were not in possession, and he came running over with the tails of his duster streaming out behind him, his hands held out, his face a study of childish joy. He shook hands with us all around, and called us the saviors of Piegan and such rot. When he got through with his first transports, he started centering his attack on me, but I tried to shut him up by telling him in detail just what Charlie Butcher had done.

Charlie cut in on me with these words, which I shall never forget:

"Brother, if you had not been with me, I would be lying dead up yonder among the Makerites!"

"It's very well to be modest, Jerry," said the colonel, "but you see that the truth will out."

I had to let it go for the moment, but I shook my head at Charlie.

Afterward, when we were alone for a moment, he put his big bony hand on my arm and said:

"Tell them whatever you want to. Men only believe what they wish to believe. Between you and me, there is nothing owing. You saved my life, for which I have no value. I gave you a little reputation, which you'll die before you enjoy."

There was a sour conviction behind his words that quite took out from me any thrill that I might have been feeling at the moment. It gave me no pleasure to feel the glance of Harry resting on me, a moment later, with a profound and silent worship.

Young Steve Cole had a different attitude. He looked at me with bewilderment. He could not feel that I was such a conjurer, but he was puzzled. For his own part, he had done his share with the rest, and suddenly he was accepted by the entire lot of those fellows, both the ones who had ridden with him from Piegan, and those who came over afterward with the colonel.

His mistakes were forgotten, more or less. It's that way with people in the West. In the East, if you slip once, your neck is broken forever, but in the West, we have a feeling that every man has a right to make a fool of himself now and again. It's the best quality to be found in the entire country. So now the lad was taken wholeheartedly into the respect of all the community that was represented by the men from Piegan. I could even from a distance tell how he was blossoming under the new atmosphere.

While the colonel was making his final arrangements, I had a chance to chat for a moment with Steve, and I told him point-blank how well he had impressed every one, and how he would stand shoulder to shoulder, in public estimation, with every man in Piegan, from this time forth. He was so pleased that he turned red, but like a good fellow he tried to dodge the praise and turned back the talk to me, the last subject that I wanted.

He said that the lot of them, as they slipped in among the horses, and began to cut the hobbles, had been able to look down onto the road and to make out, dimly, the form of the stage, but they could not see what Charlie and I were doing, and only were aware that the devil was loose when the stage began to rush and roar, careening down the valley. And then he asked me if I really took pleasure in that sort of work, and if I really were trying to throw my life away as soon as possible, because he said that that was what the rest of the men from Piegan said about me, and that they all declared that there must be some terrible mystery connected with my early life which had soured me, and made me indifferent to anything that might come into my life.

I said: "Steve, listen to me. I like life as well as the next fellow. To-night, it was Charlie Butcher who dragged me into this affair. I didn't even know what he intended to do with the coach. Otherwise I wouldn't have gone. But Piegan has determined to turn me into a hero. It'll be a sick town when it finds out how far its pet gunman and wild man falls short of the mark."

Steve surprised me by smiling only a little, and remarking: "Jerry, some people never know themselves even when their pictures are in the newspapers every day!"

Then the colonel came over, and I was glad to be able to talk of something else.

CHAPTER XXXV

A Real Hero

WHAT cut me up was the continual expectation of the day when I should be cornered and show the white feather in front of the entire town. That was what I prayed against; that was why I kept swearing to myself that I would leave Piegan soon and stay away forever. Every day that I remained, I was apt to be rounded up for some such affair as this!

Well, Colonel Riggs came up, his arrangements all made for the return journey, and the arrangements were showy, but amusing. Ahead and behind the coach were to ride a special bodyguard of the Piegan fighters. The driver was to be Charlie Butcher, who it appeared had an old reputation for handling horses on reins. And since the visiting party consisted of three, the colonel wanted to have three Piegan men in the coach with them. He would be one, he insisted that I should be the second, and when I wanted to get out of it, he said that I was the only man in Piegan, outside of himself, who could speak good English. I said then that he ought to include Steve Cole, who spoke better English than either of us.

The colonel balked at the thought of Cole. He said that I was too young, as a matter of fact, and the only reason he really could afford to have me in the coach was because even Tracy Dixon might have heard about me and my exploits. But I insisted that Cole would be a good member of the reception committee, youth or not, and that he would make the visitors think that we had a few gentlemen in Piegan. At last Riggs agreed and went off to speak to Steve.

You should have seen the pleased and astonished face of Steve Cole! He came over to me, a little later, and grabbed my arm, and said that Colonel Riggs had asked him to be one of the three on the reception committee.

"Of course," said I. "You're a marked man in Piegan, Steve!"

He laughed happily.

"Jerry," he added, a minute later, "I'll tell you what! I'm going to show Piegan that I'm worth while, after all. You've shoved me into this job."

"Not at all."

"You have, though. I know that you are behind it, but I'll try to manage things so that Piegan will be glad I'm in the party!"

There were other and bigger resolves shining in his eyes, and I began to see more clearly than ever that my friend Steve Cole was going to be a fellow to be proud of!

A little later, the train came slowly down to the end of the branch track, and the colonel had us all grouped about. The boys waved their hats and yelled and whooped and cheered, while the visiting party of three men got off the train. I saw right away that there was nothing pompous about them. They simply looked like ordinary farmers, or cattlemen. Two of them were biggish fellows, one middle-aged, one not more than thirty. The third was Tracy Dixon. One could pick him out from a distance in spite of his size by the silver shine of his hair, and something resolute and grim in his face. He had cut throats in business. He looked ready to cut some more.

Well, when I had watched that gang of three arrive, and saw the boys gathering up their bags, and watched the old rascal of a colonel greeting the men and shaking their hands, and with his hat off waving them toward the waiting stage, my heart went sliding and slipping down to my boots, for I suddenly was sure that all the wiles of a thousand such as Riggs would never impose upon one weather-beaten old fox like Tracy Dixon.

I was introduced in turn, along with Steve, and then we got into the stage. The young engineer, whose name was Bridges, I think, called Dixon's attention to the stage, saying that he never had seen a finer turnout. The great man climbed down from the stage again, and looked it over, and got down on his knees to examine the underpinning, and came in again all dusty and soiled, with a splotch of axle grease on one hand. But he said not one word in praise of the big stage!

I saw the colonel bite his lip, and guessed that he would have occasion to bite it again, before that day was over. Events proved that I was perfectly right, too.

We got away from the railroad in good time, for as we went winding up over the brow of the first hill, on the way toward Piegan, off to the left we could see a mass of men come streaking through the dust up the Makerville trail. They saw us, and halted, and some guns were fired in the air. I got a glass from the colonel, and through the glass I could see those Makerites doing a war dance of sheerest fury! It gave me cold chills of pleasure and terror to watch them. I felt like a small boy who is bound to get his thrashing sooner or later.

But then we rolled along our way, and presently the colonel got up and from the head of a mountain, where the stage had halted at his command, he started a long speech, whooping up the glories of the valley, and peopling it with farmers, and filling up the cities with thousands, and splitting the mountains apart and making rivers of gold and silver flow out from them.

He shot along for five minutes without drawing his breath, and when he paused, Tracy Dixon said coldly:

"What we see will mean a good deal more than what we hear!"

The colonel sat down with a jolt. He had barely breath left in him to tell the driver to go, and I never in my life saw a man that I pitied more than I did the colonel at that moment. His wind and gilt had done a great deal for him, during his career, but now he was up against a man to whom facts counted, and nothing but facts. Riggs recognized it in a flash, and he was gray with pain and fear. His eyes shifted. He looked like a caught fox.

Those three, for an instant, looked on him like so many judges, and before they had finished their glance at him, I knew that the entire project was looked into and damned. Then they exchanged glances, and Tracy Dixon shrugged his shoulders, as much as to say that since they had embarked so far on the job, they might as well go through with it.

Well, I've never seen atmosphere change so suddenly. A moment before, all had been radiant hope, and the three of the committee had been up on their toes to take in everything. Now the colonel was a wet rag, and the three sat back with dull, tired eyes, and looked straight ahead of them at the front end of the coach instead of sparing an eye for the glories of Riggs's paradise. I was sad, ashamed, and a little amused, too. I rather despised Riggs, but I was surprised to find that there was a good deal of affection for the old rascal tucked away in my heart.

I don't like to think about most of that day, and how we sat there stewing in the infernal heat of the sun, and how the wind would not blow, and how the dust poured in on us like a sea fog, and how Cole and I were like mute stumps, and how the poor colonel gradually trotted out his best stories, and how he could not win even a semblance of a smile from the wooden faces of the three railroad men.

But one thing must be put in.

We had come to the last long down grade on the way to the town, and as we turned at the top of the slope, something went wrong. There was a squeal from one of the leading horses, a hearty curse from Charlie Butcher, and then that stage went down the grade a mile a minute.

The brake was slammed on. The rear wheels were skidding at every turn. But brakes couldn't hold us. The surface of that road was like ice, and I jumped up and looked to see what was wrong.

It was easily seen.

Sid Maker had picked out the finest animals in Makerville for that team, and the most beautiful of the lot was the off leader, eleven hundred pounds of lightning, a cream-colored beautiful devil with never more than one ear forward at a time. He had been dancing and prancing all the time, and now, in some way, his rein had jerked out of the hold of the driver, though what Charlie meant by not securing the ends of all the reins to the seat, I can't tell to this day. However, there the mischief was done. There was no control at all of that demon, and there was only a one-sided pull on the near leader; which had gone mad, in turn. The whole team had caught the frenzy in an instant—none of the lot were more than half broken to the work—and I had a pretty sight of eight crazed horses bolting down a sharp slope where there was only a semblance of a road, with a deep ravine ravening for us on one side, and sharp-toothed rocks reaching for us from the other.

We skidded and slithered around a terrible bend; the coach seemed to leap out into thin air, and I knew we

212

would have been gone had not Charlie, with superhuman skill, managed to turn the wheelers sharply in.

So the front wheels hit the road again, the stage gave a crazy, groaning wrench and heave, and away we went bowling, once more. It was only a question of time, however, before we went to smash. I knew it. In fact, we all knew it. I heard Tracy Dixon call out loudly to Bridges:

"Bridges, I'm too old and brittle to live through it, but you may. If you do, make those directors buy the Cresswell-Hampton line. We've got to have it. Tell 'em it's my dying request!"

About this time, I saw that Steve Cole had climbed onto the driver's seat. He helped haul upon the reins for a time. Then suddenly he pitched forward in a wild leap. Charlie Butcher cursed again. I looked back, fearing to see Steve lying on the road, smashed by the heavy wheels. But he hadn't hit the road. No, there he was on the back of the off wheeler. The horse began to buck, but Steve hung on by the back strap, and bending away over inside, he reached, straightened, and he had the lost rein in his hand again!

I let out a yell of joy, then closed my eyes as we shuddered at full speed around a hairpin turn, the leaders out of sight. However, we didn't quite go over the cliff, and now I could see the mouths of the leaders being pulled wide open by the strength that was leaning back on the reins. Pretty soon their traces were hanging limp. Then the swingers and the wheelers came under control. The stage no longer rolled on freely, like an avalanche, but the brakes were taking hold. And now the stage was in the hands of Charlie, where it should have been.

I sat down, very sick, with a chill of sweat running on my face, and I heard Tracy Dixon saying:

"We owe our lives to that young man, I believe!"

It was true. At one stroke, Steve Cole had showed more real heroism, more natural courage, than I ever would show in my life.

CHAPTER XXXVI

A Bombshell

WE pulled up, now, and took stock of things. Nothing was damaged. The tough running gear of the stage was as good as ever, and yet we needed that pause to take breath.

When we started on again, the ice seemed to be broken. The committee had thanked Steve one by one, and he had blushed and waved their gratitude aside. He was so embarrassed by it that he climbed back onto the driver's seat and remained there all the rest of the way into Piegan.

But now the colonel had an entrance wedge; and he drove it in with talk about other close staging escapes, and proved how many lives a year the railroad would save—to Makerville!

It had been Makerville, of course, all the way from the railroad to Piegan. Makerville was the town of which the colonel talked, and Maker was the name he gave himself. How he was going to make the switch to Piegan I could not tell. That was something for him to shudder over. However, we were in a much better atmosphere all around when we pulled into the town. And young Bridges stood up, just before we came in, and heartened us by exclaiming:

"A glorious valley, Dixon. Simply glorious!"

I was amazed. I looked in my turn. A veil fell from

before my eyes. In spite of all the smoke of words that the colonel had sent up, in spite of all of his lies and camouflage, suddenly I saw that Bridges was right. It *was* a glorious valley. Those broad acres one day might be green with crops; those mountains *might* send down their hidden treasures; and perhaps the colonel was more prophet than scoundrel!

That was a most amazing idea for me, and I suddenly half expected that everything would go all right. We reached the hotel, which was done up in bunting like the Fourth of July, and our three distinguished guests were taken to their rooms. Then the colonel embraced and practically wept over me and Steve. He said we between us had saved Piegan. He didn't care, he said, about his own life, but he knew that the fate of Piegan still depended upon his schemes and the courage, et cetera, of the gallant young men who, et cetera. It was a lot of bunk, but it hit Steve hard, and he was in the clouds.

Then a bombshell dropped. Just as we were celebrating, and as I was beginning to get ready for a dive into bed, with the intention of staying there for about a week, down came the three railroaders, Tracy Dixon walking first and stepping high. He sailed straight up to the colonel and said:

"Your name is not Sidney Maker. Your name is Riggs. And you're a rascal. This town is Piegan. You've committed a crime, besides wasting invaluable time for me, and I'll have you behind bars, you second-rate fraud!"

You can judge a blow by the sound it makes, and the way the other fellow drops. The colonel slumped against a wall, otherwise I'm sure that he would have fallen to the ground.

Where had the visitors picked up their information?

To this very day it remains a mystery. Some rascal of a servant in the hotel may have planted the news in the wrong spot. We never were able to tell.

Tracy Dixon turned on me:

"I've heard of your record, too, young man," said he, "and it appears that this excellent town of Piegan is filled with thieves and blackguards and gunmen."

He gave me the cold shoulder and whirled toward Steve Cole, grasping his hand.

"My boy," said he, "I thanked you before for your glorious conduct to-day. I thank you again, and forever. I want you to come away with me. I'll show you doors of life that may be opened; I'll show you a future, my friend. But to begin with, I've never heard your name, I believe."

"My name is Steven Cole," said Steve, dazed and uncertain.

"What's that? What's that?" snapped Tracy Dixon. "Parker Cole has a son named Steven!"

"He's my father," said Steve.

"Ha?" cried Dixon. "You're the son of Parker Cole! Oh, blood will tell, blood will tell! Give me your hand again. Parker Cole's son? You are, too. You're the image of him when he went to college with me. Did he ever tell you about the day I gave him fifteen pounds and a licking? I'll wager he never did. He was always a proud young devil; a proud old one, too. Steven, what are you doing in this nest of brigands?"

Steve was pretty badly stunned by this reception, but suddenly I saw that blood *did* tell. He reached out his hand and touched my arm.

"I'm here with my best friend, sir," says he. "This is Jeremiah Ash, Mr. Dixon."

It was a very neat stroke. Old Dixon blinked a couple of times and turned red, but he swallowed the insults he had just fired at my head and held out his hand.

"Mr. Ash," said he, "I don't know your father, but I take Steven's word that I've made a mistake. Forgive me. I'm a hothead. And that's a great handicap to a railroad man. Forget what I said before, like a good fellow. Steven, do you mean to tell me that your father is actually interested in this part of the world? Are we going to have the Cole money slipping in here? Well, he always had a long arm in boxing, and a long arm in business, too. If he's found something in Piegan that's worth while, I'm going to stay here long enough to see what it is!"

You can see how he rushed along, making his own conclusions, and most of them wrong. Here he had stumbled

216

onto the belief that Parker Cole was ready to do financing in Piegan, and instantly that unheard of little town was on the Tracy Dixon map with a vengeance.

He got young Steve by the arm and said: "You come up to my room and talk to me. Tell me about things. I want to talk about a great many things. Bridges—Davison —we're going to stop over here, after all. That is, if Colonel Riggs is willing to let us. Eh, colonel? Words are air. They don't scalp a man, Riggs. We'll have a new look at everything."

A new look?

Yes, everything was newly made, in that instant. Away went Tracy Dixon,.and his two men with him, and young Steve Cole still beside him, up the stairs.

I got the colonel into his office and poured a shot of brandy down his throat. He lay back in his chair with his eyes fixed on the ceiling for a long time, and his face was a bad, splotchy purple.

The day was dying. The sunset rose flushed across the ceiling, and a cool evening wind came through the window and revived the old boy a little.

"Parker Cole!" he murmured. "Parker Cole! Oh, that was a narrow shave, a narrow shave! Jerry, you rascal, why didn't you tell me that Parker Cole is interested in this town?"

"He isn't," said I. "He hardly knows that it exists."

"Hey?" said the colonel, sitting up. "Then what will young Cole be saying to Tracy Dixon by this time? We'll be sunk again!"

"I don't think so," said I. "Steve doesn't yet know how to play with the cards very close to his chest, but I gave him a sign as he went off with Dixon, and I think that he understood. He won't let Piegan down if he can help it."

The colonel leaned back with a groan of relief. He closed his eyes, and said in a tone of fervent prayer:

"I'll build a statue in bronze to him. And to you. Clasping hands. Jerry Ash and Steve Cole, the saviors of Piegan! And now, my boy," said he, sitting suddenly upright and rubbing his hands together, "I'll give you a more solid testimonial of my gratitude. You have several square blocks of ground here in Piegan. Worthless, naked ground. But I have hopes in the future of the community. I'll tell you what I'll do. I'll write you out a check for fifty thousand dollars. D'you hear me? I'll pay you fifty thousand for that patch of land, my son! I'll give you your start in life."

I looked calmly on the colonel. I was so tired that nothing mattered a great deal, and his foxlike meanness of nature did not revolt me. I merely said:

"Colonel, I may be wrong, but I have a queer idea that in spite of the trick we've played on Tracy Dixon, he's going to build his line into Piegan. And then my land will be worth—well, fifty thousand a block, I take it. At least that much. You're working on the same idea. Why try to cut my throat?"

He had showed me the shady side of his nature so many times before that now he was not ashamed. He merely laughed.

"Did you think that I meant it, Jerry, my son?" said he. "Not for an instant! I simply wanted to see if you have the makings of a business man in you. That's all. And you have. I see that you're not a fool, by any means. You're going to go far. Very far! And I'll be beside you every step of the way, helping you, advising you, giving you all the strength that I have on the upward—"

I smiled at him a little and got out of the office. He meant well enough, but he was simply—well, a shyster.

Up in my room, I lay flat on my back and stared at the darkening ceiling, and felt a pulse thudding in my temple, with a steady pounding.

I was tired, very tired. It seemed to me that I could still feel the electric shock go through my heart when Tracy Dixon came down the hall and raged at us. Yes, I was tired, but the dreadful sense of falling, floating, sinking through space toward death was not in me. Instead, it was the sort of fatigue that any man might have felt, after the last few days of rough riding that I had been through.

So I counted the throb of the pulse in my temple, and suddenly an idea came to me that almost lifted the roof off my brain. It made me leap into the center of my room.

There came a knock at my door, and the voice of Steve.

"Come in!" I managed to gasp.

He came in.

"What's the matter? Are you sick?" he exclaimed. "The old heart staggering again?"

He ran to me, with an exclamation.

"Listen to my heart!" I ordered him huskily.

He bent his head and pressed it against my breast.

"It's going mighty fast, but steady and regular as a clock," said he.

I lifted up my head. I knew that the miracle had happened. Or was it a miracle, after all? Through a shock the disease had come upon me; through a shock might it not have been brushed away? So I stood there with my face turned up. I wanted to give thanks. But my throat was bound with a band of iron. I dared not try to speak! But I knew that once more I was a real man, not a frail shadow, a mere pretense!

CHAPTER XXXVII

The Boom

THE days that followed were about the happiest in my life, in many ways. I could not tell that the great blow was coming, and I only knew that my body was sound again, and that things were booming in Piegan.

And how they were booming!

Of course it was nine tenths dependent upon the coming of the great Tracy Dixon and his long stay. Because he remained for more than a week in the place, and every minute of the time he was busy. He rode ten hours a day through the valley and into the mountains. He estimated timber, mineral wealth, all the possibilities of the district, and then he sat up half the night doing figures, making plans with his two engineers. That man was a tiger for work. Piegan was a busy place, just then, but compared with Dixon, every one was standing still.

You can lay your money that we didn't allow the news to die on our hands. We sent fast riders relaying over to the two railroads, north and south, and they carried batches of written matter for Eastern newspapers, and Western, too. Piegan had been barely a scratch on the map. Now it was to be a complete picture.

After two days, Dixon told the colonel that he had made up his mind; the line would run straight through to Piegan. And the colonel almost died with joy. I found him looking bowed and white, his face all tense, and I asked him what was the matter.

"I'm carrying a terrible burden, Jerry," said he.

"A burden of what?" I asked him.

"Money," said he, with a sudden grin. "Tracy Dixon has just dumped a million dollars into my pockets! Boy, the line is coming through our town!"

He said it faintly, staring at a dream, and then he added hastily: "Not that I'll forget you, Jerry. No, no, I understand exactly what you've done for me. You'll have your fair share, all right. Not of money, only, but of glory, too. The statue—"

I got away from him as soon as I could, because he was disgusting to me in that humor. I knew that he hated to part with money to men, though he would water his schemes with all the gold he could beg or borrow after he had spent his own.

The lots which I possessed—two whole blocks in the middle of things!—were a constant weight upon the mind of the colonel. He tried every day or so to get them away from me. He offered me seventy-five thousand in spot cash for them, the day after the railroad was definitely given to Piegan. But I refused. For people were beginning to pour into Piegan from all sides. The mountaineers came down, the prospectors, the outlying cattlemen, the miners, the lumbermen. We were crowded. The stage line quadrupled its service and battered the road to pieces, and still could not fetch in the passengers from the growing pool of them at the railroad.

This was only the beginning of the rush. The word had gone far and wide. I think that there was something in the very name "Piegan" that hung in the imaginations of men, and the colonel's lying reports, plus the knowledge that the railroad was coming, did the rest. Lots that had been worth twenty dollars sold for a hundred, a thousand! And the prices were still going up. It was crazy, and I knew that it was crazy, but I hung on until the regular Thursday auction, which commenced just before the first stage of the day came in from the railroad. Then I offered not a scattering of my lots, but a whole block, and the auctioneer could turn and point to the ground.

The speculators got excited, at that. They began to fight one another in their bidding, and in half an hour that block was sold for sixty-two thousand, five hundred dollars!

I felt I was rich. I stood transfixed in my place, and could not realize what had happened, but the crowd understood, and it yelled and cheered in a wild way. It knew that with prices going up like that, fortunes were hanging in the air, so to speak, and any man might grab them off. Then I remembered that I had another block just like this one—and my head swam!

In the midst of this, a young man crushed his way to me, a big fellow, and slapped my shoulder. It was my friend Harry, and he hooked a thumb over his shoulder.

"She said that she wanted to see you," he said.

Looking over his shoulder, I saw Betty Cole, her face brown and rose, her eyes flashing at me. I got hold of her hand and asked her how she managed to get there.

"I dropped out of the sky to see you get rich, Jerry," she said. "I'm glad for you. Not so much the money, but the way the crowd cheered you. That was sweet to my ears!"

"I'll get you out of this jam," said I.

"Before I move," said she, "tell me where they've locked up poor, foolish, crazy Steve!"

"Locked him up?" said I, not remembering for a moment what must be in her mind. "If anybody tried to lock Steve up, this town would split the earth in two to get him out again!"

She stared at me.

"Then he's not in jail?" said she.

I laughed a little, the whole thing coming back over me, but it seemed as though seven years had passed since Steve arrived in Piegan and started out to make a fool of himself. His first day in town was forgotten, now. I was still laughing a bit when the auctioneer helped me out with an odd coincidence, for just then he announced a lot which was being offered for sale by Steve himself.

The auctioneer was pretty flowery about it. He pointed out that the lot was on the corner of C and Fifth Streets, and he said: "It is offered by one of our youngest but most distinguished townsmen, a man whom Piegan will never forget, a man who helped to make Piegan possible— Steven Cole! Let me have a cheer for him first, boys, and then we'll hear the bidding on his lot!"

Oh, they gave him the cheer, well enough. There wasn't a rascally speculator in the bunch who didn't know quite well that Steve's heroism in the stagecoach runaway was the real source of Piegan's present prosperity. So they strained their throats for Steve Cole, and then they whooped up the bidding on that lot, and I heard it knocked down for twenty-five hundred dollars.

Yes, the colonel had given Steve half a dozen lots; he hadn't realized how the prices would soar!

While that cheering and bidding was going on, I worked the girl to the back of the crowd, and then we walked down the street together. Charlie Butcher, his face horribly yellow and white, his eyes red with whisky, came by, and I sang out to him to find Steve Cole and send him to the hotel, pronto. Charlie saluted, and went on.

"Are you running this town, Jerry?" she asked me, tilting up her face.

"No, but I'm a charter member," I told her, fairly enough. "I want to tell you about Steve, though."

"You don't have to," she said. "It was all told to me when I heard them cheer. He's found himself. That's what you wanted to say, isn't it? He's on his feet, and able to make his own way."

"And way for another, too," said I. "He's the gamest and the straightest fellow in town. He had a bad start, but he's making a great finish."

"It's you, Jerry, that I want to find out about," said she. "You've lost that gray look you used to have."

"My heart's gone right," said I.

She stopped short.

"Do you mean it?" she asked me.

"I mean it. It's true."

She gasped with pleasure. It nearly sent my heart bad again to see the shine of her eyes.

"And are you going back into the ring again, Jerry?" she asked me.

The question was a shock. I don't know why, exactly, but the shock was there. I had to look for a moment far away into my own mind before I could answer her. Once nothing in the world had mattered except that I wanted to be middleweight champion of the world. And that championship had been fairly near, I thought. The hope of it had filled my days with electricity and fire. But now that was changed.

Somehow all of those old triumphs inside the ropes were dim and childish. They were a lifetime away. Perhaps I could get back into training, but that was not in my mind, at all.

"No," I told her. "I'll never go back to that. I've graduated from that business."

"And what's the business to be, then?" she asked.

I looked around me—not particularly at the shacks and the dusty streets of Piegan, but beyond, at the blue ranges of mountains.

"This!" said I, with a wave of my hand.

She gave me a good, hard look, and then she said, in a matter-of-fact way, "I understand!"

That made me like her better than ever. I stepped into a seventh heaven. I hardly know how we reached the hotel, but when we walked into the lobby, we were just in time to see Steve Cole run up and grab a tall, dignified fellow of sixty. And the dignity melted out of that man, and he caught Steve and hugged him before all the people.

No one had to tell me that I was watching a family reunion. I started to fade out of the picture, but Betty Cole caught my hand and held me there. She even dragged me up to the pair of them, and she introduced me to Parker Cole, himself!

They said that Parker Cole was a hard business man, and I could believe it. He had an eye that went through me with one glance, like the flicker of a rapier. Then he shook hands with me. I felt a good deal like a fool, for Steve was blurting out things he might have saved until I was out of hearing.

However, it was a pretty proud moment for me, and off yonder in the corner, Colonel Riggs and Tracy Dixon, and the two engineers were on tiptoe with eagerness to meet the great Cole. But just then a bomb dropped into the lobby of the Riggs Hotel. A bomb in human flesh and blood.

It still takes my breath when I think of it, the consummate nerve and coolness of the fellow in coming singly into our town, but nerve and coolness were overplus in him. For into the lobby walked the bulldog form of Sidney Maker himself!

CHAPTER XXXVIII

Vengeance

EVERYTHING else was forgotten, of course. Twenty men rose silently around the lobby, and twenty hands were gripping the same number of guns, not too covertly.

Riggs showed a good deal of courage, I must say. He stalked up to his rival and said:

"I'm glad to see you here, Maker, under pleasanter auspices than during your last little visit!"

He stretched out his hand. Maker did not hesitate. He took the hand and gave it a grip that brought a howl from the colonel's mouth.

"I ought to wreck your little village for you," said Maker, in his heavy, bawling voice, "but it's not worth while. If you've kept the thing on the map, remember that it's not your credit. That goes to Jerry Ash. He's a *man!* As for the railroad, when you see that idiot, Dixon, tell him that Makerville doesn't care anything about him. We'll buy his line, if we want it, or else we'll build one of our own and put him out of business. We've struck hundred-and-twenty-dollar silver in the hills three miles from town. Tell that to Dixon, too. It'll make him feel pretty good when he tries to load his freight trains with the sort of hot air that feeds a town like Piegan!"

It was all true. They had struck the great Cavendish lode. People know how many fortunes came out of that.

After he had blasted the others, Maker came across the lobby straight to me. I almost thought that he was going to use his fists on me, his look was so threatening. But when he came up, he stuck out his hand. I gave him mine, and met the pressure of his hold. He stood there holding my hand and staring into my face earnestly.

"Kid," he said, "it was a grand trick. It ought to win the game for you. But remember that out here a lot of games are lost and winnings wiped out in the last play. I don't mind. My town is on the map. We don't have to come to the railroad; the railroad has to come to us. I say that I don't mind, but some of my boys do. They mind badly. They want your scalp and they mean to have it. I'm trying to hold them back, but they want blood. Kid, beat it out of Piegan and get some distance between you and this part of the country, will you? Whether you will or not, I'm giving you the best advice. You know why I give it, too!"

When he had said that, he turned on his heel and walked out of the lobby, and I was plenty ready to sit down and think things over!

I faded right out of that cheerful family group and got off into my own room, and stayed there until night. I had dinner brought up on a tray, and then I lay down to decide what I should do.

There was no doubt that this was a serious business. Maker was taking his life in his hands when he rode into Piegan, and he knew it perfectly well. He had come because he felt under a serious obligation to me. He would not have come unless he felt that it were a matter of life or death.

And it was my life and death that were concerned!

You can imagine that my nerves were not exactly smooth, at that time. Still, it was the worst moment in the world, for me. If I left, I would be leaving Betty Cole, at the very moment when she had arrived!

In the midst of these thoughts, there was a rap at my door, and when I sang out, Steve and Betty came in. He stood back, looking worried and dark with trouble. She did the talking. And what she said was begging me to get out of Piegan, get fast, and get far.

I looked straight back at her and said:

"It's pretty hard for me to go."

"It ought not to be," she said.

"It is, though," said I.

I kept on looking straight at her, and suddenly she flushed to the forehead.

"If you go now, you can always come back, Jerry," said she.

"Look," said Steve Cole, "if you two are going to be— Well, let me get out of this."

"We're not going to be any way at all," said she, redder than before. "Jerry, I want you to say that you'll leave Piegan! The man meant what he said, when he told you that your life was in danger."

"If you want me to go, Betty," said I, putting all the emphasis I could on the words, "I'll do as you say."

And all this while, I was not budging my eyes from her, of course. She could have pretended to misunderstand, but she was not small enough for that. She met my eye like a soldier, and she went on:

"I want you to go, Jerry. I want you to go at once."

"Good-bye, then," said I.

She shook hands with me, and enough was in our eyes to settle our future as clearly as words could have managed the trick.

When she and Steve went from the room, I only half saw them go. I was in a haze, and a trance, and couldn't see straight.

It was partly that haze which caused what happened immediately afterwards.

I went over and dragged out my war bag, when something creaked behind me. I turned, carelessly both hands full, and there I saw a small man standing between me and the window, a small man with his head thrusting forward and canted a bit to one side as he looked down a pair of big Colts at my head and heart.

It was Chuck.

That was a thunderclap. But habit is a strange thing.

Even then, while I felt the awful shock of the thing, I was listening to my heart, waiting for it to begin to stagger and go crazy. I sighed with relief when it raced, to be sure, but with a firm and rhythmic beat.

I was my old self!

I said: "What is it, Chuck? Murder?"

"Not murder," said he. "But we're taking our turn with you, Poker-face. You've had plenty of turns before this."

"That's true," I answered. "In fact, you seem to be dealing yourself a hand out of my own pack!"

He did not smile. There was a horrible hunger in his eyes. They shifted just a little, as they traveled over me. He seemed to be hunting for the best places to send his bullets home.

I heard the door swish softly behind me, and a sudden hope jumped—and died as I heard Chuck say:

"It's all right, boys. He hasn't got a gun on him. I almost wish that he had! Bert, do up his hands. You might as well do them up behind him."

"I'll do 'em up," said the snarling voice of Bert, which I remembered so well.

They were all there.

Swede stood in front of me, grinning till his scalp twitched. Three more were back in the shadow by the door. The six mighty men of Sid Maker had come for me and have me they would.

I thought of everything. Of trying to grab a gun and make a fight of it. Of yelling out. Of doing anything to attract attention.

Then they would fill me full of lead, and they would die for it afterwards, every one of them, horribly, at the hands of the Piegan mob.

Perhaps Chuck read what was in my mind.

"Not murder, Poker-face," said he. "That's not our idea. You haven't gone that low, and we won't cut lower than you've done. But you'll face us one at a time. We'll draw lots. All we want is a quiet place, to have the thing out."

Then they marched me out of the hotel.

Yes, just as easily as I write the words, they took me out

of that place and not a soul saw us, not a word was spoken to us. We simply went down the back stairs and out through the yard, and in the grove where I had hidden horses for Maker and Chuck, on that other night, they had their own mounts waiting.

I climbed into a saddle, helped by Chuck and Swede. Then we rode at a walk away from Piegan and into the hills.

I remember that clouds were blowing across the stars, and gusts of rain whipped us, now and again. But though I felt the sting of the drops, they did not seem either cold or wet to me.

I supposed that was because part of my nervous system had gone to sleep.

Swede rode beside me, my horse's lead rope over the pommel of his saddle.

"You and the gal, kind of sweet on each other, ain't you?" he said, chuckling, sneering at the same time.

Chuck snarled in his bull-terrier's voice from the head of the line: "Cut that out, Swede! Leave him be!"

I was grateful to Chuck for that. I was grateful, but all the while, I was knowing that Chuck's gun would be the one to down me. I felt it. I mean, I almost could feel the crash and the rending of the bullet as it tore through flesh and bone.

We got up to a hollow where trees were growing dense all around the edge, and as we worked through them, Swede said:

"This is far enough. Bert, you got the lanterns?"

"It's not far enough," insisted Chuck. "You know that the chief will be on our trail, before very long."

"Maker'll never find us here," said Bert.

"We won't stop here. It's too close. I know a better place farther on," declared Chuck. "Maker would rather lose an arm than have anything serious happen to Poker-face. He owes the kid his life, and he don't forget that, as you all know. Didn't he come into Piegan to-day to warn him? Wasn't he taking his own life in his hands when he did that? He'll work out our trail as soon as he misses us from his camp, this evening!"

I began to have a small hope. If it were true—if Maker really were apt to come on our trail—well, he was the one person in the world who could handle these gunmen with a word.

In spite of what Chuck said, the others were firm.

"You've had your own way too much, Chuck," said Bert. "Let's get the dirty work over with. This is where we stop."

Chuck gave in, and as a signal of his giving way, he dropped from his stirrups to the ground.

But he said: "There's to be no dirty work. Mind that, Bert. The first fellow who tries to murder the kid will have to murder me afterwards. I mean what I say!"

This did not go without another argument.

"Look at here," said Bert. "He's made us the laughing-stock of the whole range. He's made fools of us. I had a kind of a reputation. It's gone, since Poker-face come along. I say: Sock him, and finish the job."

"That's what I say, too," said Swede.

And the others agreed, heartily. The work might be too dangerous, they said. Why should they spill their own blood, when they had me entirely helpless?

"He never dealt cards off the bottom of the pack," Chuck said. "You can't do it to him. If you do, my guns are on his side."

That was final. They wanted my scalp, but they feared those deadly guns of Chuck about as much as I did.

Bert gave up the dispute with a groan, and lighted the lanterns. They were hung on the low side branches of a tree, and gave a very fair light, except when a guest of wind set them swinging. Then the plan of the fight was explained to me by Chuck, who had thought the whole thing out in detail.

With free hands, and a gun in my thigh holster, I was to take a position under the tree, and ten paces away my opponent would stand. We would have our backs to one another, and at the word of command, we would whirl and commence shooting until one of us fell or begged for mercy.

When he used that word, I had a sudden picture of

230

myself groveling, begging for my·life! It made me half sick. I started to pray, not for life, but for the courage to meet my death like a man.

Because there was no real hope for me, unless it lay in the hardly to be hoped for arrival of Maker himself. There was hardly a man of the six, I well knew, who was not a faster and a surer hand with a revolver than I. One, even two, I might down by luck. But six such warriors I could never dream of flattening, one after the other.

Perhaps there was one grisly ghost of a hope left to me —a terrible wound that might lay me out, and yet leave a spark of life that could be nursed back into a flame.

You can see how far my hopes had sunk, when I thought of that!

They were to draw lots for their turns.

In the meantime, my hands were set free. Then they proceeded to draw the lots. I looked them over, with a vague wonder, while I kneaded my wrists to get the blood and life and strength back into them.

Perhaps it would be Chuck—and then my troubles would soon be over, of course.

But it was Bert.

Well, I was almost glad of that. I had no liking for that man. He was as bitter and vengeful as a wolf, and as he stood there before me, his thin lips twisting with a hatred, and his eyes bright and small as the eyes of a beast, I had no hesitation in wanting to put an end to him.

I had a gun, now. It was a Colt with the usual good balance. It had a hair trigger, and would shoot, Chuck assured me, for it was his gun, as easily as breathing.

Chuck stood off to one side, to give the signal. Before we turned our back on one another, he said:

"Is there anything you want to say, Poker-face?"

I said: "No, not a thing. Only, get on with this business, because I'm scared cold, already."

Swede laughed, a loud, horrible, bawling sound.

"He's got the cold nerve, ain't he?" said Swede.

But it wasn't nerve. It was telling them the truth. Yet that laughter, that bit of praise, went like wine through my blood, and steadied me.

"How about you, Bert?" asked Chuck. "You want to say anything we could remember for you?"

"Not a single thing," said Bert. "Lemme at him. That's all. I'm goin' to eat him. I can feel it in my bones."

"Turn your backs, then," said Chuck.

I turned about.

"When I say, 'Start,'" said Chuck, "you turn and begin shooting."

And, almost instantly, he added: "Start!"

I spun and drew in the same instant. I had in mind not to turn too far, for fear the impetus of the swing about would throw my gun out of line with its mark. So I only made a quarter turn with my feet, and twisted my shoulders around. This presented the side line of my body to the bullets of the other fellow. I didn't try to aim, either. I just threw the gun out of half-arm distance, and fired at the blur of Bert as the form of him jumped into line with my vision.

He was around, too, and fully facing me. Perhaps he had lost a part of a second in making so full a turn. At any rate, he only fired his weapon into the ground, a spasmodic, natural contraction of the hand. For my bullet had gone home. I heard the spat of it against his face like the clapping of hands together. He threw a forearm across his forehead, covering the wound, and dropped straight forward. His body hit with a loose, jostling sound, then he lay still.

"Didn't I go and tell you?" said Swede. "Poker-face was too good for Bert. He'll be too good for anybody else, excepting me! I'm the one that'll finish him. You wait and see, if any of you are left to look!"

And he laughed, his bawling, brutal laughter again!

They took the body of Bert away. Their lips were tight, all of them except that beast, Swede.

In the meantime, I was thinking of various devices. I might run for the horses, for instance, and try to break away. I might step behind the trunk of the tree and use it as a fort.

No, I saw that both of those ideas were worthless.

There were too many of them, and the rest could not all have the bad luck of the first to fall.

Bad luck was what it was, too. I knew that. My turn, I thought, had been figured out perfectly. But I knew that the head was not what I had aimed for. I had intended that shot to fly for the center of the body, the only sure target in snap shooting. Instead of that, the slug had gone home almost three feet higher. They thought it was wonderful marksmanship, wonderful steadiness of nerve. It wasn't, though. And I knew it, and was cold with the knowledge.

I had to try something else. I wondered what it would be, as I saw them drawing the lots again. I was a little sick, too, thinking of the way that Bert had fallen—the sound of it, I mean. My mind was confused. And I remembered looking with a scowl at the lanterns and wishing that they would burn brighter.

Then I saw Chuck take his place opposite me!

Well, of course I would have to face him, sooner or later. But somehow it was a shock to see him there, cool, steady, purposeful. There was a look on his face not savage, but deeply and quietly contented. He meant business; his business was my death.

Swede stood by to give the signal. The other two were shadows. They hardly mattered.

"Bill," said Chuck, very calmly, "if he drops me, don't forget to send my watch to the girl. You know her address. Write her a note along with it. Tell her I was thinking about her at the finish. Are you ready, Poker-face?"

I was not ready, I never would be ready to face that calmly determined gunman. But I nodded.

I had made a new plan, this time. Somehow, I told myself that in shooting for the head lay my luck. I would shoot for it this time, but not a chance shot. No, this time I would take my time and draw a bead. I would be prepared to have one, two, even three bullets tear through my body, while I drew my bead, and then finished off my man. I set my jaw and told myself that this was the only way. I must banish all feeling from my body. Whatever agony I felt, I must not let it shake my gun hand.

Now I stood with back turned to Chuck. People say that all their past flowed before them, at such a time. None of my past flowed before me. I saw nothing but the dark of the night, the loom of a mountain, the glistening of wet leaves in the lantern light.

Then—"Start!" roared Swede.

I turned to the right, just as I had turned before, but swinging my arm straight out, shoulder-high, to sight down the barrel, and by the grace of fortune, I got the head of Chuck right in line!

At the same instant, I saw the muzzle of his gun jerk upwards. In fact, he was standing there as though he had not had to turn at all. He seemed to be taking his deliberate time.

The gun jerked in his hand, which was held hardly more than hip-high, and at the same time a bullet struck me a violent blow on the hip and then glanced up through my entire body.

Some lucky devils are numbed all over by a bullet wound. So they say, at least. But I felt, or thought I felt, the terrible crunching of bones. My flesh was one compact of nerves, ripping before the lead. The agony threw a red sheet of flame across my brain. But through that red I saw my mark, and fired.

I knew that I was falling as I pulled the trigger, but still I watched, and saw my bullet knock Chuck flat!

Then I was lying gasping. I remember feeling that the thing was unfair, that the pain alone was enough, but that I ought to be able to catch my breath. No, I could not breathe. Then I was sure that I would never again draw that breath I prayed for.

This was death! This was the end!

My legs were drawing up and kicking out slowly. One foot struck against the trunk of the tree, and the pressure that resulted sent a twisting, tearing spasm of agony through me. I screamed in the throes of it!

Well, I hate to think of that yell of pain that was torn

from my lips. But the truth has to come out. I screeched like a hurt boy.

Then I heard a roaring, furious, and yet exultant voice that was bellowing at me, in the familiar accents of Swede:

"Fill your hand, Poker-face! Fill your hand, you sneaking varmint, because now you're goin' to fight your last fight!"

I looked across at him. He was standing erect, a gun in either hand, poised, his feet spread, a look of fiendish, animal joy on his wide face. Chuck was gone; fair play had ended; murder remained.

CHAPTER XXXIX

A Pair of Riders

THE gun lay close to my hand. I grasped it, but I felt that there was hardly strength in my shaking hand to raise it.

I looked down. The ground was red; my left hand, as I tried to push myself up, slipped in mud.

"Hurry up!" roared Swede. "You got your gun. Hurry up, and fight like a man, will you? Count him out, Bill! Count to ten on him!"

I heard the voice begin.

It flung me back into the old ring days. That fourth round, and I down, and the voice booming distantly in my ears.

So it boomed now: "One, two, three, four, five, six—"

My wits leaped off to the garden of the Parker Cole house, and Betty Cole, in the garden, under the dappling of the shadows.

"Eight," the voice was saying, "nine, and—"

"Drop that gun!" yelled a voice behind Swede.

He leaped into the air, and whirled.

I, still half prone, my weight in my hands, could look across and see beyond Swede a figure rising out of the ground, as it were. It was Chuck, and the lantern light showed his face bathed in crimson, and glinted upon the gun he had recovered.

Was it only a glancing blow of the bullet that had knocked him prone?

"Drop that gun!" shouted Chuck again, now coming from his knees toward his feet. "You hound, you murdering swine!"

"Murder?" snarled Swede. "I'll finish him first, and you second! You been comin' pretty big, over me, Chuck. It's the last time. You got your hand filled, and now—"

There was a crashing through the brush at the side of the hollow, the beating of hoofs.

"They're here! Piegan!" screeched Bill, and bolted toward the horses.

Swede did not wait. He let out a similar howl of fear, and bounded after his confederates.

Onto their horses they bounded, and away they went into the night.

But it was not a group of Piegan men that poured onto us. It was only a pair of riders. One was Sidney Maker, and the other was none other than Richardson, the detective, whom I never expected to see again. Glad enough to see him this night, you may be sure!

"Your work, Chuck, and you'll pay me for it!" I heard Maker saying.

Then he was on his knees beside me. I looked up at him through darkening eyes.

"I'm going to die, Sid," said I, "but Chuck was fair and square. Fair stand-up fight. But Swede—murder—"

I got out no more. I wanted to speak more words. But the breath went out of me; a spasm choked my throat. I saw the lanterns spin, and the cold of death seemed to be freezing my brain. Then that horror was shut away.

When I got back my wits, I thought that somebody was driving a red-hot knife through my body, with a monotonously regular rhythm. It was only the throb of the pulse against my wound.

I put my hand down to it, and found that my body was gripped hard by an immense bandage. I put my hand out farther, and touched blankets, then the cold of a sheet. I opened my eyes, and I was looking up through the branches of the lantern-lighted tree.

They had brought a mattress and springs, and fixed me a bed under that tree. If they had moved me, I should not be scratching these words on paper, now. It was a close enough shave as the thing finally worked out.

But now, when I turned my head a little, I saw the circle, and counted them over, one by one—Sid Maker, and his bulldog face, first of all; and Richardson, the detective, looking sullen and bored; Chuck, with a white bandage around his head, making his face seem unusually dark; Colonel Riggs; Tracy Dixon, drawing lines on the ground; big-shouldered Harry; Charlie Butcher, just then drinking from a flask; Parker Cole, patting the hand of Betty; Steve standing in the background, his arms folded, his face twisted; the auctioneer; the hotel clerk; the stage driver biting off a chew of tobacco.

"This is quite a show, boys," said I, and regretted speaking, such a pang stabbed me.

"Shut your mouth!" said a rough voice.

A man whom I had not seen before stood over me. His sleeves were rolled up. His hands were stained with red. Suddenly I knew that this fellow who looked like a butcher was the doctor who might save my life.

I gazed at him with mild surrender.

"You got a breath and a half left in you," said he. "You ought to die. You probably won't. A man who's lucky enough to have as many friends as you have, is too lucky to be killed by one bullet."

He was right.

For two weeks, it was nip and tuck. Two weeks of consummate hell, I tell you. Every time I breathed, it was agony. All that saved me was the purity of that cold, clear, mountain air, I know. I did not have to get much of that into my lungs in order to sustain life.

Then, at the end of two weeks, I was carried down to Piegan. They made a ceremony of the thing. That was the colonel's fault, of course, and confound him for it.

He had the litter prepared, and he picked out two relays of men, who carried me down bit by bit, as gently as though they were carrying nitroglycerin. And finally they bore me up the main street, because that was really the shortest way to the hotel. And the people lined he street and took off their hats. The colonel had arranged that, too! He was a showman to the finish. That silence ate in on me. I began to pity myself, and the only way I could possibly keep the tears from flowing down my face was to start cursing.

That was the only sound that broke the silence, my steady cursing, as they went on toward the hotel.

Charlie Butcher swore to me afterwards that I said things that made him blush, even him, as he walked beside me, carrying a portion of my weight.

But I dare say that Charlie was stretching things a little. However, that litter ride is one of the things that I least care to remember out of my life.

It ended in the hotel, at last. Going up the stairs was a torment, because the litter tipped down a good deal, but finally I was in a room, and being slipped between a pair of cold sheets.

I was only about half conscious, by that time, but I could hear the rough voice of the doctor saying:

"He's pulling through. I told you he would. If the mean streak in a man is wide enough and deep enough, one bullet simply can't kill him. I remember a fellow who put the muzzle of a gun against his temple and—"

I did not hear the rest of it, because I was sinking into a profound sleep.

When I wakened, all was right. There was still a considerable distance for me to go, but that day I cared nothing about distances because Parker Cole stood at my bedside and said:

"I have to return to my business. But Steve and Betty are staying on, Steve for a month or so, and Betty, it appears, is going to remain almost indefinitely, if that meets with your wishes, young man!"

I said faintly: "A man with a criminal record, Mr. Cole, is—"

He raised a hand and stopped me.

"There is no criminal record," he declared. "That has been expunged from the books. And I dare say that it will never be written in again on the blank pages. There's no law court in the world that wants to pass on you just now, Jerry."

So he went away, and left me climbing, climbing, climbing toward a blue zenith of joy. Even when Betty came in, I hardly looked at her, but upwards and wondered how God could give so much happiness to one poor human.

Well, there have been ups and downs in the years between, but as I write this, I can look from my window across the rolling acres of my land, dotted with cattle, red, white-splashed, their fat sides gleaming in the sun. And I can look far down into the valley, where the windows of Piegan blink in the glittering light of the day. It is only a small town. Even the railroad could not bring to it enough of the vital blood to turn it into a city, Makerville has grown big. It flourishes. It throws a black cloud from the stacks of its furnaces. But I would not trade Piegan for ten such rich cities. For Betty agrees with me that Piegan is just big enough to fit into my heart.

Max Brand is the best-known pen name of Frederick Faust, creator of Dr. Kildare, Destry, and many other fictional characters popular with readers and viewers worldwide. Faust wrote for a variety of audiences in many genres. His enormous output, totaling approximately thirty million words or the equivalent of 530 ordinary books, covered nearly every field: crime, fantasy, historical romance, espionage, Westerns, science fiction, adventure, animal stories, love, war, and fashionable society, big business and big medicine. Eighty motion pictures have been based on his work along with many radio and television programs. For good measure he also published four volumes of poetry. Perhaps no other author has reached more people in more different ways.

Born in Seattle in 1892, orphaned early, Faust grew up in the rural San Joaquin Valley of California. At Berkeley he became a student rebel and one-man literary movement, contributing prodigiously to all campus publications. Denied a degree because of unconventional conduct, he embarked on a series of adventures culminating in New York City where, after a period of near starvation, he received simultaneous recognition as a serious poet and successful popular-prose writer. Later, he traveled widely, making his home in New York, then in Florence, and finally in Los Angeles.

Once the United States entered the Second World War, Faust abandoned his lucrative writing career and his work as a screenwriter to serve as a war correspondent with the infantry in Italy, despite his fifty-one years and a bad heart. He was killed during a night attack on a hilltop village held by the German army. New books based on magazine serials or unpublished manuscripts continue to appear. Alive and dead he has averaged a new one every four months for seventy-five years. In the U.S. alone nine publishers issue his work, plus many more in foreign countries. Yet, only recently have the full dimensions of this extraordinarily versatile and prolific writer come to be recognized and his stature as a protean literary figure in the 20th Century acknowledged. His popularity continues to grow throughout the world.